THE SECRET PRINCESS

RETURN TO THE FOUR KINGDOMS

THE SECRET PRINCESS

A RETELLING OF THE GOOSE GIRL

MELANIE CELLIER

LUMINANT PUBLICATIONS

Luminant Publications
PO Box 203
Glen Osmond, South Australia 5064

melaniecellier@internode.on.net
http://www.melaniecellier.com

Cover Design by Karri Klawiter
Editing by Mary Novak
Proofreading by Deborah Grace White

For Marieke Adele,
and your infectious smile

ROYAL FAMILY TREES

THE FOUR KINGDOMS

KINGDOM OF ARCADIA

King Henry—Queen Eleanor

Parents of

Prince Maximilian (Max)—Alyssa of Arcadia
    Parents of
    Prince Henry (Harry)
    Princess Rose

Princess Lily—Prince Jon of Marin
    Parents of
    Prince Owen
    Princess Hope

Princess Sophie—King Dominic of Palinar
    Parents of
    Prince Arthur
    Princess Grace

(Missing: Princess Mina, younger sister of King Henry, married to Prince Friedrich of Rangmere)

KINGDOM OF RANGMERE

King Josef (deceased)—Queen Charlotte (deceased)

Parents of

Prince Konrad (deceased)—Princess Clarisse of Lanover

Queen Ava—King Hans
 Parents of
 Princess Ellery

(Missing: Prince Friedrich, older brother of King Josef, married to Princess Mina of Arcadia)

KINGDOM OF NORTHHELM

King Richard—Queen Louise

Parents of

Prince William—Princess Celeste of Lanover
 Parents of
 Princess Danielle

Princess Marie—Prince Raphael of Lanover
 Parents of
 Prince Benjamin
 Prince Emmett

KINGDOM OF LANOVER

King Leonardo—Queen Viktoria

Parents of

Prince Frederic—Evangeline (Evie) of Lanover
 Parents of

Prince Leo
Princess Beatrice

Princess Clarisse—Charles of Rangmere
Parents of
Princess Isabella
Prince Danton

Prince Cassian—Tillara (Tillie) of the Nomadic Desert Traders
Parents of
Prince Luca
Princess Iris
Princess Violet

Prince Raphael—Princess Marie of Northhelm
Parents of
Prince Benjamin
Prince Emmett

Princess Celeste—Prince William of Northhelm
Parents of
Princess Danielle

Princess Cordelia—Ferdinand of Northhelm
Parents of
Princess Arabella
Prince Andrew

Princess Celine—Prince Oliver of Eldon

BEYOND THE FOUR KINGDOMS

DUCHY OF MARIN

Duke Philip—Duchess Aurelia

Parents of

Prince Jonathan—Princess Lily of Arcadia
   Parents of
   Prince Owen
   Princess Hope

Princess Lilac

Princess Hazel

Princess Marigold

KINGDOM OF TRIONE

King Edward—Queen Juliette

Parents of

Prince Theodore (Teddy)—Princess Isla of Merrita

Princess Millicent (Millie)—Nereus of Merrita

Princess Margaret (Daisy)

KINGDOM OF PALINAR

King Dominic—Queen Sophie
   Parents of
   Prince Arthur
   Princess Grace

KINGDOM OF TALINOS

King Clarence—Queen Sapphira

Parents of

Prince Gabriel (Gabe)—Princess Adelaide of Palinar

Prince Percival (Percy)

Princess Pearl

Princess Opal

KINGDOM OF ELDON

King Leopold—Queen Camille

Parents of

Prince Oliver—Princess Celine

Princess Emmeline

Princess Giselle

KINGDOM OF ELIAM

King George (deceased)—Queen Alida (deceased)

Father of

Queen Blanche (Snow)—King Alexander

KINGDOM OF MERRITA

King Morgan—Queen Nerida (deceased)

Parents of

Princess Oceana—Lyon of Merrita
    Parents of
    Prince Edmund
    Princess Eloise

Princess Coral

Princess Marine

Princess Avalon

Princess Waverly

Princess Isla—Prince Teddy of Trione

(General Nerissa and Captain Nereus—brother and sister of Queen Nerida)

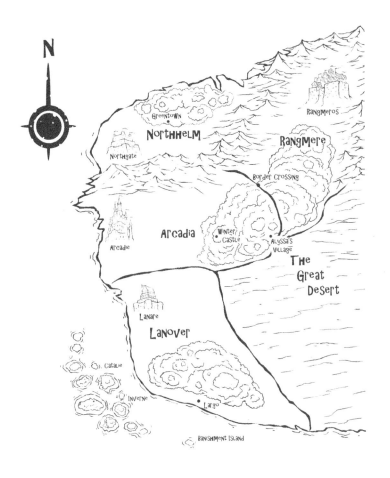

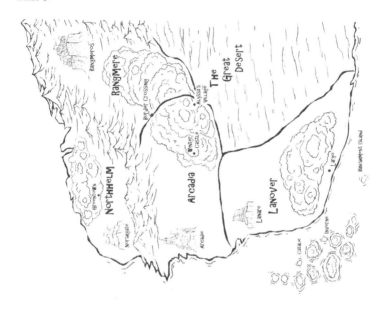

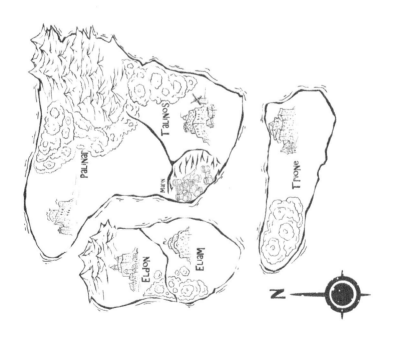

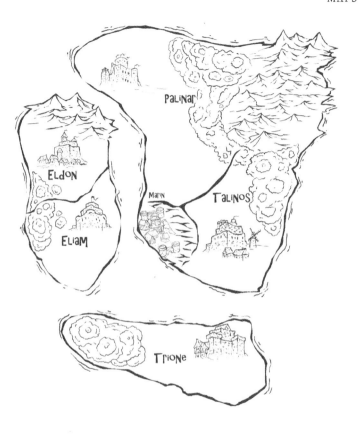

PART I
THE GEESE

PROLOGUE

A wave, larger than the ones preceding it, slapped against the hull of the ship. The deck beneath my feet lurched, sending me staggering against the rail. I managed to get a firm grip before it swung back the other way, the tilt sharper than it had been before. Several sailors called to each other, but a breathless voice shouting my name distracted me from their words.

"Giselle! Giselle!" Daisy, a thirteen-year-old wearing an elegant gown which she had hitched up to give her freer movement, scrambled up the steps from below decks. "There's something wrong with Arvin. He's screaming and neighing, and it sounds like he's going to smash his way out of his stall."

"Arvin?" I let go of the rail and dashed across to meet her at the top of the stairs.

When the ship pitched again, I nearly lost my footing and sent us both tumbling into the depths of the ship. I managed to stop myself just in time, Daisy steadying me on one side.

"Is he injured?" I asked.

"Not that I could see. But he was kicking up such a fuss, I couldn't get a good look at him. I didn't know what else to do but come and get you."

Like everyone else on board, Daisy had noticed the connection between me and my horse—the only mount brought along for the voyage. What she didn't know was that he was a recent gift from my godmother.

I half-climbed, half-slid down the steps, racing toward the horse's stall as quickly as I could given the increased tilt of the ship. I didn't have to make it all the way, however, before I could hear him.

Giselle! Get those useless sailors down here. There's a leak. Starboard. Aft. Where is that useless girl? GISELLE!!

I pulled myself to a stop. At first I had been surprised to learn no one else could hear his equine sounds as words, but I had given up attempting to get any answers out of Arvin. The godmother had given him to me, and I alone could understand him. His manner and behavior made me fairly sure it was an enchantment on him rather than me though.

I reversed direction, Daisy slipping and sliding a few steps behind me. The ship tipped again, and a thin stream of water rushed over our feet.

"There's a leak," I said, hoping she couldn't hear the fear in my voice. "We have to get the sailors—"

Bodies tumbled down the stairs, their voices filling the space below decks as they crowded after each other. I grabbed the closest one.

"There's a hole—or something. Starboard. Aft." I pointed in the right direction.

He hesitated for only a second, before calling to the others to follow him. Daisy and I flattened ourselves against the wooden walls, trying to get out of their way as they rushed past. As soon as they reached Arvin, the horse instantly calmed, and I could no longer hear his shouts.

The yells of the sailors soon replaced them, however, the location of the leak evidently discovered. Daisy looked like she wanted to go after them, curiosity all over her face, so I herded her back toward the deck.

"Giselle! Daisy! There you are. Do you know what's going on?" My older brother Oliver, crown prince of Eldon, appeared from the door of the great cabin. "Everyone else is in here."

"There's a leak," Daisy announced, a little too much relish in her voice.

The ship tilted steeply to the side, and Oliver caught me before I stumbled into the door. His grip didn't loosen, but he glanced back over his shoulder into the cabin, concern on his face.

Someone barreled into him from behind, pushing us both away from the door.

"Sorry!" Celine gasped as she flew past us and up the steps to the deck.

Oliver abandoned us to dash after his wife, both of them disappearing up the steps. I peered through the still open doorway at two more girls. Daria's concerned eyes flitted from me to Daisy.

"What should we do, Giselle?" she asked.

"I think we should all head up on deck," I said, conscious of the continuing shouts of the sailors from the depths of the ship and the increasing tilt at each wave.

"I second that," said Cassandra, hurrying forward to join me. "I don't fancy being caught below decks if the ship's going down."

Daria's worried eyes flashed back to Daisy, the youngest of us. "I'm sure it won't come to that."

"Imagine if it did!" Daisy's eyes were shining. "I've never been shipwrecked before. We could all cling to pieces of wreckage and kick our way to shore."

"Perhaps we could try the longboats before we're reduced to scrounging for flotsam," I said, ushering the others ahead of me toward the steps.

But privately I admitted to some relief that we had been sailing north along the Arcadian shoreline since sunrise. We had been traveling through open ocean for some time now, and I wouldn't have liked to go down days from any land. I had grown up with the closely clustered continents and island of my home lands, where no sea voyage took you far from shore. So this voyage to the distant Four Kingdoms was my first true experience of that vast, open ocean.

For most of my life, any ships that sailed east from our lands encountered a solid wall of impassable storms. Legends held they had been placed there by the High King to protect our people when they fled from their original kingdoms to the uninhabited lands that we would build into kingdoms of our own. But that was countless generations in the past, and few believed or even remembered the legends—until five years ago when the storms stilled.

Daisy, Daria, Cassandra, and I came from the lands of my childhood, but my sister-in-law Celine had grown up in Lanover, one of the original Four Kingdoms. She had come with the first delegation sent by the Old Kingdoms and had stayed to rescue my kingdom of Eldon from a vast enchantment, gaining fire powers and falling in love with my brother in the process.

They had been married for nearly four years now, and she had been promising to take Oliver and me to see her kingdom for at least three of those years. A leak in the boat before we even reached the Arcadian capital didn't seem an auspicious start to the long-awaited journey.

I climbed the steps last, gripping tightly with both hands to keep from losing my footing. When I emerged back into the sunshine, I staggered my way over to the railing to join the others.

Celine, looking pale, managed a smile in greeting. Apparently she had finished being sick over the edge. I gave her a sympathetic wince in return.

"Does it feel like the ship is steadying a little?" Cassie asked, gazing across the deck.

Oliver frowned. "Perhaps a little."

"My men have plugged the hole with their hammocks." The captain appeared beside us, looking grim. "And now they're hard at work at the pumps. But a lot of water got in, and it's only a temporary solution."

Oliver and Celine, the official heads of our delegation, exchanged looks.

"Will we make it to the port at Arcadie?" Oliver asked, naming the Arcadian capital.

The captain's frown deepened, and he rubbed his chin, eyeing the six of us. Daisy was the youngest princess from Trione which meant we consisted of four royals, as well as Cassie, the niece of a minor noble from my kingdom of Eldon, and Daria, a close friend of the queen of Eliam. I could understand why our presence on his damaged ship was making him uneasy.

"It's not ideal conditions," he said at last. "You've seen how slow our progress has been this morning. That storm three days ago drove us slightly off course, and we've hit the coast too far south. Now we've got the wind and the current working against us. An hour ago, I wasn't concerned, steady going would get us there eventually. But now..."

"We have to put to shore," said a panicked voice behind us. "At once."

I turned to my personal maid, Sierra, with a flash of guilt. I hadn't even thought of her since the crisis began. She had always been a diligent and attentive maid but had been strangely absent and distracted since we started the voyage. It hadn't occurred to me her strange behavior might be motivated by a fear of the ocean, but I couldn't mistake her terror now.

She leaned forward. "I can't swim," she whispered to me.

I frowned across the water at a gleaming stretch of sand, picturing the map of the Four Kingdoms. We were working our way northward, toward Arcadie, our planned first stop in our tour. But southward lay Lanover, Celine's home kingdom, and its capital of Lanare. Putting a comforting hand on my maid's arm, I turned to the captain.

"So you're saying even though Lanare is further away than Arcadie, you could reach it faster and with less strain on the damaged ship?" I asked.

The captain rubbed his chin again, looking at Oliver uneasily before turning back to me. "That would be correct, Your Highness."

I faced my brother. "You've already decided Celine can't stay in Arcadie. You were planning to beg a carriage to take her to Lanare as soon as we arrived. But that just means more travel for her. It makes far more sense for you to take the ship south now."

Celine made a noise of protest, but since she had to break it off to be sick over the side of the rail, it didn't carry much weight. Oliver rubbed her back, murmuring about staying cool. Celine had strong feelings about being sick, but she couldn't afford to lose control of her emotions and overheat the baby. At least that was the theory. No one—including the ship doctor—had any experience with the combination of fire powers and pregnancy, but everyone agreed it was better not to take any risks.

She had only just discovered the pregnancy before we set sail and had been determined to proceed as planned. Our trip had already been delayed for years, delegations traveling back and forth to finalize various trade treaties with only officials to represent Eldon. When Celine said she wanted to tell her family the happy news in person, my parents had agreed. At that point, Daisy, Daria, and Cassie had already joined us at our palace to prepare for the voyage, and the Arcadian royal family were expecting our arrival. After so many delays, my parents were uneasy about how it would appear if we canceled at such a late point.

But no sooner did we hit the open seas than Celine began to

feel ill. And the further into the voyage we got, the sicker she became. We had intended to finish our tour in Lanover, rather than starting there, but Oliver now wanted Celine settled with her family as soon as possible.

They didn't know if the illness would last the whole pregnancy, and my sister-in-law was in no fit state to conduct official visits. Oliver hadn't said whether he was more concerned about the risk of her causing a diplomatic incident by losing control and blasting part of the Arcadian palace, or whether he just wanted her calm and comfortable in familiar environments. And it didn't matter. Both were valid.

I pointed at the shoreline. "There seems to be some sort of beach there. Put me ashore with the longboat, along with Sierra, and Arvin, and a few guards. We can continue on to Arcadie while the ship takes the rest of you south to Lanover. I'm sure once I explain the situation, King Henry and Queen Eleanor will understand."

CHAPTER 1

I stood on the beach, watching the longboat row away from me, back to the ship. Our haphazard and somewhat damp disembarkation on a deserted beach wasn't the arrival in Arcadia I had been expecting when we set out from Eldon.

"Your Highness!" Sierra waved for me to join her further back from the water.

The slim girl, slightly older than me, beckoned again, and I slipped through the milling guards toward her. I had no trouble keeping sight of my maid since the sunlight bounced, almost painfully bright, off the blond braid that hung down her back.

There had been debate, of course, but eventually everyone had agreed to my plan—with some modifications. Daisy, Daria, and Cassie had all insisted on accompanying me, driven by varying mixtures of responsibility to our original diplomatic mission and desire for adventure. Oliver capitulated only when Celine reminded him we had pigeons on board and could send a message to the Arcadian capital. Given how long it had taken us to make the necessary arrangements and get all the relevant people to the beach, I hoped the carriages Arcadia had been requested to send wouldn't be far away.

I waved at the distant figures on the ship as the sails were slowly raised again. Soon they would be in Lanare, and Celine could have some relief from her illness. Once the repairs had been completed, the captain would return to Eldon as fast as he could sail to bring our family's personal doctor back to attend her. The two of them had been conducting experiments on Celine's power for years now, and there was no one better to attend her given this turn of events.

From the captain's dire mutterings as we prepared for departure, he was looking forward to being home again so he could have some hard words with the shipbuilders responsible for checking the vessel before the expedition and declaring it seaworthy.

I tugged at my left sleeve, feeling the lump of material I had wedged in there. Now we had stepped foot in Arcadia, I didn't mean to let the family heirloom out of my possession for a moment. The handkerchief—the only working godmother object my family had left from past generations—was not only a useful tool, but a sign of my mother's trust. She had passed it down to me, not Oliver. And now circumstances had proven her right. I would be taking responsibility for the delegation—primarily an Eldonian one, despite the presence of Daisy and Daria from Trione and Eliam—and representing our family without my brother by my side.

And I was more than ready for the chance to stand alone.

"Your Highness!" Sierra appeared beside me, apparently determined we remain glued to each other's sides. A surprising development given her absence on board ship.

I nodded to her, but my attention was focused on locating the other girls. They had been sent with the delegation so they could experience the Four Kingdoms—a small adventure away from their familiar homes. I couldn't help but be conscious it had already become something more of an adventure than their families had likely been expecting.

I eventually spotted them together, Daria their calm center as always. Her brown skin shone warmly in the sunlight, her demeanor reserved. You wouldn't guess she was several years younger than me—not given the way she expertly managed the terrifyingly adventurous Princess Daisy. The thirteen-year-old Trionian princess currently hung off Daria's arm, saying something to her at a fast pace, her whole body quivering with the excitement that was only hinted at in Daria's eyes. I suspected Daisy's family, at least, wouldn't be surprised to hear she had catapulted herself into unexpected adventure.

Cassandra, standing beside them, looked up and caught my gaze. Smiling, she pointed toward Arvin, who stood calmly several steps away. He regarded her pointed finger with an expression of contempt that should have been impossible on the face of a horse before following her gaze to me and tossing his head.

I grinned and started toward them. I had insisted Arvin accompany us, despite the difficulties of getting him to shore. Leaving him behind hadn't been an option. I had no doubt he would have kicked open his stall, trotted up the stairs, jumped overboard and swum to shore on his own if we had dared to forget him.

The young one seems to be greatly excited, he whickered at me, as if it was somehow a personal insult directed at him.

I slung an arm around his neck. "Well, it is all rather exciting."

Is it? I can't say I've seen anything I would label exciting.

"Yes, I am sorry about the awkward trip to shore."

I don't know what you're talking about, he said, with great dignity. *I am always happy to be of service. I am not in the habit of putting others out with my own needs and wishes.*

I snorted. "Of course not. How foolish of me."

"It's strange the way you talk to your horse," Daisy said at my elbow. "Almost as if he talks back." Behind her I could see Sierra watching us, the same confused expression on her face.

I swallowed a grin. "I can't help it."

If the small one wishes to ride me, tell her no, Arvin neighed.

"I thought you were happy to be of service?" I asked innocently.

He whipped his head around, turning the full force of his baleful left eye on me instead of Daisy.

You misunderstand. I think only of her safety. I am not saddled.

I raised an eyebrow, smothering a laugh. "Oh, of course. See, there I go, being foolish again."

It is certainly something you should work on, he said gravely.

I rolled my eyes and turned back to the other girls. "I hope you don't regret coming with me instead of staying with the ship."

Cassie grinned at me. "Of course we wanted to come."

In all honesty, I liked the idea of having the other Eldonian girl at my side. Cassie had proven herself many times over—she had the ability to blend in anywhere she found herself, and the smarts to make the best of every situation.

"Plus, Cassie had to come," Daisy piped up, a disconcerting gleam in her eye. "Eldon might still need her. What if Percy's taste doesn't run to blond hair? He might find he likes Cassie here better than you, Giselle."

Cassie and I groaned in unison. Prince Percival of Talinos was the one remaining eligible prince from our set of kingdoms, but he had led his own delegation across the seas weeks before we left. The Arcadian court had claimed to be delighted to host us all at once, and my parents had been no less delighted at the prospect of throwing me and Percy together. Now from Daisy's comments, it appeared Eldon's interest in an alliance with Percy's kingdom of Talinos was a more open secret than I realized.

Not that anything formal had been arranged or even

discussed. But I knew his presence in Arcadia was the reason my parents had made the kingdom the first stop on our itinerary. A marriage alliance with any of the Four Kingdoms was unlikely for either Percy or me since none of the distant kingdoms had any available royalty of marriageable age. Eldon would have to rely on trade treaties and the alliance Oliver had already secured with Lanover—the richest of the Four Kingdoms. Hence the reason my parents had turned their eyes to our close neighbor of Talinos.

Personally I still wasn't sure what I thought about the scheme. Given both our kingdoms had spent years under separate curses, Percy and I hadn't seen each other since the days when all the royal children of our six kingdoms played together at royal functions. All I remembered from those days was a young boy, olive skin darkened by the sun, running headlong into trouble in his efforts to keep up with the older princes—including his older brother, Prince Gabe. But I had promised my parents I would keep an open mind on the matter, at least.

I turned my mind back to the present as the squad of guards accompanying us began to form up. Oliver had insisted the message sent with the pigeons include a request for two Arcadian squads to meet us along with the carriages, although Celine had assured him the roads in the Four Kingdoms were safe these days.

I think my brother expected us to wait in place for the Arcadians to arrive, but I had already given the order that we were to start toward Arcadie on foot. I had no intention of sitting around on a remote beach when everyone in our party was perfectly capable of walking. Meeting our escort part way might be the difference between reaching Arcadie before nightfall or being caught still on the road at dark.

The spring weather and the solid ground under our feet made the coming journey a pleasant prospect, and I almost wished we had further to travel. Turning, I nearly tripped over Sierra who continued to stick to my side. I bit back an unkind rebuke and scanned the group.

Daisy's maid, a sensible, older woman, stood several paces behind her mistress. Two ceremonial Trionian guards stood with her. After some discussion, it had been decided that there was no need for Trione to send more than two as we did not wish to be discourteous to our hosts by overwhelming their hospitality or suggesting distrust. The Eldonian squads had therefore been instructed to consider all the delegation members to be equally under their protection.

I was the only one with a mount, of course, if Arvin could truly be called that. He only let me on his back when he was in the best of moods, and even then, only bareback.

I knew that many in the party considered it a foolish indulgence to allow me to bring such a useless horse, but they didn't know Arvin's origin. If the godmothers gifted you a talking horse from the Palace of Light—the mysterious and powerful domain of the High King—you didn't leave him behind, however useless he might appear to be.

My right hand drifted to my left wrist, touching the handkerchief tucked safely inside my sleeve. I had two gifts from the godmothers—even if the handkerchief had been given to one of my distant ancestors rather than me. Its power to reveal the truth would serve me all the same.

One of the other guards strode toward us, the familiar look that passed between him and Sierra helping me place his face. More than two years ago, an Eldonian ship had discovered and rescued a small ship-wrecked community from a remote island. Most had chosen to stay in our kingdom when they were offered positions in the palace, my maid and this guard among them.

Sierra had been an exemplary maid since then, her recent distraction on the ship my first complaint. Perhaps it had been the presence of this guard rather than fear of the ocean that had caused her abstraction?

I would let her know she could have extra time off to go walking with him during our time in Arcadia—as long as she stopped disappearing at crucial moments when I needed her services. I didn't want to disgrace Eldon by failing to present myself appropriately as both princess and diplomatic envoy.

The guard addressed himself to me rather than my maid, however.

"We're ready to move out, if Your Highness is agreeable."

"Certainly," I replied. "Lead the way." I attempted a small smile. "You will find royal feet as capable of walking as any others."

He gave a half-bow. "Of course, Your Highness. We have all heard the stories."

He glanced sideways at Sierra before hurrying back to the front of the group, directing the second group of guards to form up behind us. I bit my lip. I hadn't meant to reference the famous trek up the mountains by Oliver, Celine, and me to defeat the Snow Queen four years ago. But apparently my attempt at being approachable had failed dismally.

I groaned silently. This trip was supposed to be my chance to move past that history. Everyone acted as if I had been some sort of heroic savior—and Celine and Oliver were always generous enough to share the credit. But it had been Celine who saved us. She had saved me from freezing twice—first from a frozen heart and then from the actual snow—and then she had saved the entire kingdom. I might not admit it to anyone, but I desperately wanted an opportunity to prove myself without Celine and her powers looking over my shoulder.

One of Daisy's guards glanced at Arvin, a crease between his eyebrows. My horse—although Arvin could be considered mine in only the loosest sense of the word—was bare of so much as a lead rope. I patted his neck and smiled at the guard.

"Don't be concerned, he won't have any trouble keeping up. And he's not prone to wandering away."

The guard gave a quick head bob and turned his attention back to the front.

"Don't make me into a liar," I muttered to Arvin.

I never get lost, he said, and I couldn't help but note it wasn't much of a reassurance.

We began to move, Daisy chattering about something to Cassandra in a voice too low for me to comprehend. The warm sun and the soft call of birds made the walk pleasant despite the ground rolling strangely beneath my feet. I had completed enough sea voyages to know it was a temporary sensation.

The road passed through vast stretches of fields, many populated by farmers busy planting seeds. A line of trees along its length kept the sun from becoming unpleasant, and before long we approached a thicker copse.

Entering the small wood, I turned to make sure no stragglers were falling behind. For a moment I couldn't find Daisy. A frantic glance around revealed her brunette head off the path, examining something on a tree to the side of the road.

I hurried over to shoo her back to the group, but she was already turning toward us again. For a moment our eyes locked, hers full of energy and enthusiasm, and then something jerked her roughly back into the trees.

She didn't have time to scream, her shocked expression still fixed on me as she disappeared from view completely.

I screamed for her, shrieking her name. But my voice was cut off as something large collided with me, knocking me to the ground and stealing the rest of my breath.

CHAPTER 2

I twisted, looking for my attacker, but all I could see were long legs and flashing hooves. Shouts and screams had broken out behind me, but I couldn't see any of the others.

I scrambled to my feet as Arvin attempted to herd me into the trees. Pushing past him, I surveyed the road.

The small group had erupted into chaos. Struggling figures fought each other, but I couldn't work out who the attackers were, or where they had come from in what looked like a mass of moving bodies. Daisy's maid streaked past me, pursuing the vanished girl, the two Trionian guards on her heels. From the corner of my eye, I saw someone lunge toward Daria.

I opened my mouth to scream a warning, but Cassandra was already there, kicking the man in the stomach. He doubled over, gasping, as the Eldonian girl fled for the trees on the opposite side of the road, dragging Daria behind her. She paused, just off the path, her eyes finding me before flitting to Arvin behind me. I gestured wildly for them to keep running, and the two of them disappeared into the wood.

My eyes caught on another female figure, standing just inside

19

the opposite tree line. Sierra. Her eyes latched onto me, and she gestured frantically for me to join her. I shifted to my toes, preparing to dash through the battle on the road, but something wrenched me backward.

I almost tripped, fighting to keep my feet as Arvin's firm grip on the back of my dress pulled me away from the road.

"Let me go!" I snapped at the horse, my eyes still on Sierra.

Don't make me knock you down again, he neighed, finally releasing his bite.

My maid, her eyes grown even wider, gave one desperate glance at the raging battle and dashed across the road toward me.

Get on my back, Arvin said. *Now.*

I gripped his mane, my hands trembling and slipping in my haste, and swung myself onto his back.

"Wait," I yelled, as I settled myself in place. "Sierra. We can't leave her."

Arvin said nothing, but neither did he race into the trees, so I leaned down, holding out my hand to my maid. She reached us, panting heavily, and grabbed at my wrist, swinging up behind me with more agility than I'd expected.

Arvin didn't wait for her to balance herself, launching into movement so quickly she nearly fell straight back off. She didn't scream, however, and when I cast an anxious glance back, no one appeared to be following us.

"Who are they?" I gasped.

Neither Arvin nor Sierra answered.

"We have to find the others," I said. "Someone took Daisy. And Cassie and Daria could be anywhere by now."

They are not my charges. Arvin continued to move with almost impossible speed through the trees. *You are.*

"You stopped for Sierra," I said.

I was momentarily infected by your foolishness. I will no doubt come to regret it.

I sighed. I wasn't going to get any help from Arvin, and I didn't dare throw myself from his back.

"Whatever the beast is saying, listen to him, Your Highness," Sierra said sharply. "We must consider your safety now."

Arvin gave an indignant snort, although whether it was a protest against being called *the beast* or disgust at finding himself in agreement with Sierra, I wasn't sure.

Somewhere in the back of my mind it registered that my maid apparently knew my horse could talk, but more urgent matters consumed my immediate thoughts.

"We can't just abandon them, though. They came to this land under our care."

Not under your care, Arvin neighed, not seeming in the least fatigued or discomfited by our unnaturally fast flight. *Celine was supposed to be in charge. It is not your fault that you have lost them. I would even be willing to back you up,* he added, as if conferring a great favor.

"Fat lot of good that will do when no one else can understand you," I muttered and then groaned aloud. His words only reminded me that the attack on the road would have played out differently if Celine had been there to come to our aid with fire balls. I was hours into my chance to prove myself, and I was already wishing for Celine to come and save us all.

The trees in front of us thinned, revealing distant fields. Apparently we were nearing the far edge of the copse. Arvin slowed and came to a stop, apparently unwilling to venture out into the open.

I immediately slid from his back, only to hesitate, one hand still on his flank. We had traveled too far for it to make any sense for me to go dashing off into the trees alone. For all I knew, the others were just as likely to find me if I stayed put as I was to find them by stumbling around alone.

"What is the use in being a princess if you can't even get your horse to obey your orders?" I muttered in frustration.

I am neither yours nor a horse, Arvin snorted.

I pointedly looked him up and down. "What are you then? A unicorn with a misplaced horn?"

He huffed and spoke with great dignity. *Unicorns? Really? Naturally I am not an imaginary creature. I merely meant I am not just a horse. A horse from the Palace of Light should not be compared to an ordinary steed.*

"No, you're right," I said. "There's no comparison at all. I liked my last mount far better than you."

Arvin huffed out what sounded surprisingly like a laugh. Apparently he cared too little for the good opinion of a mere human to take offense at my words.

Reluctantly a smile spread over my own face, turning into a chuckle that I abruptly cut off before it could edge toward hysteria. I had been in dangerous situations before, and I wasn't going to lose my wits now.

Sierra had followed my lead and also slid down, proving surprisingly adept at dismounting without a saddle. She ignored my conversation with Arvin while she carefully examined our surroundings, but she now fixed her attention back on me.

"The roads of Arcadia are supposed to be safe," she said. "Which means those may not have been ordinary bandits. If they were targeting you specifically, then we have to make sure you stay safe."

I regarded her with a creased brow. "And how exactly are we going to manage that? We're two girls and a talking horse. We aren't even armed." I omitted mentioning the small dagger in my boot since I didn't think it would do us much good in the case of a bandit attack.

"We swap clothes," she said. "Swap places completely. I will be Princess Giselle, and you can pose as my maid."

"What?" I stared at her. "So that they kill you instead of me? No indeed! I couldn't possibly allow you to take such a risk."

"You believe their aim is to kill you?" Sierra frowned at me.

"Surely ransom is more likely or some political intrigue. They could have opened their ambush with an arrow to your heart if that had been their aim. I should be safe enough—for a while at least. This way, if they do find us, you may be able to slip away to get help." She sounded grim. "They will soon discover that having me in their custody does them little good."

"At which point they may well decide to kill you," I pointed out.

She smiled. "I'll assure them you hold me dear and that I would make excellent bait."

A reluctant chuckle escaped me. The Sierra of the boat had changed again, the girl in front of me showing a spirit and determination I hadn't seen before.

"I almost believe you would be able to convince them of the scheme," I said.

"I always succeed at what I set my mind to." Her eyes gleamed with strength and certainty.

"Very well," I said, still reluctant. "I'll admit I can't come up with any other plan."

Her hand whipped up in a silencing gesture. "What was that?"

She looked into the trees and then back to me with wide eyes.

"Quickly," she whispered. "I think there's someone coming."

I glanced at Arvin, but he was staring uneasily in the direction Sierra had pointed. I hesitated for another moment, but she was already starting to unfasten the back of my dress. Her outfit was a much simpler design, crafted to be easily removed without assistance, and a moment later I was slipping it on, my ears straining for any further sounds.

I heard nothing further, but then I hadn't heard the first sound either. Twice, Sierra's head whipped up, her hearing apparently better than mine. By the time we'd completed the transformation, keeping only our own boots, I was jumping at the slightest whisper of the breeze in the leaves above us.

"If they're coming, we can't stay here," I said. "We'll have to risk riding on. It will be easy enough to find the road again among those fields, and the Arcadian guards must be somewhere along its length. They may even be near. If we could find them, we could bring them back here to search for the others. They would no doubt make a much better job of it than we possibly could on our own."

Sierra nodded silent agreement, so I turned to Arvin.

"Will you carry us again?"

He regarded me for a moment. *I don't like this plan.*

I rolled my eyes. "Next time, if you want your vote counted, make it before any changing of clothes happens."

He gave a haughty huff.

"Will you let us ride?" I pressed again.

He regarded me with one large eye before blowing out a breath and giving a single nod. A fallen log nearby allowed for a much more graceful mounting than our previous one, and we had soon broken free of the last of the trees.

A small trot across a fallow field returned us to the road. Arvin increased his pace to a canter without complaint. It shouldn't have been a sustainable pace, given he carried two passengers, but just as in the wood, he showed no sign of tiring. The ride was so smooth, in fact, that Sierra managed to rearrange my hair from her position behind me. She soon had my pins free and the careful arrangement replaced with the same simple braid she wore every day.

When I glanced behind me not long later, I found she had managed to put the pins to use in her own hair, pinning her braid to her head in some basic semblance of a formal style.

"It's the details that give you away," she said when she saw me looking.

I almost started chuckling again at that and barely refrained from asking if she had a lot of experience impersonating royalty. But the fleeting amusement instantly dried up, replaced with the same circling worries about Daria, Cassie, and Daisy. What had the attackers done to Daisy? Had Cassie and Daria managed to escape as we had done?

Sierra thought the attackers had been after me, but Daisy or even Daria could as easily have been targets. And I knew they had Daisy at least. I shivered at the thought, and Arvin responded to my unspoken message, increasing his pace even more.

No matter how many times I looked behind us, no pursuers materialized, but soon enough we caught sight of a dust haze in the distance ahead. Arvin was already checking his pace, apparently having seen them before I did. He slowed to a walk and veered off to stand by the side of the road.

The three of us waited in silence as the haze became two carriages and a group of riders, most in what looked like guard uniforms.

"It must be the Arcadians coming to meet us," I said.

"Don't forget, you are the maid," Sierra hissed. "We must be sure they are not in league with the attackers before we reveal your true identity."

We were in a great deal of trouble if it was the Arcadian crown who had attacked us, but I held my silence. A little circumspection would not go amiss.

Sierra commanded Arvin to return to the road, but he ignored her. She dug her heel into his side, trying to propel him forward, and I half expected him to throw us both off. After a pointed moment of stillness, however, he took several steps forward to stand in the path of the approaching group.

A shout and a raised arm from the lead rider caused them all to slow. Every eye fixed on us, some filled with surprise and others concern.

"Excuse our disheveled state," Sierra said in stately tones. "I am Princess Giselle of Eldon, and this is my maid. Our party has come under attack, and we barely escaped with our lives."

Murmurs rippled down the line of guards at her words, with a single shout of surprise quickly stifled.

"Attacked?" The guard at the front of the column sounded horrified. "Who can have dared such a thing? And so close to the capital!"

"That I cannot answer," Sierra said. "But it occurred in the small wood behind us, and I beseech you to accompany us back to check on the safety of my traveling companions."

The guard, an older man with a commanding presence, frowned. "Naturally we will go to their rescue, but I cannot permit you to ride back into potential danger." He rose in his saddle, surveying the riders behind him. "I will take one carriage on, while you make use of the other for the rest of your journey to Arcadie. One squad shall accompany you, of course, although I cannot imagine even these criminals would be so brazen as to attack a royal carriage on its approach to the city."

"In that case," I whispered to Sierra, "tell him to take more of the guards with him. The rest of our people will have more need of them than us."

Sierra hesitated for a moment, glancing at me before speaking again.

"Surely two or three guards will be a sufficient escort for us. Please take the others to assist in finding and protecting my delegation."

The man gave a partial bow from his saddle. "Your concern for your people does you credit, Your Highness, but I cannot allow it. Once my squad has seen you safely to the palace, they will return, with reinforcements, in case I find myself in need of greater numbers."

I worried at my bottom lip. The return journey would take considerable time, but I was in no position to argue the matter. Not least because of our charade.

The guard barked a series of orders and his followers had soon split into two equal groups, each with a carriage. Sierra nudged me, and I dismounted. She hesitated, not sliding down after me, and I realized she was waiting for my assistance. She was better at this game than I was.

Offering a hand, I helped her reach the ground, falling into step behind her as we were directed to climb into one of the carriages. As we passed the guard in charge, I looked up at him.

"They took Princess Daisy, I saw them. But Daria and Cassandra might have gotten away. You may need to comb the forest for them."

Sierra paused, her brow creasing slightly before clearing.

"Yes, indeed, thank you, Sierra," she said to me. "This whole ordeal has quite disordered my mind. I was traveling with three other young girls, Captain, and I fear greatly for their safety."

He bowed again. "It is I and my people who must apologize, Your Highness. I can assure you that everything in our power will be done to find them."

And with that assurance I had to be content and follow Sierra into the carriage. As galling as it was to abandon them all, any further protests would only slow the rescuers from departure. With a sharp cry, the captain wheeled his mount and took off down the road at speed, his squad hard on his heels, and the second carriage trailing more slowly behind.

Our own vehicle did not begin to move, however, and when I stuck my head out the window, I could see why. I hurried back down onto the road as a puzzled looking guard edged his mount toward Arvin. The poor man held a lead rope but had clearly been thrown into confusion by the lack of either halter or bridle.

"He's a magnificent animal." The admiring voice came from slightly above me. I looked up to see our coachman regarding Arvin with an intrigued expression. "And he doesn't look in the least fatigued from carrying two riders."

"He's quite the most elegant and noble horse anyone has ever seen," I said. "But don't let him hear you saying so. He has quite a high enough opinion of himself already."

The coachman let out a surprised laugh. He neither looked

nor spoke like the coachmen I was used to, being considerably younger, for a start. Perhaps they did things differently in Arcadia and coachman was not a senior position, acquired with age.

For all his youth, he held the reins with competent ease, despite his attention remaining on Arvin. His golden skin glowed in the afternoon sun, his brown eyes warm, and his dark hair tousled in the wind. My mind had no business thinking of such things during a crisis, but I had to admit to myself he was also a great deal more handsome than the average coachman.

Sierra stuck her head out the window of the carriage and took in the scene.

"Arvin is a special horse," she said. "He doesn't need to be restrained." She looked at the horse, a strange expression of concentration on her face. "Isn't that right, Arvin?"

Arvin disdained to even glance in her direction, continuing to pretend he was unaware of the scene he was causing. Her eyes narrowed.

"He is a troublesome creature. Pay him no mind. If he doesn't make it back to the palace with us, it will be no great loss, I assure you."

I glanced at her, startled, as the coachman also twisted to look down at her. Apparently the events of the day were beginning to strain Sierra, something I could hardly blame her for—especially since Arvin was rather trying at the best of times.

"There is no need to restrain him," I said to the guard. "He will stay with us."

Arvin tossed his head. *We should definitely have left her back in the woods.*

"Be nice," I told him sternly. "We've all had enough excitement for today."

He whuffed but didn't protest, which I took as agreement. When I turned back to the carriage, I found the coachman's attention had now turned to me.

"I'm Philip." He gave me a friendly nod.

"I'm…" I hesitated. "Sierra," I said in a rush.

"It's a pleasure to meet you," he said, "despite the circumstances. And I promise you, if it's possible to find your friends, Captain Markus and his guards will do it. King Henry and Queen Eleanor sent the captain of the king's guard to meet you, along with some of his finest troops."

"Thank you." I wished his words were enough to ease the constant feeling of dread which had settled in my middle.

They did spur me to action, however, since the faster we could get to the capital, the faster reinforcements could start back for the wood. As soon as I was settled on the well-padded seat, the carriage began to move, picking up speed faster than seemed possible.

I sighed and closed my eyes, my hand drifting to my left sleeve. I froze, my eyes snapping open. *My handkerchief.*

I sat bolt upright, sliding along the seat toward the door, as I tried to remember the distracted, terrifying moments while Sierra and I swapped dresses. How could I have forgotten about the object tucked into my sleeve?

"We have to turn back," I said, breathlessly. "I've lost something very important. We have to return to the woods."

"No, I don't think so," Sierra said.

I frowned, out of patience with my maid's strange mood.

"Yes," I snapped, "we do." My mother had entrusted the family heirloom to me, and I had lost it before I even made it to the Arcadian palace. I had to recover it.

Sierra leaned forward, her eyes suddenly intense on mine. "No, *Sierra*, we don't. I think you've forgotten that it is the princess who gives the orders, not the maid. We will be continuing on to Arcadie so I can be presented to King Henry, Queen Eleanor, and Prince Percival."

CHAPTER 3

I gaped at her, frozen in place by my shock. What in the kingdoms was going on?

"Besides, there's no need." She sat back against her seat, a smug smile transforming her face. "At least, not if you're concerned about having lost this." She pulled my missing object out of her sleeve.

I gasped and lunged toward it, but she quickly stuffed it back out of sight.

"You should be more careful with such valuable items, you know." She chuckled. "You really did make it ridiculously easy for me."

"What are you doing, Sierra?" I asked, a dangerous edge to my voice.

"That's Your Highness to you," she corrected in an amused tone that set my teeth on edge. "You should start practicing now."

My eyes stayed focused on her sleeve and the treasure I now knew it carried. "If you think I'm permanently swapping places with you—"

"Then I would be completely right," she said. "While you were so busy worrying about those tiresome girls, I was occupied with more important matters."

My eyes flashed to her face, momentarily distracted. "What have you done to the others?"

"Me? Whatever do you mean?" she asked in a voice of over-done innocence. "I've been with you the whole time, as you well know."

I growled at her. *"What have you done with them?"*

She shrugged. "I have no idea. They might have all gotten away for all I know. But you can be certain if they did, my men will ensure they keep running and they don't look back." She smiled sweetly. "It wouldn't do at all to have anyone around Arcadia who actually knows what you look like."

"Percy's there," I snapped.

"Ah, yes." Her smile didn't falter. "Dear Percy. Who I haven't seen since I was a small child." She batted her eyelashes coquettishly at me. "It's remarkable how people change as they age, isn't it? I wouldn't have even recognized him. But I have such fond memories of the trouble we all got up to as children."

My heart sank. All those times she had asked me to tell her stories about my childhood, exclaiming at how different life was in Eldon and the surrounding kingdoms compared to her island home. Whatever was going on here went much further than a moment of crazed rebellion by my maid. She must have been planning it since she came into my employ. Or before. I remembered recognizing one of my guards as her fellow islander.

A rush of cold down my spine brought back a flood of bad memories. I shivered and reminded myself I was no longer frozen by an enchantment as I had once been years ago. I was not helpless now as I had been then. Whatever Sierra wanted from me, I wasn't going to let my friends pay the price. The Arcadians would capture her men, and I would make them tell us where to find the others.

As I recreated the scene of the attack in my mind, I noticed something I should have noticed at the time. The number of people on the road hadn't increased. The unexpected fighting had made me assume we'd been attacked, but it had been treachery from within our own number. Which meant Sierra didn't have a great many men, and the Arcadians should have no trouble capturing them.

"I know who I am," I said. "And I remember far more about my childhood than I ever told you. I can be quite convincing, too."

Sierra shook her head. "You can't imagine I would leave you free to question my identity? Why do you think I needed this?" She lightly touched her sleeve.

I frowned. "That handkerchief is a family heirloom passed down for generations, but I'm not going to let you usurp my identity just to prevent you from destroying it."

"Destroy it?" She sounded genuinely surprised. "I wouldn't do such a wasteful thing. I intend to use it. Just not for its original purpose." She paused. "Well, not only for its original purpose."

I narrowed my eyes. "It can't just be used to cast any enchantment. That's not how godmother objects work. That handkerchief lets the owner know whether or not someone is telling the truth. That's all."

"Such narrow thinking. It's no wonder you got yourself into such difficulties."

I glared at her. "What have you done to it?"

"Nothing that will harm its original purpose," she said. "At least, I don't think so. I have merely...expanded it somewhat."

"What's that supposed to mean?"

"It means," she said, her voice turning brisk, "that you may not communicate the truth about our identities to any living soul. Not now, not ever. The enchantment will prevent you from doing so."

"I don't believe you," I said, injecting more confidence into the statement than I really felt.

"Nevertheless," Sierra said calmly, "it's true. Your mother kindly sewed one of your hairs into the border of the handkerchief, thus extending its enchantment to you. However, I used a more powerful binding agent."

She pulled it out again, holding it tightly this time, and showed me three reddish-brown drops on the white material. The handkerchief around the small stains had gone stiff and yellowed as if with great age. It looked, if such a thing were possible, as if it had been poisoned.

Bile rose in my throat. The unnatural appearance of the object convinced me far more than her words—perhaps she truly had twisted the object's enchantment after all. It wouldn't be the first time I had encountered a corrupted godmother object being used for evil. It was the way I had been trapped in an enchantment before. Celine had fought against a whole collection of such twisted objects.

"These aren't just ordinary drops of blood," Sierra continued. "They were made with a second object, enchanted long ago for protection. It had only a trace amount of power left, but it was enough to transfer with my blood into the handkerchief. Now this object carries the lingering remnants of its power, twined with the truth enchantment linked to you. We are connected now, and neither of us can speak the truth about our identities."

Apparently Sierra had managed more than just pinning her hair while she was behind me on Arvin's back. I revised my earlier guess. She must have been planning this for years. I could not believe she had done it all alone.

Anger clouded my mind, and my hand strayed down toward my boots where my dagger still hid. I would force her to return the handkerchief, and then, as much as it pained me to do so, I would destroy it.

"If you're thinking of doing me an injury," Sierra said, as if she could read my mind, "then I strongly urge you to reconsider. You are a maid now, and I am a princess. You would be wise not to give me a reason to order your execution."

I hesitated, struck anew by the enormity of the deception Sierra had begun. I was thinking like myself—a princess with all the power and authority of a throne to back me up. But I had let myself be introduced to the Arcadians as a maid. If I now attacked Sierra, it would appear like a betrayal against the mistress who employed me.

Although, if I could destroy the handkerchief, I could tell everyone the truth. I hoped.

Of course, I didn't actually know for sure if destroying the handkerchief would break the enchantment. And if I didn't succeed in wresting it from her and destroying it, then I wouldn't put it past her to attempt to have me executed.

Reluctantly I sat back against the seat, watching her through narrowed eyes.

"So I am to play the role of your servant? In that case, I'm giving you advanced notice of my resignation."

Sierra raised her eyebrows. "Are you sure? I have no doubt the Arcadian royal family will be more than happy to provide a replacement maid after the trauma of our attack rendered my previous maid unfit for service. For you, however, the future might not look so rosy. Where do you suppose a commoner girl without resources, friends, or references will find food and shelter in a strange kingdom?"

I glared at her. "And what will the Arcadian royal family think of you when you cast off this traumatized maid to fend for herself?" Every word out of Sierra's mouth only proved how little she understood what it meant to be a princess.

Sierra looked disappointed. "Perhaps you are right, and a different solution is needed. Never fear, I will find one. I have overcome every obstacle thus far, and you shall soon see that nothing is going to stand in my way."

I bit my lip and looked determinedly away from her, my blank eyes barely absorbing the countryside passing by the window. It seemed an age ago that I had stood on the deck of our ship, surrounded by friends and family. I chewed on the inside of my cheek. Celine and Oliver would recognize Sierra the moment they saw her, of course. And their testimony would be believed. But I could well imagine Sierra would employ every possible excuse to put off leaving Arcadia for the next stage of our trip. And she certainly wouldn't travel to Lanover when the time came. Celine and Oliver would eventually travel to us if we deferred our trip to Lanover, but how long until Celine was well enough for such a journey?

Should I attempt to travel to Lanover myself? If Sierra was right about the enchantment, I wouldn't be able to explain the situation when I got there. They would protect me, of course, but it was a long way to go. I might starve or encounter some accident before I ever made it there. I knew how to safely travel through snow, but I knew nothing of the Arcadian or Lanoverian countryside. I had never considered that I might find myself alone and friendless here.

For all my fear, a hard knot of rebellion formed inside me. I didn't want to run, cowering to Celine for shelter, unable to explain my predicament, while Sierra caused my kingdom and its reputation unknown harm in this strange land. I had faced seemingly impossible situations before. I wouldn't turn away from this one. Enchantments could always be broken, that was the way they worked. I had been a small part of breaking a much bigger enchantment than this—one that kept a whole kingdom in thrall. I just had to find out how to break this one.

Thinking about enchantments inevitably brought to mind my own godmother, and without looking away from the window, I opened my mouth to call for her. No sound emerged from my throat.

I glanced briefly at Sierra but looked away again when I saw the amused expression she had trained on me. Apparently the enchantment was clever enough to block such a simple stratagem. It seemed calling my godmother was akin to speaking my true identity.

Silence fell between us, and I began to look a little more closely at the fields which still lined the road. Were the other girls fleeing through such fields now, or had they found a place to hole up and hide in the woods? I refused to consider any other possibilities. I had to believe they would all be found safe—and not just because that would free me from my current predicament.

Sierra eventually broke the silence, her tone petulant. "I don't understand why Arvin wouldn't listen to me."

I snorted. "Arvin doesn't listen to anyone."

Her mouth pursed. "But why can't I hear him? You still seemed able to do so. And now that I'm also linked to the object, I should be able to hear him as well."

"What?" I stared at her. "You thought I could hear Arvin because of that object?"

The idea gave me some hope. She didn't know as much about the object as she thought she did, which meant there might be a weakness somewhere in the enchantment that she hadn't considered.

"Of course." She frowned. "Horses can't talk. It must be the enchantment. It must be telling you the truth of his thoughts. And now I am the princess with the connection to the enchanted horse. Arvin is no good to me if I can't understand him."

A vague feeling of foreboding filled me.

"Words or not, he's still the most elegant mount anyone has ever seen," I said. "He's obviously special, a horse fit for a princess." Arvin wasn't a prop to serve my royalty, but if that was what Sierra needed to hear, I was willing to play along—for his sake.

Her brow lightened at that, but after a moment it creased again, her eyes resting heavily on me.

"Yes, he is special. That much is obvious. And he has a connection with *you*. A maid."

The sensation of fear blossomed into full flower, and it must have shown on my face because the determination on Sierra's hardened.

"You don't intend to cooperate with me, so I think you need a demonstration of just who holds the power in this situation. I shall have the animal destroyed, and it can stand as a reminder of what will happen to you if you try to cross me."

"What?" I gaped at her, appalled. "You can't kill him just because I can hear him talk and you can't."

She raised a single eyebrow. "Why ever not? I'm a princess. I can do what I like."

"That is not what it means to be a princess. Being a princess means you sacrifice for your people and kingdom, not that you hand out death on a whim."

"It's a horse. I'm hardly slaughtering babies." She drummed her fingers on her leg, staring out the window. "Besides, I've been a maid in your palace for over a year now and working for you for most of that time. I know everything I need to know about princesses."

Responses flooded my mind, but I held them all in. She wasn't meeting my eyes which told me some part of her knew it was wrong to pronounce a death sentence on an innocent animal, but her tone communicated she was beyond argument. The more I tried, the more determined she would become. I had to place my hope in that small seed of discomfort and doubt—and in the possibility that the Arcadian guards might discover Daria, Cassie, or Daisy before she could carry out her threat.

Time passed, although my mind was in such a state that it was hard to say how much. My efforts to prove my capability could hardly be going worse. And I was starting to question them myself. Sierra claimed she knew all about being a princess— while clearly knowing nothing of the qualities my family had raised me to uphold. And yet, at the end of the day, it was only an accident of birth that gave me royal status, not Sierra. I had spent years increasingly bound by an enchantment, only to be loosed from it and hailed as a hero, despite not deserving the title. What had I ever done to deserve the role I now found myself so angry at being forced to relinquish?

My mind churned around and around in circles, and the drive seemed never-ending. Eventually, however, the road began to slope slightly upward as we approached the low hill that held the Arcadian capital city.

The afternoon sun shone too brightly for my black mood as we reached the outskirts of Arcadie, joining a wide, main road which cut through the city. Staring out the window, I saw that the city had been arranged in layers, each circular district distinct from its neighbors. I had enough experience with large cities to recognize the small, connected houses of the commoners, the bright, elaborate shops and homes of the merchants, and finally the spacious estates of the nobles, these homes built in elegant, embellished stone and surrounded by gardens.

Despite myself, a spark of interest stirred. The bustling streets of the commoners' district had a productive hum without hint of desperation that told me much about this kingdom and its rulers. And my stomach gurgled in response to the delicious smells from the marketplaces that were tucked just off the main street, their courtyards and stalls visible in brief glimpses down side streets. How long had it been since I ate?

I glanced uneasily at Sierra who watched with interest out the other window. Until now I had been more concerned with her broader plans, but my rumbling stomach made me question my immediate future. What were her intentions for me now I had made it clear I would not playact as her personal maid?

CHAPTER 4

The sun flashed off a thick wall of white stone, drawing my attention back to the window. We had climbed through the city to the peak of the hill, and our carriage now passed through an enormous archway and rolled into the vast yard of the palace.

One of the guards in our escort was already calling for reinforcements to assemble, and the space outside the window quickly turned into a chaotic confusion of bodies and voices. A footman appeared and opened our door, lowering a step and holding out his arm to assist the supposed princess to alight.

Sierra hopped down without a backward glance, but the footman remained in place to assist me as well. I gave him the first smile I had been able to muster since Sierra's treachery was revealed. His behavior toward a mere maid was another count in favor of this kingdom.

My smile fell away. Arcadia was peaceful and prosperous, just as we had been promised, but I had inadvertently brought evil into its heart. Even if I could find a way to foil Sierra, would Arcadia forgive Eldon for the deception? Sierra was being accepted among them because of their trust in my kingdom, and I had no idea how she might betray that trust.

The yard around me already looked more ordered than it had a moment before. A stream of grooms led away the horses that had been ridden in by the guards, their riders forming into an orderly group to one side. More guards hurried into the yard to swell their number, and as the first fresh mount appeared, they began to swing back into the saddle. I watched them with relief, glad to see that both the guards and the grooms were well trained enough that they would be gone again without delay.

"What goes on here?" called a commanding voice across the noise and busyness of the scene.

I swung around to see a middle-aged couple standing at the top of a short flight of stairs that led to the great doors of the palace. They made an impressive sight, framed by the white stone building, topped with soaring towers and graceful spires and accented with the dark slate of the roof. I didn't need the subtle circlets they wore to tell me I was beholding King Henry and Queen Eleanor of Arcadia.

In the back of my mind I noted the queen's beauty, her age lending her maturity and elegance without stripping away her arresting loveliness, and the way her arm rested in the king's. They stood as if they were true partners, her face reflecting the concern that echoed in his voice. They made an impressive pair, his dark hair a complement to her golden head.

"Captain Markus's orders," called back one of the guards, separating himself from the mass of guards and jogging to the foot of the stairs.

The king gestured for the guard to ascend the steps to join him, and a hushed conversation ensued, too quiet for me to follow. It didn't last long, however, and both monarchs directed thunderstruck expressions toward Sierra where she still stood beside our carriage.

The queen started down the steps toward us, her hands

outstretched, and King Henry was only a step behind her. Sierra moved forward to join them, a stricken expression on her face that hadn't been there in the carriage. I trailed behind her, not sure what else to do.

"My dear! How awful!" Queen Eleanor clasped both Sierra's hands, all thought of formal introductions forgotten. "We're so sorry that such a thing should have befallen you within our borders."

Sierra managed a brave, tremulous smile.

"Thank you, Your Majesty. I will admit I feel rather overset." She cast down her eyes. "And greatly worried for my traveling companions."

"Of course!" said the king. "But please know that Captain Markus has my full trust. We will spare no efforts to make this right."

"You are very kind," Sierra said.

"It is our duty and responsibility," the queen said gently. "You are a guest in our kingdom. Give me but a moment, and I will have a word with our housekeeper. We will cancel the evening meal we had planned for you and have food delivered to you in your room. I am sure you will wish to rest and will not wish to be meeting a roomful of people after such an ordeal."

She stepped away, beckoning for an upright older woman with an air of calm authority. The two fell into quiet conversation, heads bent close together. The king's attention was captured by the same guard who had spoken to him earlier, leaving Sierra's attention free.

She glanced around, her eyes gliding over me without stopping and latching onto a groom.

"You!" she said, calling for his attention.

The man paused, glancing around with a puzzled expression before apparently deciding the princess must be talking to him. He bobbed his head and directed an inquiring look at her.

"Your Highness?"

"My horse is here somewhere. He has a golden coat and arrived without any sort of saddle or harness."

The groom nodded. "You can be sure we'll take excellent care of him, Your Highness."

I looked around, trying to locate Arvin, but he seemed to have disappeared, whether merely obscured by all the activity in the yard or already departed for the stables, I wasn't sure.

"Well…" Sierra looked down, an assumed expression of sadness on her face as she hesitated theatrically. "I'm afraid he isn't well. I couldn't bear to part with him on the ship and have him tossed into the ocean, but now that we're on land, I cannot keep him in pain any longer." She hesitated again. "I assume you can make the necessary arrangements? It will be nice to know he is buried in such a beautiful land as this, and I will appreciate the chance to visit his grave while I am here."

The groom, visibly taken aback, didn't seem to know what to say at first. But he quickly found his voice, once again bobbing his head respectfully.

"Of course, Your Highness. You may safely leave the matter in our hands."

She nodded once, apparently dismissing the matter from her thoughts. But as her gaze skimmed back over the yard, it caught on me briefly this time, the ghost of a satisfied smile crossing her face before swiftly being suppressed.

My hands balled into fists in my skirts as I glared at her back. The queen, turning back toward Sierra, saw me, her smile faltering for a moment. I quickly schooled my expression into a semblance of calm, but her brow creased, an expression of confusion lingering on her face.

I hadn't actually tested the efficacy of Sierra's enchantment, so I opened my mouth, forming the words to tell the queen the truth. But just as in the carriage when I tried to call on my godmother, no sound emerged.

The confusion on the queen's face deepened.

Sierra followed her gaze, narrowing her eyes at me before turning back toward the queen. Stepping forward to meet her, she spoke in a voice that was just loud enough for me to hear.

"Please excuse my maid, Queen Eleanor. She wasn't the most...stable before this happened, and I'm afraid the trauma of the attack has left her mind quite disordered."

"Oh, the poor thing." The queen directed a warmer look toward me, and I realized too late how my attempt at speaking the truth had only confirmed Sierra's story. "It must have been a great ordeal for you both. I'm so glad you were able to elude your attackers."

"As are we." Sierra directed a look of sympathy at me that made me want to scream. This time I refrained, although the damage had already been done.

"I don't like to be an imposition," Sierra continued, "but I wonder if you might be able to help her? I fear that caring for me is too much for her in her current state, and the hustle and bustle of the palace will only delay her recovery. I know, however, that she would want to stay busy and useful. I don't suppose you have some quiet, solitary sort of role she could be assigned to for the duration of my stay?"

The queen looked thoughtful. "Of course we will do everything we can to help her recover. And to provide you with the care you need as well. I'm sure that something can be found..."

A genteel throat clearing attracted our attention to the return of the royal housekeeper.

"Your earlier orders have been disseminated, Your Majesty, and I couldn't help but overhear the princess's request. It just so happens that our goose boy has recently been granted leave to return to his family for a short period. The Poulterer has been asking me if I have a young person available to take on the role for a time."

She turned to me. "The gaggle is a well-trained one, and they roam within the palace park." Looking toward Sierra, she explained, "At the rear, the palace grounds extend all the way down to the city wall, providing a large stretch of greenery for the inhabitants of the palace to use for riding and other recreational purposes. It is completely safe, so your maid would have no cause for fear while herding the geese."

Sierra smiled at them both beatifically. "How perfect! Perhaps I can leave her in your hands then, Mrs…"

"Mrs. Pine." The woman gave a small curtsy. "You will have no need to fear for her well-being while in our care, Your Highness."

"You have my gratitude," Sierra said graciously, before accepting Queen Eleanor's arm and allowing herself to be guided into the palace.

I watched them go, my head reeling. So I was to become a goose girl? Mere hours ago I'd been a princess, with the responsibility of an entire delegation on my shoulders. And now my responsibility was a gaggle of geese.

I sighed. And finding a way around my enchantment, discovering the extent of Sierra's plotting, and reclaiming my true identity—and at the end of all that, restoring good relations between Eldon and Arcadia. But also a gaggle of geese.

I hadn't lost a weight of responsibility, I'd lost all the power that had come with it, making all my goals much more difficult to achieve. I couldn't even help Arvin—although I was still determined to try.

"You may follow me to the servants' wing," Mrs. Pine began, just as my stomach gurgled loudly.

I flushed with embarrassment, but Mrs. Pine's efficient air softened somewhat.

"I can imagine you must be hungry. We can make our first stop the kitchens where I am sure there is something left from lunch that you could have right away."

"Thank you," I said, relieved by her kindness as much as the promised food. "And I'm sorry to be difficult, but I also lost all my baggage."

She nodded briskly. "You are not the first person to come into the employ of the palace in need of a full kit out." She began walking, and I scrambled to keep pace. "I think in the circumstances it would be better if you had your own space to sleep. Thankfully a small alcove has just come available. I will ensure some appropriate clothing and basic supplies are left there for you before nighttime."

I breathed a quiet sigh of relief. I hadn't even considered the possibility of sharing a room, and I could only imagine that roommates would end up asking the kind of questions I couldn't answer. No doubt they would be utterly bemused at my ineptitude. I was used to thinking of myself as a capable person, but even that had been stripped away. The sort of skills I had spent my life learning would do me no good as a goose girl.

The wing we approached jutted out toward a building that looked like a large stable, a fact I filed away for future reference. A hum of energy and activity filled the servants' wing and the yard around it, but everyone stepped aside for Mrs. Pine. She reminded me of our own housekeeper, monarch of her own domain.

She led me into an empty dining hall, filled with long wooden tables, and directed me to take a seat.

"I will send someone back with some food as soon as possible," she said. "And I will inform the Poulterer about your arrival. He will instruct you in your duties."

I could only be grateful that as an apparent personal maid, I wasn't expected to have any experience with geese.

I nodded and thanked her again, and she swept out of the room, leaving me alone in the large, echoing space.

Within minutes a scullery maid appeared with a bowl of steaming stew and a large hunk of bread. She regarded me with large, curious eyes but merely commented that someone would come to show me to my bed once I was finished eating.

Despite all my fear and anxiety, I ate quickly, the food simple but satisfying. I was mopping up the last of the stew with the bread when a new face appeared.

"I'm Nikki," the woman, at least ten years my senior, said. "And I hear you're Sierra."

She waited, but I couldn't immediately think of a response. My situation was bad enough without having to answer to Sierra's name for an unknown length of time.

"I actually prefer Elle," I said at last, and then felt the need to add, "It's an old family nickname."

The words were true since I vastly preferred Elle to Sierra, and I had insisted my family use the shortening for the entirety of my sixth year. The day after my birthday I had made an abrupt turn and insisted they return to using the more formal Giselle. I remembered being struck by the certainty that my full name was more appropriate for my important role as a princess. Which perhaps meant Elle was the perfect choice for my new, decidedly not formal, role as goose girl.

"Elle, then," Nikki said cheerfully. "Mrs. Pine has assigned you a sleeping alcove. I can take you to it if you're finished."

"Yes, thank you." I glanced in the direction of the stables. I was far more interested in returning outside than in seeing my bed, but I didn't wish to offend these people or make a fuss. I would lose any chance I had of influencing them if I confirmed Sierra's words about my disordered mind.

"Attacked on the road," Nikki said as we exited the dining hall. "I never heard of such a thing!" She glanced at me sideways before continuing. "Our roads have been safe for years now. Ever since Alyssa came."

"Princess Alyssa?" I couldn't quite keep the surprise out of my voice. "Ever since she married Prince Maximilian, you mean?"

"Yes, I should use her title." Nikki grinned. "But even after all these years it's hard to remember sometimes." She couldn't quite hide the note of pride in her voice. "For those of us who knew her before, I mean."

She looked vaguely disappointed when I didn't question her further, but Celine had told me the stories about how Alyssa had once been a woodcutter's daughter who stumbled upon the Arcadian winter castle in a storm. That she had finished by marrying the prince would once have astonished me beyond belief, but when the High King opened up the way between our two sets of kingdoms, the godmothers—always active in the Four Kingdoms —had returned to our lands as well. Now we were relearning the old ways.

Prince Maximilian was the crown prince, and a land ruled by true love prospered for all. There was a reason godmothers aided princes and princesses as they did.

"I hope no new darkness is coming," I said heavily, "after so many years of peace."

Nikki gaped at me, and I realized too late that my words were hardly promoting the impression I was unaffected by the attack.

"Gracious, I hope not!" she said. "Why? Do you think there might be a darkness coming? Weren't they just robbers, then?" She gave me another intense sideways glance.

For a moment I was tempted to try telling her the truth that they had been Eldonian traitors. But I didn't want to risk her seeing me babbling soundlessly as the queen had done.

"I don't know," I said instead.

She looked disappointed. Her age and familiarity with the princess suggested she was far too senior a staff member to be assigned to showing me my bed. And I knew full well how fast information spread in a palace. Had she heard about me and volunteered for the task in the hope that she would find me full of interesting information—or at least excitingly deranged? I could only hope that since I was forced to disappoint her on one count, I would also succeed at disappointing her on the other. I forced myself to make an effort.

"The palace is beautiful," I said. "Are the staff happy working here?"

"Oh, yes. There's a few who prefer a different sort of hustle and bustle, like you can find at the Blue Arrow Inn, but for most, you can't find a better place to work than the palace. We get paid fair and all have time off—even the scullery maids and messenger boys. And Mrs. Pine and Dorkins don't hold with no trouble."

I nodded appreciatively. We had already passed a number of people hurrying to and fro, and all seemed full of energy and good cheer, even if they did all give me looks of undisguised curiosity.

"Ah, here we are," Nikki said, pushing open a plain wooden door.

I blinked at it. *Alcove,* Mrs. Pine had said, but it looked remarkably like a broom cupboard to me. Peering through the doorway, I saw a bed had somehow been wedged inside, leaving a narrow strip of space beside it. Only the small window made me question my initial impression of a storage closet. I had slept in caves on a snow-covered mountain, but I had never slept in a room like this. My twinge of distaste made me feel guilty. I had told Sierra she didn't understand the true role of a princess, but perhaps I had forgotten as well if I thought it was about sleeping in nice beds and having lots of space to move.

"There's tubs under the bed for your things," Nikki said. "Once they've been delivered, that is. I'm sure they will be along any time now. Annice is in charge of the servants' uniforms, and she's not one to dally. She'll have something your size sitting by, you mark my words."

She surveyed the neat bed with a satisfied look. "You're mighty near the kitchens here, so there might be some noise, but better than a roommate who snores, eh?" She grinned. "Most of us have rooms on the next floor up, but you have to work for years to get seniority for a single one."

Her satisfied look told me that she currently enjoyed the privilege.

"I'm very grateful to Mrs. Pine." It was certainly a better situation than some I had envisioned in the last few hours, and I was determined to be comfortable in it. I would prove to myself, along with Sierra, that being a princess wasn't about the life of luxury and power she seemed to think it.

"Well, I suppose I should leave you now," Nikki said slowly, giving me a hopeful look.

I made no effort to convince her to stay, nor to ask her for a tour, so she completed her farewell. Pointing further down the corridor, she told me where to find the kitchens, adding that many of the servants gathered in the dining hall in the evenings.

As soon as she had disappeared from sight, I abandoned my room—if it could be called that—without a backward glance, heading in the direction of the kitchens.

CHAPTER 5

*E*very palace kitchen I had ever seen had a door out into the yard, and the Arcadian one was no different.

I slipped through the chaos of the huge room, full of people laboring over the evening meal. Someone rushed by, nearly colliding with me, too intent on her task to either apologize or upbraid me.

I was more prepared for the second near collision, sidestepping the servant as she rushed back in the other direction. The smells made me want to linger, but thoughts of Arvin drove me on.

Coming out into the yard, I paused for a moment to get my bearings. It only took a moment to orient myself and identify the vast stables. Breaking into a run, I crossed the small open space and burst through the doors.

Long rows of stalls stretched out before me, full of familiar smells and the sound of stomping hooves and whuffing breaths. Somewhere down the row, a horse neighed, and another answered.

I looked around wildly before forcing myself to take a deep breath. More than ever it was important that I present a calm and reasoned presence. But my heart beat too fast, reflecting back my fear that I might already be too late. Surely they wouldn't have acted with such speed? Would they?

"Can I help you?" a vaguely familiar voice asked.

My eyes found Philip, leaning against the doorway of a small storage room wedged between two stalls. I walked down the row toward him.

"I'm looking for my horse. Have you seen him? The one without saddle or bridle?"

He raised an eyebrow. "Your horse?"

"Oh, well..." I floundered. "I mean Princess Giselle's horse, of course. Arvin."

"Ah, yes, I know how it can be with royals." He began to chew on a long strand of straw, something almost like amusement in his eyes. "Every mount is interchangeable to them, and it's left up to us poor servants to love the beasts."

"I don't know what royals he's talking about," said a new voice. "But it isn't ours." A groom popped out of a nearby stall. "Our princess still visits old Starfire whenever she gets the chance, although she has a younger mount for everyday riding now. And the young princesses cried for a week when their old ponies passed."

It took me a moment to untangle the various princesses he referenced. 'Our princess' must be Princess Alyssa, the only adult princess left in Arcadia. And when he spoke of the young princesses, he must mean Lily and Sophie—Prince Max's younger twin sisters, now happily married and living across the sea in two of my own group of kingdoms. I wished I could tell him I knew the twins and ask for stories about their childhood. But that was the sort of thing I would have done as Princess Giselle. I was Elle the goose girl now, and I had no business knowing princesses.

Looking at the man more closely, I realized I recognized him.

"You!" I said. "You're the one she spoke to. I'm looking for Arvin. Princess Giselle's horse. Did you find him?"

Philip removed the straw from his mouth. "Lark here has come to make a farewell visit to that magnificent steed she rode into our kingdom."

The amusement still laced his voice, so I glared at him.

"My name isn't Lark."

"No, but I heard you don't like your real one," he said, undaunted by my cold tone.

I bit my lip. Word really did spread fast in this palace.

"Do I look like I have wings to you?" I snapped, still galled that he could find Arvin's fate amusing.

"Short for Larkspur," he said, returning the straw to his mouth, his eyes laughing at me. "Your eyes are the exact same shade of blue as the larkspur my grandmother has in her garden back home."

I put my hands on my hips. "So you've named me for a poisonous weed, then?"

"You wound me, Lark," he said, looking entirely unperturbed. "I wouldn't call it a weed."

I narrowed my eyes, but before I could say anything, the groom stepped in.

"Ignore Philip. The rest of us do. He should have started by reassuring you that we are not in the business of putting down perfectly healthy animals here in Arcadia."

I let out a long, shaky breath, gripping a nearby stall door for support.

"I will say he's rather an odd animal, though," the groom added.

I laughed, my relief making it sound slightly hysterical. "That would be putting it mildly."

"Harry, by the way," he said.

"Lark," Philip interjected, before I could respond.

"Elle," I said firmly, keeping my attention on Harry.

"It seems someone on that ship of yours doesn't know horses very well," Harry said. "I can't imagine how they came to the conclusion he was dying."

"Although it's a little easier to see how they thought he was in pain," Philip said, surprising a reluctant snort of amusement out of me. How Arvin would love to hear his haughty aloofness compared to a stomachache.

"I didn't think he could be so very ill," I said, trying to choose my words carefully to avoid being silenced by the enchantment.

"I'm sure your princess will be overjoyed by the news," Philip said, still watching me with that strange look of amusement. "I suppose you'll want to run off immediately to tell her?"

"Oh, didn't you hear?" I asked innocently. "I look after geese now, not princesses."

"An upgrade then." His eyes laughed at me.

I glared back, although he could hardly be expected to guess I was a princess myself.

"I suppose the next one of us to see her will have to pass on the good news," Harry said in an utterly bland voice.

"Yes, indeed. We wouldn't want to keep her in grieving suspense," Philip replied in grave tones.

I looked at Harry and then back to Philip.

"An excellent plan." A smile twitched at my lips, pulling them upward, my irritation with Philip fading away.

Clearly these men had a loyalty to their horses that transcended even royalty, and they knew when something was off, even if they didn't know what it was. It might be weeks before Sierra discovered Arvin was still alive. And there was little she could do when that moment came. She couldn't order her horse killed for no reason—not when she had a character to maintain.

"Is he in here?" I asked. "Can I see him?"

Philip laughed. "You should have seen the look of disdain he gave the first stall we offered him. In the end, poor Harry had to give him one of the larger stalls they normally reserve for brooding mares."

I chuckled. "That sounds about right. Is it down the end?"

I began walking, eager to see Arvin with my own eyes, and the two men trailed behind. I had thought Arvin might hear us and put his head out to greet me, but there was no sign of him.

I found him two stalls before the end of the building. He was focused on munching his way through a bucket of oats, and when I called his name, he merely flicked an ear back in my direction.

"Let me guess," I said. "He refused the hay?"

"We know not to offer such an insult again," Philip said wryly.

"If you put him out to pasture, he'll eat grass," I said.

Reluctantly, Arvin huffed.

"But he'll only accept oats, corn, and apples from humans," I finished before turning back to the horse. "Greetings to you too."

You're forgetting sugar cubes.

I let myself into his stall, closing the half-door behind me. The two men immediately leaned against it, watching us with interest.

That worm tried to have me killed, Arvin said. *I told you we should have left her behind.*

I sighed. "You were right, as it turned out."

I believe I've mentioned before that you should accept I'm always *right. It's for your own good.*

I laughed shakily, burying my face in his mane to hide the tears suddenly filling my eyes. I never thought I would be so glad to hear his strange voice.

What are you blubbering about? he asked. *You can't imagine I would have let them kill me, do you?*

Hearing him say it filled me with a certainty that he was right, however illogical it seemed, which only succeeded in making me feel like a fool. I pulled away, my tears gone.

"For all his temperament, he's an impressive animal," Harry said, looking over Arvin's form appreciatively. "Are all horses like that in Eldon? There'd be a market for them here in the Four Kingdoms if they are."

I shook my head. "No, Arvin is one of a kind, I'm afraid."

"Where did he come from?" Philip asked.

"You'd have to ask the princess about that," I said, with perverse satisfaction. The knowledge of Arvin's origins hadn't been shared outside of my immediate family. Let Sierra struggle to come up with an answer.

I turned back to whisper my news to Arvin. "Tomorrow I start my new role as a goose girl. So I'm not sure when I'll be able to visit you."

He paused in his eating and directed a repressive eye toward me.

I think you're forgetting who is in whose charge. I will visit you if needful.

"What, not even a little surprise at hearing I've become a goose girl?" I asked.

He returned to his oats. *I could smell the enchantment on you as soon as you walked into the stables. I would have smelled it as soon as you got out of the carriage, but I was forced to contend with a number of pesky grooms who were attempting to herd me. Me! Can you imagine?*

I could imagine, and I had to stifle a chuckle of amusement at the mental image. Not that his explanation made much sense. I hadn't been enchanted to become a goose girl. But it didn't seem worth the bother of pointing that out. Arvin didn't like to acknowledge any fallibility, and apparently only imminent danger to my life was enough to rouse his concern.

"Well, if you're happy here, I'll leave you be, then," I said.

He flicked his tail. *Happy would be a stretch.*

I rolled my eyes. "Have a good night, Arvin."

I stepped out of the stall and started back down the aisle. Philip fell into step beside me.

"You talk to your horse like he can actually understand you."

I shrugged. "Can't your horses?"

He grinned. "I like you, Lark. I would hate to discover you were up to something nefarious."

I glared at him. "Nefarious? Is that what you think about every new arrival at the palace—or am I special?"

"Oh, you're definitely special," he said, with a dangerous grin. "I can sense it. I'm good at sensing that sort of thing. I just haven't made up my mind what kind of special."

"I haven't made up my mind about you, yet, either," I said. "You don't seem at all like a regular coachman."

That surprised a laugh out of him. "Maybe that's because I'm not a coachman."

I faltered mid-stride, turning to stare at him. "Not a coachman? What's that supposed to mean?"

He had an amused smile on his face that I didn't like at all. "It's been most interesting meeting you and your impressive horse, Lark. I hope you find Arcadia to your liking." He nodded and sauntered away while I continued to stare at him.

Growling to myself, I turned and stalked out of the stables. I had enough mysteries on my hands without adding Philip to them.

I had almost succeeded in putting the irritating man out of my mind when I arrived back at my storage cupboard and all thought of him disappeared.

"What are you doing here?" I snapped at Sierra, glaring at her as I closed the door behind me, shutting us both into the tiny space.

She stood up from where she had been sitting on the edge of my bed and smiled.

"Lovely room you have here. Do you want to hear about mine?"

I rolled my eyes. "If you think I care about my room in the middle of all this, then you don't know me at all."

"Actually, so far it seems I know you quite well enough," she said, the satisfaction in her voice nearly tipping me over the edge.

"Percy was delighted to renew our old friendship and has already begged me to join him on his daily rides through the park. Clearly I'm well able to pass for a princess."

I snorted. If Percy had taken to *begging* young ladies to accompany him for exercise then he definitely hadn't improved with age. I tried to imagine his older brother Gabe saying anything like that and failed.

"Have fun with that," I said. "I hope you *begged* him to provide you with a mount."

"Are you still upset about Arvin?" Sierra asked with faux sympathy. "I can't imagine why. He was the most useless horse I ever saw."

She paused for a moment and looked disappointed when I didn't burst into tears or lash out at her. I let the silence draw out. I certainly wasn't going to tell her Arvin was safe.

"Did you want something?" I asked, ice in my voice.

"Just to check on you, of course."

"What, worried your enchantment is failing already?"

She shuffled forward, standing almost toe-to-toe with me.

"Of course not, don't get your hopes up. I'm just making sure you know you're to stay out of my way. If you interfere with me —if I so much as see you—I will use my new position to make sure you don't bother me again."

"I'm the palace goose girl now, remember? And you're planning to go riding in the palace park every day. I'm afraid there's every chance your delicate sensibilities will be forced to endure the sight of me from time to time."

Sierra glared at me with narrowed eyes. "Just stay out of my way."

She spun around and attempted to wrench open the door for a dramatic exit, but nearly tripped over me in the process. I made no effort to assist her, and she barely caught herself.

With a single, angry sniff, she managed to get the door open and disappeared. I took a deep breath of my own and collapsed onto the bed. The day felt like it would never end.

And yet, as I lay there, I didn't feel in the least sleepy. Sierra's unexpected visit worried at me. She had already bound me by enchantment not to reveal her identity—why her desperation to keep me away? Had Percy been less convinced than she claimed? Did she still fear he would recognize me?

The idea held a kernel of hope, but I couldn't escape the feeling that something else was going on—that Sierra wanted me to stay away because she hadn't yet achieved her true purpose here. And if my former maid wanted more in life than becoming a princess, what could it possibly be?

CHAPTER 6

$\mathcal{T}$he bell that rang through the servants' wing the next morning clanged far too loudly. I groaned and rolled over, the deluge of memories from the day before flooding over me.

Thankfully my uniform and basic supplies had been delivered as promised, so I was soon dressed in a simple, hard-wearing dress and eating breakfast in the dining hall. A crowd of servants surrounded me. Some ate silently, their surly expressions clearly communicating their dislike of early mornings. Others called cheery greetings and chatted over their bowls of porridge.

When the bell rang, I had bitterly missed a quiet maid bringing a tray of breakfast to my room. But now that I was up, I found I quite enjoyed the communal atmosphere of the dining hall, everyone starting their day together. I hadn't expected to find any enjoyment in my circumstances, and it buoyed me up.

Nikki spotted me and waved. I smiled back but didn't attempt to join the group around her. I had too much on my mind to want company with my meal. Merely sitting among the crowd was enough for now.

But even as I thought it, my eyes were searching the crowd of their own volition. When I realized I was looking for Philip, I sternly trained my gaze back on my bowl. My curiosity about him could wait until after I discovered if I was going to survive my first day of goose herding.

A grizzled older man found me as I was returning my bowl to one of the trays laid out for dishes.

"You my new herder?" he barked out.

I swallowed and nodded, and when his expression turned thunderous, quickly murmured, "Yes, sir."

His eyes narrowed, but otherwise his face returned to calm.

"I'm told you've no experience, but it seems no one has the inclination to find me a proper replacement. Not for a temporary position. Which means I'll have to accept you. However unsatisfactory you may be."

I had never experienced such a complete dismissal, but I found myself amused rather than offended. The emotion was a relief—as if I had passed the first test set by myself.

"I'm a quick study," I told him.

"I'll be the judge of that, young lady."

"It's Elle," I offered, but he merely narrowed his eyes again and stomped off toward the exit.

After a brief moment of uncertainty, I ran after him, quickly catching up. I found him mid-instruction and struggled to catch the import of his words. Something about startling easily? But whether he meant me or the geese I couldn't be sure and didn't dare ask.

"We have six ganders, and I try to keep them to three geese each, but every now and then one of them manages to attract himself a fourth," he said next. "But the flock also has goslings at the moment, so you'll need to move slowly and be ready to defend them—and yourself until the adults get used to you."

I stared at his back with wide eyes. That sounded terrifying.

We left the building, circling around past the stables to the back of the palace. Stretching before us was a large area of green with small copses of trees dotting the expanse. It was a larger area than I had been expecting, the city wall too distant to disturb the effect of the park.

On the near edge of the green stood a large wooden pen. Honking and rustling sounded from inside, and I approached slowly, falling behind the Poulterer. But he unlatched the gate and disappeared inside, leaving me little choice but to follow.

The smell hit me first, making me gasp. I drew back instinctively at the onslaught of flapping white and gray feathers. But when none of them flew forward to attack me, I took a fortifying breath—instantly regretting it and resolving to breathe only through my mouth—and stepped forward.

"Oi, you lot!" the Poulterer shouted.

Somehow, miraculously, the noise and fluttering actually abated to a noticeable degree. Unfortunately the smell was not so easily addressed. A fluffy, moving carpet seemed to stretch across the floor of the pen, between the full-sized geese. How many goslings were there?

"This is your new herder," he said. "Just til Colin gets back from his ma's. You listen to her, and she'll keep you safe." He glanced sideways at me and added in a mutter, "I hope."

"Can they actually understand you?" I asked, astonished.

He stared at me as if I was daft and shook his head. "Sent me the dregs, have they? Of course they can't understand me, girl." He shrugged. "But it never hurts to try. All of these lot were raised here at the palace, and they've known me since they flopped out of their shells."

"Oh, right…" I bit my lip, surveying the birds. I'd spent too much time around Arvin.

"Here." The Poulterer retrieved a long, straight wooden staff from where it leaned against the inside of the pen, near the gate. "Take this. You use it to herd them, like I was saying. Just sort of sweep them along with it, guiding 'em, sorta. First one side, then the other."

He eyed me uneasily. "Think you can manage that?"

A large part of me wanted to say no, but I squared my shoulders and nodded confidently. I would not be defeated by a gaggle of geese.

"Very well, off you go, then." He opened the gate again and stepped through, holding it open behind him and handing me the staff. It was nearly as tall as me and more solid than I had been expecting.

The honking resumed, the geese surging toward the opening while I scrambled to get out of their way. That was it? I wasn't to receive any further instruction?

"But…what do I actually do with them all day?"

He shook his head. "Let them eat, girl, let them eat. What else? When they've eaten the grass right down in one area, move them to another. And don't let any predators at them. Especially the goslings." He nodded toward the staff gripped uncertainly in my hand. "Another use for that."

Thank goodness we were in a walled park. I couldn't imagine any predators of serious size getting near us. A fortunate situation since there seemed to be about four times as many goslings as adults.

The birds took off, waddling forward in a pack, and I hurried after them, making no attempt to control their direction. They were heading into the green park, and that was enough for me.

One of the goslings started to veer away, but urgent honking recalled it, and it rejoined the group before I remembered the staff I carried. I glanced back to see if my lapse had been witnessed, but thankfully the Poulterer had already disappeared.

Two geese moved further to the left, separating from the group, and this time I was ready. Sweeping the long wooden pole in front of me, I shooed them back toward the others. They changed course, rejoining the group, and I let out a relieved breath.

Several minutes later, I had almost gotten the hang of the

staff, swinging it first to one side, then the other in a wide v shape, keeping the gaggle together. But I still wasn't actually directing them, and I began to wonder if I was supposed to do so. Surely they wouldn't wander the park endlessly if left to themselves?

A minute later, I had my answer. The birds' progress slowed and halted as we reached the edge of one of the small clusters of trees. Here the grass was noticeably longer than it had been closer to the pen, and the birds spread out, honking as they each found a place to eat.

Looking around, I found a flat-topped rock and took a seat, surveying the birds. Now that they were more or less stationary, I could count them. I spotted twenty-five adult birds. I knew from the Poulterer that six of them were ganders, but I couldn't do more than guess at which ones. The number of goslings was harder to pin down since there were more of them, and they kept shifting before I had finished counting. But after a number of failed attempts, I settled on one hundred and two.

No sooner had I determined the total number, than I began obsessively counting them again. What would happen if one of them wandered away, and I didn't notice?

I attempted the futile exercise over and over, each time losing count part way through. But as the morning wore on, I grew more familiar with their behavior, and my anxiety lessened.

When the goslings began to wander away, one of the adult geese would call them back to the group, just as they had done to the wandering gosling on our walk here. At one point, such a honking and flapping broke out from several of the geese that I launched off my rock and went running. I discovered a fox who, while undaunted by the angry geese, took one look at me and my solid staff and turned tail.

I remained vigilant for another minute, standing guard where the fox had approached, before returning thoughtfully to my rock. It seemed my task would be a little easier than I had feared.

As long as I made sure I hadn't lost any of the adult birds, they would watch over their own babies. Which made perfect sense now I thought about it.

The hours dragged on until the sun reached its zenith, and I at last gave myself permission to open the packet of food I had been handed by someone from the kitchens. I had carried it with me in a small satchel, alongside the water skin I had been given.

Inside, I found bread, cheese, and an apple. It was simple fare but appealing enough after waiting so many hours for it. Any internal fears that I might find myself holding my nose up at it were dispelled as soon as the smell hit me. I already suspected that boredom was likely to be my greatest suffering in this job, with the midday meal a major moment of interest during the day. I had seen several groups of nobles go riding past, but all kept their distance from the gaggle.

As I finished the bread and cheese, another group rode into sight. I glanced at them idly before stiffening and rising to my feet. Sierra trotted past, accompanied by three other riders. A small escort of guards rode behind at a respectful distance.

For an unthinking moment, I thought the group included Oliver's friend, Gabe. But I immediately realized it must actually be Percy, his younger brother. The two looked remarkably similar.

The guards with them wore local uniforms, not the colors of Gabe and Percy's kingdom of Talinos, so they weren't part of Percy's entourage. Were the other riders with them local royalty, then? Crown Prince Maximilian and Princess Alyssa, perhaps?

They rode on, out of sight, and I resumed my seat on the grass. I was still working on the apple—which turned out to be juicy with the perfect hint of tartness—when a friendly voice hailed me.

Twisting around, I spotted Philip crossing the grass toward me in long, easy strides. I began to scramble to my feet, but he waved me back down.

"Don't get up. I'll join you." He threw himself to the ground beside me and gave me a broad smile. "How goes the goose herding, Lark?"

"There seems to be a lot more sitting than herding involved."

He laughed.

I surreptitiously examined him. He looked different from the day before, now wearing the standard outdoor uniform I'd seen a couple of gardeners wearing.

"The palace park seems a strange place to meet a not-coachman," I said. "Unless you're actually a gardener. In which case the driving seat of a carriage was a strange place to meet a gardener."

"I'm not a gardener, either."

I put my hands on my hips. "Then what are you?"

He shrugged. "I suppose I'm a sort of jack of all trades. I help out wherever I'm needed."

I raised an eyebrow. "So what are you doing here?"

He grinned at me. "Checking that the new goose girl hasn't lost any of the geese."

"Well, then?" I stared him down. "Go on, count them. Are they all there?"

He stared briefly at the gaggle before turning back to me.

"All accounted for. Well done."

I narrowed my eyes. "There's no way you counted all of them."

"I counted the ones that matter."

I bit my lip. It was a hard strategy to fault since it was the one I had decided to adopt myself.

"Rumor is that you're mentally disturbed by the attack on the road." His tone didn't indicate what he thought about these apparent rumors.

"Do I look unbalanced?" I snapped.

"No, not in the least," he said calmly, and I relaxed.

"Which leads me to wonder," he continued, "what you're doing out here herding geese."

I stiffened. I'd fallen into that trap far too easily.

"Maybe I prefer it," I said.

"Do you?" he asked.

"Would you want to work for her?" I muttered under my breath, but he must have caught my words because he chuckled.

"No, I can't say I would."

I looked at him sideways, wishing I could see inside his head. What did Philip know of Sierra?

"Personally, I'm not one for serving at the beck and call of royalty," he said, as if in answer to my thoughts.

"Isn't that what you're doing now? I could have sworn you were a servant just like the rest of us."

"Oh, but this is different." He stretched out his legs. "I don't see any royalty."

I glanced around, but he was right, there were no riders in sight. I nearly pointed out that he'd only just missed them, but something made me pause.

"Exactly how much oversight does a new goose girl need?" I asked instead.

He raised an eyebrow. "Why do you ask?"

I shrugged and played with a blade of grass. "I just thought if you're going to come out to check on me again tomorrow, you might as well come a little earlier and join me for lunch."

I looked up in time to catch a hint of surprise on his face, although it was quickly replaced by a pleased smile.

"Perhaps I will."

"But you'll have to bring your own food," I added quickly. "I don't intend to share my own rations."

He stood and gave me a deep bow. "A gentleman would do no less, of course. Tomorrow, then."

He loped away without further farewell. I watched him go, my brows knit. I couldn't deny it felt lonelier now, and colder, without his presence and warm smile. But I felt uneasy as well.

I had grown up in a palace, so I knew something of their

ways. Servants who were accepted in the stables—sent on important missions as coachman, even—didn't tend to check on geese the next day. He had said he helped out where needed, but those sort of servants—when they existed at all—sat at the bottom of the hierarchy. They didn't carry themselves with Philip's confidence, or talk to senior grooms as equals.

There was something strange about Philip, something he wasn't telling me. And I couldn't help but remember that Sierra and her men had implanted themselves in my own palace. Was it possible Sierra had men positioned here in Arcadia as well? Philip certainly seemed to be showing undue interest in me, but I hated to think it was at Sierra's orders.

I sighed. I had no way to force him to tell me the truth. I could just hope that Sierra and Percy intended to ride at the same time every day. Observing Sierra and Philip together might give me the answer I needed.

$\mathcal{I}$n the afternoon, grown overconfident by the smooth progress of the morning, I decided to herd the geese to a new spot. I reasoned it would provide them with fresh grass and myself with new environs to observe.

However, no sooner did I start calling to them and waving my staff around, than the largest of the birds rushed at me, honking and hissing. He flapped his wings, suddenly appearing at least twice as large as before, and I quickly retreated.

I hovered for a moment at a safe distance before giving up and plonking back onto the ground. We had moved slightly during the course of the day, leaving close-cropped grass behind us, and apparently that was sufficient for the birds. I began to think apprehensively about the coming evening and the need to return to the shed. Why hadn't the Poulterer given me more instruction?

The afternoon passed slowly, my mind revolving endlessly between rage at Sierra's betrayal, growing concern for the safety of Daria, Cassie, and Daisy, and constant, fruitless speculation about Philip. Sierra had made me doubt myself, but already I was disproving my fears that I was reliant on a life of luxury and ease. But it wasn't enough. A true princess put her kingdom first, and she always found a way. I couldn't sit here, tamely tending geese while Sierra caused untold damage to our kingdom's standing.

Thankfully, as the sun began to dip lower and lower in the sky, the most immediate of my problems solved itself. With a sudden loud honking and rustling of wings, the geese all gathered themselves up and turned for home. I scrambled to my feet and fell in behind them. The sweeping motion of the staff came easily after the morning's practice, but I still felt like a fraud. I couldn't actually direct the gaggle with it, merely prevent the occasional stray from wandering free.

I counted the adults three times as we walked, relief making me light as a feather when the pen finally came into view. The Poulterer stood by the gate, waiting for me, arms crossed, so I quickly counted them again. Still twenty-five adults. The birds streamed into the pen, honking loudly, and I ducked inside to replace the staff where it had been leaning against the inside wall.

As soon as I was back out, the Poulterer whipped the gate closed and glared at me.

"You seem to have done well enough."

"Oh...I..." I struggled to find a response, thrown off by the contradiction between his face and words. "I did my best," I managed at last.

He grunted, nodded, and strode off quickly enough that I concluded he didn't mean me to follow. As a princess I had learned to read people and diplomatic situations, but it seemed reading people was a skill servants had need of as well. Did they study their masters with as much dedication as I studied the ambassadors and royals my family negotiated with?

I hurried back toward my cupboard, eager to be out of my dress which already smelled of goose. I had been given three dresses and had already decided to designate one of them to be worn only in the evenings or on days off. The dirty dress I hung half out the window, hoping the breeze would blow away some of the stench.

Despite my physical inactivity, I thought myself tired enough to fall straight into bed, but my stomach wasn't so easily satisfied. And once I had finished the evening meal, I found my strength returning.

Most of the servants lingered in the dining hall after they finished eating as Nikki had told me. Everyone helped to clear the tables, and then instruments appeared from some hidden corner of the room. People called out competing requests, stomping their feet and banging the tables in good-natured enthusiasm. Soon a rollicking tune had begun, the haphazard collection of instruments blending surprisingly well. The relaxed camaraderie was even more appealing than the bustle of breakfast had been.

Many of those around me sang enthusiastically to the unfamiliar songs, no one seeming to find lack of musical ability a barrier to participation. So when, to my surprise, they started on a tune I recognized—an ancient folk song—I got up the courage to sing with them. I quickly had to stop, however, discovering this version contained subtle differences in both wording and tune compared to the song I had grown up with. Apparently it had evolved differently in the generations our two groups of kingdoms had been separated by the High King's wall of storms.

But perhaps, by the time my own children were old enough to sing, enough ties would have been formed between our kingdoms that these songs would be as familiar in Eldon as they were in Arcadia. That was the hope that had brought me here, and I clung to it, despite my changed circumstances.

The next morning, Philip found me as I was finishing my breakfast. The bowl he held was already empty, and he didn't sit.

"I'm sorry, Lark, I won't be able to join you today, after all," he said.

I tried to hide my disappointment. And tried to tell myself it was purely because I wished to uncover his secrets sooner rather than later.

"But I promise to be there tomorrow," he added, "if you'll still have me."

I nodded, and he was gone before I had a chance to wonder if his words meant we were dropping the charade of him checking on the geese. It took me most of the morning to decide how I felt about that, and even when I concluded it was suspicious, a small part of me held on to the idea it was a compliment.

I yanked at the sensible braid that ran down my back. As a princess, I had never had a shortage of suitors, but apparently my mind needed the combination of sparkling eyes and mystery to lose all sense. Given my current situation, it would be just my luck for him to turn out to be in league with Sierra and toying with me for some evil purpose.

I kept a close eye on my surroundings as I ate my midday meal. Having learned my lesson, I had made no attempt to guide the geese, and they had chosen a spot close to the day before. Sure enough, as I was eating, I spotted Sierra and Percy riding across the grass. This time they were alone, but for a single guard trailing behind, this one in Percy's colors. Sierra must be making at least some headway with the Talinosian prince if they were continuing to ride together in the absence of the local royals.

A wild impulse to leap up and call to them filled me. I hadn't quite been able to eradicate the hope that Percy would recognize me. But I quashed the instinct down. If I called, Sierra would almost certainly have to respond, but I couldn't guess her reaction. There was every chance attracting their attention would be something I could do only once. Which meant I needed to wait until I could make best use of the opportunity. I needed to wait for Philip's presence.

The day dragged on, and I nearly attempted moving the geese again, only talking myself out of it at the last moment. I completed a number of exercises, using my staff in place of the blade I should have held for my practice sword dance. The piece of wood was much too long, but I managed to fumble my way through the solo training, glad Celine and Oliver couldn't see my awkward moves. Celine had fought hard to get both of us included in Oliver's sword training.

That evening I visited Arvin instead of remaining with the other servants.

There you are. He removed his head from his bucket of oats. *I was starting to think you'd come to a bad end.*

I shook my head. "I can see you were moved to great lengths by this fear."

He eyed me, unimpressed. *Just because you are apparently too irresponsible to check on me, do not assume the same is true of me.*

I was extremely tempted to press him on this statement and ask exactly how he had checked after my welfare but decided that since I had brought him into this situation, I should allow him some ill temper.

"Do you not find this stable to your liking?" I asked instead. "I could try talking to one of the grooms. The one who was here the other night seemed nice enough. Harry, I think he was called."

Arvin snorted. *They do their best, I suppose. One can only expect so much.*

I bit back a smile. Arvin wasn't usually one to temper his expectations.

But you should watch yourself, he added, his tone more serious than I had ever heard it. All desire to smile left me. *That Arcadian captain has returned. They didn't find any sign of the other girls, but they've brought back the guards. Those who are still alive are all claiming loyalty to the princess.*

He gave me an intense stare. *None of them have raised the alarm, so it's the false princess they follow. They're claiming they were attempting to track the four of you without success.* He paused, and his voice sounded unnaturally heavy. *Counting the bodies, all the guards are accounted for, including the two from Trione, so we can expect no assistance from that quarter.*

I swallowed, tears pricking my eyes. Daisy's family had trusted us, and we had failed them—as we had failed any of the guards in the squad who had been loyal, although I now suspected they had been few in number. Determination surged through my core, driving away the tears. I wouldn't now fail my kingdom. I would get to the bottom of this plot. I would prove to everyone—including myself—that I could fulfill the role I had been born into. I was more than a useless ice princess, or a tag-along hero. This time I would rescue myself from the enchantment.

I hugged Arvin, throwing my arms around his neck despite his exasperated noises. After his warning, I almost did believe that he'd somehow found a way to check on me.

"If I can possibly get us safely out of this, I will," I promised.

He whuffed at me in a less than confidence-inspiring manner, but I merely gave him an extra squeeze.

The next morning I spotted Philip moving toward me in the dining hall, and my heart sank. However, he merely winked as he strode past on the way to return his bowl. I frowned after him. Was that supposed to be a confirmation that he would visit me today? The man was infuriating.

Nikki caught me before I left the dining hall, grabbing my arm. "I'm not due upstairs for a few minutes yet. Do you want to see if we can get a glimpse of the Lanoverians leaving? Annice was going to come with me because they always have the best clothes, but one of the other servants must have had an issue with their uniform because she's been called away."

"What do you mean? What Lanoverians?" I hadn't made much sense of her rush of words, but my mind caught eagerly on the idea of Lanoverians here in Arcadia.

"You know," she said impatiently, "the Lanoverian delegation on their way to Northhelm. They arrived yesterday and spent the night here. Surely you heard about it."

Now that she mentioned it, I had overheard some vague talk at the evening meal about the king and queen having guests, but I hadn't paid it much mind. If I'd realized they were from Lanover, I would have been a great deal more interested. But I had sat alone the night before since many of the servants still seemed unsure of me. Unlike Nikki, their fear of my potential instability seemed to outweigh their curiosity.

"And they're leaving already?" I asked, sudden alarm seizing me.

Nikki gave me an odd look. "They're only passing through."

Now I was the one grabbing at her arm, towing her along behind me. "Come on then! Let's go!"

Two of Celine's sisters had married Northhelmians and lived there now. Perhaps Celine's parents, or her oldest brother, were on their way to visit them. If so, I could imagine Sierra had developed a nasty stomachache and retired to bed early yesterday because any of them would recognize me. Most of the Lanoverian royal family had made a lengthy stay in Eldon for Celine's wedding.

This was a completely unlooked for chance to expose Sierra. And if it hadn't been for Nikki, I might have missed it entirely. Clearly I should have been making more effort to mingle with the other servants.

We burst out into the bustling palace yard. People swarmed everywhere, preparing a line of carriages and a whole mass of horses. Servants and guards in Lanoverian colors mixed with the familiar Arcadian uniforms, loading carriages and issuing directions. I scanned the moving crowd, looking for familiar faces.

My eyes found King Henry and Queen Eleanor, the Arcadian rulers, standing at the top of the shallow steps down into the yard. An older woman stood beside them. I surged forward, Nikki trailing behind murmuring questions I didn't hear.

But my steps slowed and stopped before I made it all the way across the yard. Now that I was closer, I could clearly see it wasn't Celine's mother, Queen Viktoria, who stood with the Arcadian royals. The woman was dressed as elegantly as any monarch, but there was more gray in her black hair, and her features were sharper. Her expression, too, was unlike the queen I remembered. She looked alert, like she didn't miss a thing, despite her age.

"Who's that?" I asked, unable to keep the disappointment out of my voice. "Where are the royals?"

Nikki pulled me back, out of the way of a groom passing with a horse. "One of the Lanoverian princesses lives in Eldon now, doesn't she? I suppose you get lots of visits from them. But this isn't a royal visit. That's the Duchess of Sessily. The Lanoverians always send her to negotiate their treaties."

"Oh." I deflated, the excitement that had carried me here leaking out slowly and leaving me utterly flat. I had heard the name. She was supposed to be brilliant, and even Celine was a little afraid of her—which was saying something. But as the most trusted advisor to the Lanoverian throne, she had been left behind when the royal family crossed the seas for their daughter's wedding. I had never met her.

The thought of Sierra's relief only made the blow worse. I forced myself to give the crowd another look, in case I recognized some minor official, but I could see no familiar faces. Dejected, I started back toward the servants' wing.

"Where are you going?" Nikki asked.

I turned back to her, remembering we were supposed to be observing the delegation's departure.

"You're an odd one, Elle," the maid said cheerfully, and I hid my wince. My erratic behavior was hardly helping me to appear stable.

We stationed ourselves out of the way and watched as the carriages filled and the horses were wheeled into line. Nikki kept up a stream of comments on their uniforms, gowns, horses, and the rumors of how they had all behaved during the brief visit.

I let her words wash over me, making the occasional noise of agreement when it seemed expected. The duchess was the last to enter her carriage, and she paused before doing so, close enough for me to hear her final words with the king and queen.

"Don't worry," she said. "I shall carry your message to North-helm. If the missing girls have made it that far, they'll be found."

I stiffened, stepping forward to hear the rest of the conversation, but King Henry merely murmured his thanks and their final farewells. Nothing more of interest was said. Before I could step back, however, a tall, thin man in the clothing of a noble shouldered past me as he strode through the yard, unheeding of the crowd that filled it.

I stumbled, only just catching myself from falling, and glared at his retreating back. A clear look at him, however, revealed him to be older even than the duchess. My irritation subsided. Perhaps he hadn't seen me, although he had seemed strong for his age.

"Don't mind him," Nikki said. "That's Viscount Edgewaring. He's a grumpy old man who thinks being Lord Chamberlain is just as important as being king." She rolled her eyes.

I tried to find his back in the crowd, but he'd disappeared from view. "He seems very elderly for an official position like that."

Nikki chuckled. "Do you want to be the one to tell him that? He's had the role for as long as anyone can remember at this point, and I'm guessing he'll have it until he collapses into his eggs one morning."

I grimaced, but I couldn't dispute that the Arcadian palace seemed to run exceptionally smoothly from everything I had seen. Either the old viscount had excellent assistants, or his age had yet to slow him down.

I said goodbye to Nikki and gathered the geese, my mind returning to the overheard words between the duchess and the king. The relief of knowing they were still actively looking for my missing friends balanced against the disappointment of the delegation. And I believed the duchess when she said that if they had made it to Northhelm, they would be found.

According to Celine, her older sister Celeste was the only one more brilliant than the duchess. Her marriage to the crown prince of Northhelm had removed her from the spy network she spent her youth building in Lanover, but she had no doubt become just as familiar with her new home by now. If only she had married Prince Max of Arcadia instead, perhaps my friends would already be found.

CHAPTER 8

$\mathcal{I}$ was still stewing on the sharp emotional turns of the morning when Philip joined me in the park. He lowered himself to the grass and unwrapped an identical lunch parcel to mine. I sat a few feet away and began to eat, my eyes jumping between him and the rest of the park. Now that he was here, I was worried that Sierra and Percy might not ride by at the right time after all.

"You seem twitchy today," he said, after a few mouthfuls.

I forced myself to focus on him and smile. "Apologies. I'm just watching for my mistress. She takes a midday ride each day, and I like to check on her well-being." I smiled sweetly, as if I hoped to find her well rather than my true desire for the opposite.

"You are most diligent…considering." He gestured toward the geese, watching me nearly as closely as I was watching him.

"The world could do with some more diligence, don't you think?" I asked.

"That depends on who we're talking about." He smiled at me. "I would indeed appreciate due diligence from the doctor stitching up my wounds—but I would appreciate a little less from the bandit robbing me on the road."

If he expected that last reference to get a rise from me, he was due for disappointment. They hadn't been bandits, even if the Arcadians still thought them so.

"You often need wounds stitched up, do you?"

He chuckled. "Let's just say I was the kind of child who was a sore trial to my mother."

I couldn't help laughing in return, easily able to picture a youthful Philip getting up to mischief.

"You remind me of—" My voice went silent, my mouth continuing for half a second before I snapped it closed.

A few minutes with this man, and I was already forgetting myself and talking as my true self. But the enchantment didn't intend to let me say that he reminded me of Percy and his older brother, Gabe. A goose girl had no business talking of princes so casually, even if she had first been introduced as a lady's maid.

"Of someone back at home," I finished lamely when Philip's eyes narrowed at my abrupt silence.

He didn't look impressed at my attempt, but neither did he press further. Instead he launched into several amusing anecdotes of his own pranks and subsequent trips to the doctor, and I was so entertained that I nearly forgot to keep an eye out for Sierra.

When I did see her, already halfway through our section of the park, I leaped to my feet. Thankfully she was once again riding with only Percy, a single guard trailing them.

"Your Highness!" I yelled, jumping up and down and waving both arms. "Your Highness!"

They both turned their heads in our direction. Sierra hesitated, but her glance at Percy clearly communicated the bind I had placed her in. She couldn't ignore me in front of him. The two of them exchanged words I couldn't hear and both directed their horses toward us.

Philip looked from me to the approaching riders, curiosity all over his face. I ignored his unspoken questions, smoothing out my rumpled skirts, and straightening my hair as best I could. Now that I had forced their attention, I preferred to appear as calm and collected as possible.

The geese honked at the horses as they approached but neither attacked nor ran, apparently deciding they weren't a threat. Sierra and Percy stopped beside us, looking down at where we both now stood.

My attention was divided, my eyes flicking frantically between Percy, Sierra, and Philip, desperate to see who recognized who. Percy was gazing at me, his face reflecting the same curiosity for my odd behavior as Philip's had done a moment before. Or maybe he just wanted to hear about the infamous deranged maid.

Did he know me, now that he saw Sierra and me side by side? When I saw no flicker of recognition or even unease in his eyes, I dismissed him, turning my full concentration to Sierra and Philip.

Dropping into a light curtsy, I looked up at the false princess.

"Are you well, Your Highness?" I asked her. "I hear your companions haven't been found." I couldn't entirely keep my voice light for the final sentence. Hopefully the two men would attribute it to natural emotions about the missing girls. At least their bodies had not been found with the missing guards. That thought had brought me considerable comfort.

"No, indeed." Sierra assumed a mournful expression. "It weighs greatly on my mind."

"On all our minds," Percy said. "I can't imagine young Daisy alone or captured." I remembered that they still thought other, external attackers were involved. "We have sent letters back to their kingdoms, but it will be many weeks before our messages will arrive and answers can be received."

His brow creased, and his hands formed into fists. "The blackguards who did this must be found and punished." He looked down at me. "Their Majesties are greatly concerned—both for the safety of the girls and the reaction of their kingdoms. Do not fear that they are taking this matter lightly."

"Thank you," I said to him. From him, at least, I knew the emotion was sincere. Daisy used to drive us all crazy, but none of us would ever want any real harm to come to her.

"It is very kind of you to inquire as to my well-being," Sierra said, "but you may assure yourself I am being most well cared for." She threw a veiled glance of triumph at Percy. Did she think herself on her way to securing a marriage with him? At the very least, she seemed to somehow think him a measure of her success at being a princess.

As if hearing her own words and realizing they reflected better on me than her, she quickly spoke again.

"I do not need to inquire as to how you are, as I have had regular reports from Mrs. Pine."

I barely refrained from glaring at her. So she was having me monitored, was she? For a moment my indignation made me lose sight of my true purpose, but a slight shifting from Philip beside me brought it rushing back. This meeting wasn't about Sierra and me.

I glanced sideways at him. He looked relaxed and interested, closely examining both Percy and Sierra impartially. As for the two of them, they had both given him only the briefest of glances, focusing their attention on me. There was no more a spark of recognition in Philip's or Sierra's eyes than there was in Percy's toward me.

I shouldn't have felt so relieved at that. Discovering a connection between them would have given me an excellent avenue of investigation. But the relief continued to bloom, filling up my insides.

"I'm sorry for disturbing you, Your Highnesses." I bobbed another quick curtsy. Now that I had the information I'd been after, there was no purpose in further irritating Sierra.

My words brought an inquisitive gleam to Philip's eyes, and I wondered fleetingly how I had mis-stepped. His glance toward Percy gave me my answer. I had no reason to know the identity of Sierra's companion. The not-coachman was altogether too quick. Although I told myself he was wrong—as Sierra's supposed personal maid, I could have recognized Percy from a state visit back in one of our own kingdoms.

Percy murmured something polite, and the two of them resumed their ride without a backward glance. Philip, however, watched them until they were out of sight.

"That was interesting," he said when they disappeared. "So that's Princess Giselle."

I busied myself sitting back down, hiding my shock at hearing him speak my true name.

"What's she really like?" he asked.

I considered the question as dispassionately as I could. What would a lady's maid say about Princess Giselle?

"Four years ago, she went up the mountain with Prince Oliver and Princess Celine and saved Eldon."

I winced internally. Could I blame everyone else for constantly harping on that one non-achievement when even I couldn't think of anything more distinctive about myself?

"We heard about that," he said. "So she's brave, then." His eyes focused on the distant spot where the riders had disappeared.

"Well," I said quickly, "it was mostly Princess Celine, truth be told. Princess Giselle was just along for the walk, so to speak." The enchantment prevented me from telling him the truth—that it had been fear as much as bravery that drove me up that mountain. Fear of being left alone in a castle full of enchanted ice people slowly losing all will to live.

He turned to me, raising an eyebrow, a slight lift to one side of his mouth.

"So, you're not impressed with her, then?"

I shrugged, struggling to put my feelings into words I was allowed to say. "She wasn't doing particularly well under Eldon's curse before Princess Celine turned up. She was just as enmeshed by it as everyone else, and rapidly losing herself to it. If it hadn't been for Princess Celine, Princess Giselle would have been as helpless in the castle as the rest of them. I guess I've been waiting to see how she does without Princess Celine to help her."

"And here's your chance," Philip said.

This time I didn't manage to keep the wince internal. So far I had only succeeded in losing my entire party and making even me question if I really knew what being a princess was all about.

"You don't think she's doing well?" He watched me far too closely. "You blame her for the attack and the missing members of your party?"

I forced a smile. "It's still early days. I suppose I'm just waiting to see how it all works out."

"I hope you don't blame yourself," Philip said, a trace of concern in his voice. "It's not your fault—or the princess's either. The guards who survived said they only did so by running once you had all disappeared. They lost the battle, and running was the only thing that saved you all. There was nothing you could do—your attackers would have killed all of you if you'd stayed. One of the remaining guards hid in a tree and saw the enemy. They carted off their own dead rather than leave any clues to trace them. They clearly knew what they were doing."

It took me a moment to assimilate these further details. It made sense they would have needed a cover story to account for the lack of actual attackers.

"You seem to know a lot about it," I said after a moment.

He smiled, not in the least discomfited. "You know what it's like in the servants' wing of a palace. You'd have heard about it yourself except you're still getting to know people."

I wasn't nearly as confident of that as he seemed to be. I was still something of an outsider among the servants, despite my enjoyment of their camaraderie. Being a princess might not be all about a life of luxury, but it seemed neither was being a servant merely about sharing the food and housing of one.

"They probably all think me terrifying," I said flatly.

He chuckled. "Maybe some. But I suspect more were motivated to keep their silence by sympathy. No one wanted to be the one to bring you bad news about your traveling companions." He paused. "But evidently you did hear the news. So you must be better connected than you fear."

I looked away, toward the geese. Let him wonder where I heard the information. I certainly wasn't going to tell him the truth. It seemed that, for some reason, he had decided I was mentally stable after all, and I didn't want to disabuse him of the notion by mentioning Arvin as my source.

He lingered into the afternoon, telling me more tales of his boyhood, although I noticed he said little about his recent history and nothing about the tasks that should have been filling his day. He made no mention of the day before, either, or what he had done instead of eating with me.

I let him draw out a couple of tales of my own childhood, carefully choosing ones that gave no indication of my location or status. He confessed that he was also the baby of his family, which immediately explained a number of the scrapes he had gotten himself into. I had also trailed around after my older brother and sister, although I had far too much sense to attempt physical feats beyond my capability.

When I informed him of such, he laughed and told me I sounded just like his sisters.

"Women of depth and wisdom, I'm sure," I told him gravely.

He laughed again. "They certainly like to think so. And I'm entirely happy to leave such things up to them."

I rolled my eyes, before fixing him with an inquiring look. I didn't want to drive him away, but I couldn't refrain from asking any longer.

"Is today your half-day off?"

I flushed faintly when I realized how my question sounded. I had meant to probe about his daily activities, but I sounded as if I was asking if he had chosen to spend his free time with me.

"I don't have regular half-days off," he replied. "Since I work when I'm needed. So I've learned to take advantage of the opportunities that present themselves."

It wasn't exactly an answer to either my actual query or my inadvertent one, but I wasn't going to push further.

"I should be getting back, though." He pushed himself to his feet while I tried to decide if it was reluctance I could hear in his voice.

Sternly, I told myself that it didn't matter. Philip didn't appear to be connected in any way with Sierra, which meant I had no reason to engineer further time with him. The fact that the afternoon had been far more pleasant than I had imagined any day here being shouldn't weigh with me.

After he left, I was abstracted, thoughts racing through my brain almost too fast to pin down. Just because Philip wasn't working with Sierra didn't mean no one else was. In fact, I knew that some at least of her traitorous guards had arrived at the palace. Were they staying with the Arcadian guards in the barracks?

The guards had their own mess hall, but there seemed to be plenty of off-duty interaction between them and the servants. Many of them had appeared at the first strains of music the other night. I tried to recall the faces of the guards who had traveled with us. Would I recognize them if I saw them in the dining hall?

Before I had the opportunity to consider the matter any further, one of the geese let out a loud honk, and the others quickly joined in, the cacophony growing in volume as many of them reared up and flapped their wings aggressively.

CHAPTER 9

I leaped up and spun, my staff gripped in front of me as I looked for the source of their alarm. It seemed too great a commotion for a single fox, although it was getting to the time of day when one might well appear.

Dark figures moved through the park, apparently having abandoned stealth in favor of speed when the geese sounded the alarm. They carried naked swords, and their attention was focused on me. I dropped instinctively into a defensive stance, my staff held out in front of me. But I could feel my awkwardness, my fingers longing for a sword.

I still had the knife in my boot, but the longer reach of the staff would serve me better now. There were three of them—and possibly more—and if they got close enough for me to use my knife, I was already lost.

As they approached closer, I glanced frantically around. The hour was late enough that no riders were in sight. Unfortunately, there was also no obvious shelter.

My eyes fell on a large rock, a short way behind me. It had a similar flat top to the rock I had sat on the first day in the park. I ran for it, willing to briefly expose my back for the advantage of higher ground.

Reaching it, I scrambled up, slipping on my skirts in my haste. I found my footing just as the first of the men reached me. He was swathed head to toe in black, a length of material wrapped around his face as well. He hesitated at the base of the rock, staring up at me.

Keeping my stance balanced, I struck out with the staff, whacking him across the side of the head. His sword, not positioned for an attack from above, was too slow to catch my staff. He swayed and dropped to a knee, cursing loudly and clutching his head with his free hand.

"I don't know why you're here, but I recommend you leave now," I said, in as threatening a tone as I could muster. "Their Majesties aren't going to allow masked men to roam the grounds of their palace killing their servants."

The man cursed again, but he was looking at the geese rather than me. They were still honking and flapping, their piercing calls echoing around us.

The other two attackers, slower runners than their leader, arrived beside him. They both looked from me to the geese, one of them murmuring something too quiet for me to catch.

"No!" the leader said. "We take her now. With three of us we can do it easily."

My hands tightened on my staff, fresh fear filling me. For a moment it had looked like I might succeed at driving them off with words and a single blow. But with three of them coming for me at once, they would be able to pull me down from the rock.

They circled around, surrounding me. I struck out with my staff, hoping to land another head blow, but they were prepared this time. My target jumped back out of my reach, the other two closing in even as he retreated.

Sweat made my hands slippery as I screamed silently at Sierra in my head. I had no doubt she had sent them. Likely they were the recovered guards, traitors just as she was.

I had a sudden picture of Daria and Cassie facing them down in such a manner, but without staffs to defend themselves, and my stomach heaved. I screamed, letting all my fear, defiance, and anger pour into the sound.

One of the men hesitated, and my eyes latched onto him, even while the leader pressed forward.

"Please," I managed, but the leader lunged toward me.

My second scream was more of a grunt of effort as I put everything I had into blocking his sword. It deflected off my sturdy staff just as hands grabbed at my legs.

I teetered and slipped, letting myself fall heavily on the man who had grabbed me, sending us both collapsing to the ground. I expected other hands to haul me off him, but they didn't come.

Instead a different scream rang over the honking of the geese, followed by a thud. I flailed, trying to right myself and only succeeding in becoming further entangled with the black clad arms and legs of the man beneath me.

He was cursing and pushing at me, trying to get me off, and I used his momentum to push myself up, stepping on him heedlessly. As soon as I felt ground beneath my feet, I dashed away, giving myself some space from the groaning man who was now hauling himself up as well.

Looking frantically around for the other attackers and the source of the scream, I found one man on the ground, a knife protruding from his thigh. Nearby, the leader wrestled with a fourth man. Somehow the masked man had lost his sword, and the two fought hand to hand.

For a moment of stunned silence, I stood staring at them. The third attacker, now upright several arms' lengths away from me, watched in equal stupefaction. But then our paralysis lifted. With a yell, he ran toward the wrestling men. I ran for the injured man.

I recognized him as the one who had hesitated at my plea, and

I dropped to my knees beside him. The enchantment binding me wouldn't let me mention anything about my true identity, but it wasn't myself I wanted to talk about.

I gripped him sharply by the shoulders, and he groaned, opening his eyes to stare at me.

"The other girls," I hissed in his ear. "Daria, and Cassie, and Daisy. What did you do to them?"

He made no attempt to prevaricate or claim ignorance, but he spoke so slowly that I shook him, hissing for him to hurry up.

"Are they dead? Have you killed them?" I could hardly bear the tension of waiting for him to spit out his answer.

"Dead? No..." He drew in a pained breath. "The older ones ran. We managed to split them up, but we couldn't find them. We chased them...like she instructed. They must be...long gone."

I drew in a shuddering breath of relief. Lost and alone was bad, but it was better than dead, or in the clutches of Sierra's guards.

"And Daisy?" I asked sharply. "The young one. I saw someone drag her away."

The man coughed, giving a gasp of pain at the sharp movement.

"She escaped." He winced, although whether at his words or his wound, I didn't know. "She's a fighter. Bit so hard she drew blood."

I let go of him, sinking backward onto my heels. They had escaped. All of them. Some of the underlying burden of dread I had been carrying lifted, despite my own danger.

Memory of the struggle going on nearby rushed back, and I twisted, looking for the other two attackers. My ally—who I now recognized as Philip—had managed to retrieve the leader's sword and stood panting, staring at him. The leader fell back, one hand clutching the opposite arm which hung as if broken.

He growled a series of commands at the third man, who hovered uncertainly nearby. Philip called my name, his eyes flickering briefly to me before leaping back to the injured leader. He gestured with his arm for me to come to him, and I jumped up as the third man rushed toward me. I raced for Philip, scooping up my abandoned staff on the way, but the third man made no move to intercept me.

Instead, he crouched by his injured companion. Ignoring the knife in his leg, he dragged the man up, slinging him over his shoulder. A sharp scream cut off abruptly as his burden slumped senseless and unprotesting.

The leader shouted something else, although I couldn't catch the words over the sound of the geese, and the two of them staggered into the deepening evening, their companion carried with them.

I stared after them. "Should we...I don't know—do something?"

"Like what?" Philip glanced down at me. "Chase after them, you mean? It seems they're willing to give up the fight to avoid being captured, which is good for us. If they decide they're cornered, they've still got enough fight in them to make it a dangerous situation for us."

I drew in several breaths so deep I started coughing.

"Thank you. For rescuing me. How did you know?"

He glanced toward the geese who were finally beginning to calm down. "I heard the geese. I hadn't made it all the way back yet, and I heard them start honking and screeching." He looked back at me and smiled for the first time since he had arrived to my rescue. "Better than guard dogs, geese. They've got excellent hearing and will raise a hue and cry at anything unusual."

I looked toward the birds with more affection than I had ever imagined feeling.

"I'm most grateful to them. They gave me warning, too. Although I must admit guard dogs would have been more useful when the danger actually arrived."

Philip chuckled softly, shaking his head. "You seem to be taking being attacked by masked assailants rather well."

"I'm just so relieved…I thought I was going to die." I didn't mention my other source of relief.

"Who was he?" Philip asked. "The man who was injured."

I frowned. "I don't know. His face was covered. They all were."

Philip turned and scrutinized me. "But you were speaking to him. Weren't you trying to find out who they were and what they wanted?"

"Oh. He…he didn't say," I said lamely.

Philip examined me for another moment and then turned his gaze out toward the park where the men had now disappeared.

"I don't think they'll be back anytime soon, but we should still get back as fast as we can. We need to report their presence in the palace grounds as soon as possible."

I glanced nervously at the geese. Philip was unaware of how little control I had over the birds, but I could imagine what the Poulterer would say if I abandoned them, no matter the reason. Hesitantly I approached the gaggle, and for once, they responded to my prodding, abandoning the grass and waddling away from me.

I let out a relieved sigh and focused all my attention on looking like I knew what I was doing. Whether we had been together long enough for them to start minding me, or whether it was an aftereffect of all the excitement, they stayed clumped close together, heading straight for their pen.

Philip walked beside me the whole way, and while I wouldn't have asked him to stay if he had said he needed to run ahead to sound the alarm, I was grateful for his presence. I kept glancing over my shoulder, wondering if the men would reappear.

"Who should I report it to?" I asked, once the geese were all safely shut away. I still kept hold of the staff, having decided I would keep it with me rather than leave it stored in the pen.

"Don't worry about that," Philip said. "I'll do it. I know where to find Captain Markus."

"Thank you," I said, secretly relieved. I didn't want to be asked a whole host of questions I couldn't answer.

"Why did they attack you, Lark?" he asked, as if half to himself. "And how did they get into the palace?"

I shrugged. I could make a fairly good guess at both answers, but I had no words to share them with him.

"Do robbers, or...or bandits often make it into the palace grounds?" I asked instead.

"No. And those men were far too well trained and equipped to be after the geese." He hefted the sword he still held, examining its length. "No identifying markings that I can see. But perhaps Markus will find it more informative."

He glanced back toward the park, now almost shrouded in darkness. "That man carried away my knife in his leg. It was my favorite one too."

"It will probably turn up, abandoned in the park somewhere. I can't imagine the men want to keep something so incriminating on them."

Philip brightened slightly. "You're probably right. I'll tell Markus to have his men look out for it." He nodded and began to stride away before pausing and looking back. "You're sure you're unharmed? Should I fetch Mrs. Pine? Or Nikki?"

"No, really, I'm fine. I promise. I don't need anyone." Being fussed over would almost certainly involve even more questions than the captain of the guard would ask.

He nodded again and left, leaving me to wonder how he had known to suggest Nikki. Had he been watching me? He had proved he wasn't working for Sierra beyond doubt now, but there was still something strange about Philip.

CHAPTER 10

*W*ord of the attack obviously reached either Mrs. Pine or the kitchens because my meal was delivered to my room on a tray. I appreciated not having to face the entire dining hall, although Nikki brought it herself, her curiosity once again overwhelming her sense of seniority.

I had to reassure her three times that I was unharmed and listen to her exclaim endlessly over the horror of armed attackers in the grounds of the palace itself. I could understand her alarm, especially since I wasn't free to reassure any of them that the men were unlikely to attack anyone else.

Eventually she left, and I ate my meal in peace, replaying the fight and my short conversation with the injured guard over and over in my head. If only I'd had time to ask him more—to find out something of what Sierra was planning. I was still sitting there, lost in thought, when a loud knock on my door made me jump, nearly sending my dirty dishes flying. I gathered them back onto the tray, leaving it on the bed while I answered the door.

Philip stood outside, carefully attempting to avert his eyes from my tiny bedroom, clearly visible through the open doorway. He looked more uncomfortable than he had while fighting off two assailants, and I nearly laughed. Stepping out into the corridor, I closed the door behind me, and he relaxed.

"I came to check on you," he said. "And to update you."

"Thank you. I'm fine. The only reason I wasn't in the dining hall is that Nikki brought me my meal on a tray."

He nodded. "I wasn't there myself. I've just come from the park. I've showed the captain where it happened. He's informed the king and roused the palace."

"The king? Roused the palace?" I gulped. I could imagine what Sierra would think of having her evening meal disturbed in such a way.

"Masked attackers in the palace grounds attempted to kill one of the royal servants," Philip said. "I can assure you, the king would want to be immediately informed."

It made sense, of course, and I should have predicted it. My father would feel the same way.

"Every room and outbuilding is being checked," Philip said. "And the park is almost as bright as day with all the torches out there. They will overturn the entire grounds to be sure the men aren't still lurking here, and then they'll plug the hole they used to get in."

He sounded grim and determined. "I'll join them in a minute. I just wanted to reassure you."

"Thank you," I said, touched by his thoughtfulness.

"I should get back to the search," he repeated, but he still lingered.

Taking one of my hands, he looked directly into my eyes. "Are you sure you're all right, Lark? That must have been a terrible shock for you." He smiled slightly. "Although I could see you were holding your own when I arrived."

I grimaced. "That might be going too far. I don't like to think what would have happened if you hadn't arrived when you did."

I shuddered as his face turned dark. "No indeed. You must promise me you won't think of it."

"I promise." I smiled up at him a little shyly. For all my desire to prove myself, and stand on my own, I couldn't deny the warmth of feeling a little less alone. Knowing someone cared made more of a difference than I would have expected. Even if I hadn't yet worked out Philip's motivations.

"Good girl," he said softly, squeezing my hand before disappearing down the corridor.

I watched him out of sight before firmly shutting myself in my room. He hadn't asked me to join the search, and I wouldn't volunteer. Everyone was safer with me out of sight tonight.

The next morning I further tested my new authority with the geese, driving them to a different part of the park, far from where they had grazed on previous days. They offered no rebellion, letting me guide them, and I appreciated the small swell of extra confidence.

I was going to need all the confidence I could muster since it was clear the king wasn't going to find my attackers or uncover the plot behind them. Philip had reported to me first thing in the morning. The entire palace and its grounds had been thoroughly searched. The attackers were gone, and a double guard had been posted at every door and gate, no matter how minor.

A small door on the far side of the park, rusted half shut, had been deemed their likely entry point. Given the long running peace, it had apparently been left without guard. And although it had been closed when they examined it, it was clear it had been forced open at some point recently.

I had to give Sierra's guards credit. They hadn't needed entry to the palace, they were already here, serving the apparent Eldonian princess. And they had no doubt sought refuge in her rooms. But they had been as thorough in creating their cover story here as they had been on the road. Given the telling nature of their injuries, it was fortunate for them that the thorough search of the palace had almost certainly not included the private quarters of a visiting princess—and one already subjected to indignity within Arcadia's borders.

As well as the increased guards at the doors and gates, patrols roamed the park and the grounds. They passed our new grazing spot several times, and as the morning progressed, my initial jumpiness faded. I couldn't see the traitors attempting such an attack again, not now they knew the geese would sound the alarm and bring a patrol running.

Not that I entirely relaxed, however. Sierra had shown her hand. Apparently hailing her and drawing attention to myself was worthy of a death sentence. Which told me two important things. One, I needed to tread carefully. Two, her plans weren't secure yet.

For some reason, despite the danger of the night before, the second revelation outweighed the first. I found myself filled with fresh hope. The increased presence of the guards not only offered me immediate protection, it also increased the pressure on Sierra. She had made a mistake last night. It would become increasingly difficult for her to act without revealing her hand.

A familiar whinny cut through my thoughts, setting the geese fluttering. I called reassurances to them, and they slowly resettled, eyeing both me and Arvin warily.

"What are you doing here? How did you get free?" I looked behind him, but the horse was alone.

Arvin snorted. *Free? You suggest I was a prisoner?* He eyed me up and down, walking in a wide circle around me to examine me from all angles. *I can see you still have all your arms and legs. I hear you have that irritating man with the outrageous mane to thank for it.*

I grinned at his description of Philip. The man did seem to always have a tousled look to his dark hair, as if he was perpetually short on time to manage it properly.

Arvin stomped a hoof and snorted, angrily. *Look at the effort you have made me expend just to ascertain your safety for myself.*

"I'm sorry," I said, instantly contrite. "I should have come to visit you last night."

Arvin calmed, whuffing at me. *See that you do so in future.*

"I hope there won't be a repeat!"

He eyed me, looking resigned. *I have no such high hopes. You are much too foolish a child. Why else would your godmother have decided you need me to watch over you?*

"I daresay you're right." I kept my expression serious with difficulty. "I'll bear it in mind."

Clearly it is no good trusting in these humans *to keep you safe.* His voice dripped with disdain. *From now on I shall keep you and these ridiculous birds company.*

The prospect filled me with a greater sense of security than it probably should have, but I still protested.

"What will Harry say about that?"

Arvin looked at me in astonishment. *You cannot imagine I care about such a thing, can you? Anyway, the human will no doubt just laugh it off. He seems the sort,* he added in dire tones.

I giggled. "I think you like Harry. Has he been sneaking you treats?"

Arvin adopted a haughty stance. *I don't know what you're talking about. Even the finest foods are merely the rightful fodder of a steed of my caliber. We don't have* treats.

I shook my head. "Has he worked out you aren't a proper horse yet?"

What he thinks is no concern of mine.

"Oh!" I said suddenly. "I got good news last night. I made one of my attackers admit that they didn't succeed in killing the other girls."

Killing them? Arvin sounded startled. *No indeed. Did you think it?*

I stared at him. "Of course I was afraid of it! Are you telling me you knew they were alive all this time?"

Arvin shifted slightly, a possible sign of mild discomfort which was more than I usually got from him.

I'm sure I mentioned it to you. They didn't find their bodies, or that of Daisy's maid.

I frowned, my sudden hope dwindling. "But that doesn't mean they're alive, just that they didn't die on the road."

Arvin stomped a hoof, apparently losing patience with me and whatever shred of guilt he might have been feeling. *However, I can assure you they're alive. Surely you cannot have thought they were all sent here just to follow you around meekly for many months. The godmothers have purposes for each of them. They have their own adventures to live.*

I stared at him. "But the godmothers didn't send them."

Didn't they? And what would you know of such things?

"But…" I spluttered, trying to find words. "But, Arvin…why didn't you tell me?"

Are you sure I did not?

I put my hands on my hips. "Of course I'm sure! I wouldn't forget something like that." But for all my irritation with him, I couldn't whip up any real anger. Not with the utter relief flooding through my body. If the godmothers had purposes for Daisy, Daria, and Cassie outside of Arcadia, then I could trust that they had safely escaped.

A loud series of honks interrupted us, making me look wildly in all directions. But the only "threat" I could perceive was two excited children running toward us. Apparently the geese eventually came to the same realization, resuming their meal with only the occasional honk and ruffling of feathers.

"Look, Mama! Look! She has a horse!" The piping voice of the younger of the children, a cherubic girl who looked no more than five, crossed the remaining distance between us.

"A very fine horse," the boy, who looked like her older

brother, added. "Have you ever seen such a fine one, Mama?"

The children reached us, and both crowded up to Arvin, ignoring me. The horse, who had originally looked horrified, softened enough at the boy's words to allow them to approach— merely tossing back his back and whinnying loudly.

Neither child showed any fear of his sudden movement, and the beautiful young woman approaching at a more sedate pace made no effort to herd them away from him.

"He is indeed a fine specimen," she said with a smile. "Although I must admit I have a partiality for my Starfire."

The name sparked a memory, and I looked at the woman more closely. She wore her hair pinned up in a loose arrangement, but her clothes had an expensive, elegant look, and she carried herself with confidence. A short distance away, three guards stopped and arranged themselves in a small circle, surveying the park in every direction. I had initially taken them for another patrol, but it appeared they were actually attached to this small group.

I dropped into a deep curtsy. "Your Highnesses."

Crown Prince Max was the only one of King Henry and Queen Eleanor's children remaining in Arcadia, and from what I'd heard, he and his wife, Princess Alyssa, were heavily involved in running the country. The last thing I had expected was for the princess, a dozen years my senior, to visit me in my guise as a lowly goose girl. Particularly not with her two young children in tow.

Princess Alyssa acknowledged my curtsy with a nod and another smile.

"I hope you don't mind us disturbing your peace," she said. "But Harry and Rose were desperate for a walk, and I wished to offer you the royal family's sincere apologies. That is twice now you have been attacked on Arcadian soil—once within our own palace." She frowned. "It's not at all what our kingdom is normally like, I assure you."

"I'm sure it is not," I said. "I do not blame Arcadia or you."

Alyssa beamed at me. "That is very generous of you. Your mistress has also been most understanding, and it almost makes the whole thing worse. Such gracious guests deserve far better treatment."

"Can I ride him? Can I ride him? Oh, please Mama!" Prince Henry's desperate pleas interrupted us.

"Me too! Me too!" chimed in Princess Rose.

"But he doesn't have a saddle or bridle," Alyssa pointed out.

"But we ride Starfire without either." Harry directed pleading eyes at his mother. "Just a short ride."

"Unlike Starfire, this lovely creature is not ours," Alyssa said. "It's Elle here you must ask." She turned to me. "I presume this is Princess Giselle's impressive mount? I have heard of him but not had the chance to visit. I'm told he was ailing but has made a full recovery on land. Perhaps he was merely seasick, poor thing."

She looked sympathetically at Arvin who snorted back at her.

I've never been seasick a day in my life.

Apparently whatever supply of goodwill the children had acquired from their initial compliments had already been exhausted.

But both turned their enormous eyes on me.

"Please Elle, may we ride him?"

"Please!"

I winced. Princess Alyssa was just as lovely as Celine had promised. She had sought me out, despite thinking me a mere goose girl, and she had even known to call me Elle and not Sierra. But she was wrong about it being my decision whether her children could ride Arvin. And one look at him told me what he thought about the matter.

"I'm so sorry," I told the young prince and princess. "But I'm afraid he's a rather strong-willed horse, and he isn't safe for strangers to ride. In fact, he doesn't let anyone but Princess Giselle ride him."

"Not even you?" Harry asked with wide eyes.

"Oh," I paused, momentarily thrown. "Yes, he does let me ride him, but not anyone else." And even me only rarely, but I wasn't going to draw further attention to his strange qualities.

Rose looked as if she was about to burst into tears, and her mother gathered her into her arms.

"You can go for a ride on your ponies later this afternoon," she promised them. "You know that some horses don't like children."

Is it any wonder? Arvin asked caustically. *They bounce and pull at your mane—and if you so much as turn around, they fall off. And then everyone blames you.*

I shook my head, refusing to answer him while the royals were present. I had never known him to accept a child on his back, so I was highly suspicious of these apparent bad experiences with youthful riders.

"It is good of you to bring him out for exercise along with your other duties," Alyssa said to me. "I know Giselle has preferred to borrow a mount so as not to overtax him with her daily rides, given his recent illness."

"He's company for me," I told her. "And I'm glad to have him."

"I'm so pleased you haven't been thrown into a state of fear by this second attack," Alyssa said in a sudden burst of enthusiasm. "I've been feeling terribly guilty. Max wondered if we should have written to Eldon weeks ago, suggesting you all divert your visit to Lanover, but Their Majesties were concerned such a message would be poorly received, and I was inclined to agree with…" She cut herself off. "Oh dear, listen to me rambling away. All I mean to say is that I keep thinking we might have spared you this pain, and your poor companions might now have been safe, if we'd let you know to defer your visit."

She glanced at her children, but they had gone to investigate the geese and hadn't heard her voice her concerns. She sighed and forced a smile.

"Princess Giselle is most understanding, as I said, but royals are trained to be that way—no matter what they're feeling on the inside. It can be a little disconcerting at times. And I've wondered if perhaps, underneath, your princess isn't quite as unperturbed as her words suggest."

Interesting. Princess Alyssa clearly had a good instinct about people if she could sense something of Sierra's insincerity. And when she wanted the truth of things, she came to the servants. It appeared that even twelve years as royalty weren't enough to stamp out Alyssa's roots. No wonder she knew to call me Elle.

Her words intrigued me, and I wished I could question her further about Sierra. I would also have liked to ask what it was that had made her husband suggest they defer our visit. Clearly something had been amiss in Arcadia before our arrival, and it threw all my assumptions about my current situation into question. But I was a goose girl now, and I couldn't question her as an equal—even if she liked to talk to servants.

Princess Rose called a question about one of the geese, drawing us over to them, and the rest of their visit was spent answering their questions and preventing Prince Henry from attempting to forcefully capture one of the goslings.

But the whole time, I kept sneaking sideways looks at Alyssa, watching how she interacted with her children. She seemed utterly relaxed about being here, consorting with a mere goose girl. She had been born a commoner, as Sierra had been, and yet she seemed to understand what it meant to fill the role of princess in a way my old maid did not. Perhaps even in a way I, born to the position, did not.

Why was that? Had I missed something important in the years I had been bound by my kingdom's enchantment? Or had I never been as well equipped for my role as I had always imagined myself to be?

When Alyssa gathered her children up and departed, their guards following discreetly behind them, I was left with a great deal of food for thought—and far too few answers.

CHAPTER 11

Over the next few nights, I pushed past the underlying feeling that I didn't belong and stayed in the dining hall after the evening meal, talking with the servants at every opportunity. I needed more information, and Alyssa had reminded me that servants were willing to talk about things royals were not. And I hoped, in the process, I might find out more about Princess Alyssa herself.

Now that I was paying attention, I noticed an undercurrent I had missed before. Or perhaps the latest attack had brought it closer to the surface.

My position at the center of the terrifying yet exciting occurrence meant I was now welcomed into conversations despite my previous stigma as a newcomer with a reputation for a disordered mind. I retold a simple version of the story many times, focusing on my fear and confusion and Philip's heroic rescue. The men were full of curses for the attackers and assertions that they wished they had been there to help fight them off, while the girls giggled and declared it romantic.

The first time they said it with Philip in earshot, he grinned and winked at me, and I had to fight down a flush. He often lingered close to my conversations after that. Perhaps he liked the sighs and giggles of the girls and hearing their praise of him.

I, however, was interested in the conversation that followed. I learned that there had been peace and prosperity in Arcadia for twelve years—ever since Alyssa married their prince—but that strange things had been happening of late. I had assumed everything had its origin in Sierra and the islanders among my guards, but something bigger was going on here.

Many questions were directed toward those servants who worked most closely with the royals. It seemed a matter of great concern with everyone as to the health of the relationships between both the king and queen and Alyssa and Max, and everyone seemed bewildered that the marriages appeared untroubled.

For twelve years they had experienced the prosperity of a kingdom ruled by true love, and no one could explain why the situation had changed. It didn't take many nights of hearing them talk about their crown prince's wife to realize Nikki was not alone in her feelings about her. While most of them were more respectful of her current rank than Nikki had been in our first conversation, they clearly felt a lingering ownership of the princess. She had once been just like them, and they would not forget it.

Or, perhaps, it would be more accurate to say that Alyssa had not forgotten it. The queen herself had only been born the daughter of a merchant, and she had already done much to help the commoners before Alyssa's arrival. But the young princess combined her efforts for her people with a warmth and approachability that inspired love as well as gratitude.

Arcadia had become a strong people, bound together in unity, but it seemed that strength was now under attack from the inside.

"It didn't used to be such smooth waters between the king and queen back when they were young," one of the older women told me. "And the kingdom suffered for it. But we're wiser now, and King Henry and Queen Eleanor lead us well. I can't imagine what has brought this new unrest upon us."

I bit my lip and stayed silent. But the guilt remained, even if the trouble predated my arrival. Because I couldn't believe it was all a coincidence. Somehow Sierra was at the center of whatever web was being spun. I was certain of it. And by her deception, she had bound Eldon in that web. I was still determined to bring her down, whatever it took.

I had expected to hear other tales of bandits on the roads, or attacks on other royals, perhaps, but the reports varied widely. One merchant had discovered an entire warehouse cleaned out of its stored food supplies. And at least three townhouses in the Nobles' Circle had been raided while their noble residents were away from the capital for the winter. The strange thing about the noble robberies seemed to be how little was taken.

But everyone agreed the most concerning—other than the two recent attacks—was the entire squad of guards that had gone missing and still hadn't been found. They had been traveling north along the coast, toward the mountain range that separated Arcadia and Northhelm, and no one knew what had happened to them. I knew very little about Arcadia's northern neighbor and couldn't even picture the terrain.

A delegation from Rangmere—the kingdom to the east of Arcadia—had visited us in Eldon the previous year, wanting to discuss a potential trade treaty, but I had yet to meet any North-helmians. The servants all assured me that Arcadia and North-helm had excellent relations, and that there was no treacherous geography in the area that could have swallowed the squad whole. Captain Markus himself had apparently led five squads to investigate, but they had found no trace of the missing guards.

I couldn't immediately see any connection between these events and Sierra, and I spent a number of days in the park mulling over the question from every angle. I included Arvin in my musings, when I could convince him to participate, but his strange brain—which usually seemed to perceive things differently from the rest of us—was no more able to see connections than my own.

Several times Philip appeared just as I was about to eat my midday meal, joining me without ceremony. I told myself Arvin and the geese were company enough, but I still found myself looking for him each midday.

After a week of gathering stories but no connections, I grew increasingly restless. I often saw Percy and Sierra riding in the distance, although I made no attempt to hail them again. I worried that if Sierra tricked Percy into marriage with her—under the guise of being me—his kingdom of Talinos might end up as angry with Eldon as Arcadia. Both kingdoms had accepted her because of the trust they had in Eldon, and I was still attempting to discover all the ways Sierra had broken that trust.

But it also scared me sometimes how easily I had fallen into the rhythm of my new life. I couldn't bear the thought of Celine arriving in many months' time to find I had done nothing but accept my fate.

I had been determined to prove to Sierra and myself that I was the true princess—and not because of an accident of birth. But some days it felt as if I was instead proving myself to be nothing more than a goose girl.

Driven to action, I seized on the opportunity of my first half-day break. Part of me longed to spend the morning in the servants' bath house, soaking in a steaming tub, but I needed to take advantage of the free time.

Back before Sierra stole the handkerchief from me, I had been determined to keep it on my person at all times. I assumed that Sierra had adopted the same intention, but what if I was wrong? Now that I had the chance to look, I had to at least check.

I sat next to Nikki at breakfast, carefully steering the conversation to her role as a senior maid. She happily chatted away, boasting of the senior responsibilities she was given. It took some time, but I eventually learned that the younger members of the court were to visit a nearby beach during the morning and that Nikki was responsible for both Princess Giselle's and Prince Percy's guest suites.

She informed me that she intended to start with the princess's suite because she never knew what state she would find it in.

"But you would know all about that," she said, rolling her eyes.

I hid my irritation at hearing Sierra was giving me a poor reputation among the servants, calling a cheery farewell when Nikki left to fetch her apron for the morning's jobs. But as soon as she was out of sight, I also left the dining hall, hurrying up the back stairs to where most of the servants had their rooms. I arrived just before she burst out of a plain wooden door, busily tying her apron strings.

Hanging back, I followed just close enough to keep her in sight. She made the task easy, moving swiftly through the palace corridors without glancing behind her. Dressed in my one clean palace uniform, no one stopped me or even noticed me. I had grown up with unseen servants all around me, and it felt strange to be the invisible one this time. I remembered wondering as a child if they hated it, but I found it strangely freeing. It was uncomfortable to know there were always eyes on you.

Nikki disappeared through the door of what was clearly a guest suite, but I didn't slow, walking past down the corridor. Now that I had the location of Sierra's rooms locked in my mind, I wandered aimlessly through the palace corridors. As long as I moved briskly and didn't show hesitation, no one questioned my presence.

When I had given her what seemed enough time, and then extra time again, I returned to the suite. As I approached it from the opposite direction to previously, the door swung open, and Nikki emerged. I spun around, facing into a large vase of flowers on a plinth against the wall.

Reaching out blindly, I fiddled with the flowers, my attention focused sideways on the maid. Thankfully she didn't appear to notice me, hurrying away with her head down and a disgruntled expression on her face. She had no doubt been held up in Sierra's suite longer than she hoped.

As soon as she turned into another door, I resumed my progress down the corridor, slipping into Sierra's sitting room as quickly as I could. Once the door was closed firmly behind me, I took a moment to look around.

Light filled the room from two tall windows. Pale green curtains had been drawn back with velvet rope, their color matching the comfortable-looking sofa and the bedspread I could see through the doorway that led to the bedroom. More fresh flowers stood on a side table, and a basin of clear water sat on a large tray with a soft white cloth beside it.

I closed my eyes and let out a long, soft sigh. This was the room I should have been welcomed into—a familiar space like many I had visited in the past in other palaces. It bore little resemblance to the broom cupboard I now inhabited.

But it wasn't the space I missed, or the little luxuries. Standing here felt like slipping back into my old self, with all its comfortable familiarities. Sneaking around palace corridors was new to me, but I knew what was expected of a girl who stayed in a room like this.

A noise in the corridor made my eyes fly open as I examined all the possible hiding places in the room, settling on the large chest that stood against one wall. But no hand rattled at the door, and I threw myself into the task of searching for the handkerchief.

I moved carefully, trying to return everything exactly how I had found it, although I chafed at the delays that necessitated. I tried to use my slow pace to consider all the possible hiding places for a small piece of material. If I was living in these rooms, where would I hide it?

But it hadn't been slid under the mattress, buried under the two blankets in the chest, hidden in any of the pockets of the dresses in the wardrobe, or tucked away in the writing desk. I even tested for loose floorboards or stones in the wall but found nothing. When I looked through a large bag that looked vaguely familiar, I realized it was Sierra's own luggage from our journey here. No doubt she had removed any personal items, but the dresses of a maid still filled much of it.

An angry voice sounded outside the door, and I dropped the bag. I recognized those tones although I no longer heard them every day. My plan already established, I didn't stop to think, throwing myself across the room and scrambling into the chest. The lid closed on top of me just as the door opened.

Two people entered, one the silent listener to Sierra's continued complaints. I suspected it was the new personal maid the Arcadians had provided, and I didn't envy her the role for a moment despite the nice surroundings she worked in.

"That wretch pushed me into the waves on purpose. I know she did!" Sierra cried for what I could only imagine was the tenth time if she had been complaining all the way back from the beach. "She's just jealous because I'm a princess, and she's only the daughter of an earl. And Percy never even looks at her."

"Yes, Your Highness," the maid muttered, sounding resigned and weary.

"And now there's saltwater halfway up the skirt," Sierra continued, making me roll my eyes. By the sound of it, she'd only been touched by the waves. I could remember occasions back in my own set of kingdoms when the royal children gathered on the beaches of Trione, and Gabe, Teddy, and Jon made it their mission to completely dunk every single one of us. Even Dominic had fallen to their stratagems, although most of us were half afraid of him.

"I'll make sure it's washed out, Your Highness," her maid said.

"But you won't be able to wash *that* out," Sierra said dramatically.

"Hmmm…" The maid sounded thoughtful. "The laundry staff might know a couple of tricks to try. You might be surprised."

"It's jam," Sierra wailed. "And it's red! The whole morning has been a disaster. I would have dismissed that clumsy fool of a footman on the spot if Alyssa hadn't been watching me with those eyes."

I stiffened, and this time the maid didn't respond at all. Embarrassment for Eldon washed over me. It didn't matter how many sweet, insincere words Sierra gave to Percy and the Arcadian royals if she treated the servants like this. What must they all think of my family?

When I was a child, my mother had demanded nothing but gracious words from us to servants who slipped or dropped things. She had been all too willing to trot out long lists of every youthful mistake we'd ever made if we showed even a hint of our irritation. It had been an early lesson in controlling what emotions we displayed in public. And yet it occurred to me suddenly that after so many years of practice, the appearance had become the reality. I felt only a swell of sympathy now when someone made a clumsy mistake, no matter how it affected me. Perhaps that had been the true lesson my mother was teaching?

Rage poured through me at the altogether different picture of Eldonian life that Sierra was painting for the Arcadians. But I suppressed the emotion, consumed with the desire to review the other lessons my mother had taught us growing up.

I had wondered, a little, at my relatively easy adjustment to the more physically difficult life of a goose girl, but did the credit for that belong to my mother as well? Before the curse fell on Eldon, she used to insist we take turns accompanying our father on trips up the mountain against which our palace was built. She had claimed that royals must know every part of the kingdom they ruled. But had she also wanted us to experience what it meant to walk until every muscle burned and then spend the night on a hard cave floor? Those freezing expeditions up steep mountain slopes had no obvious similarity with the life I lived now, but they had taught me to be cheerful in the face of physical hardship and not to think myself above it.

And as for the boredom of my new role, my mother had taught me plenty of tricks to combat that scourge, starting as soon as I was old enough to need to attend royal functions. I would never have guessed how the traits I had learned as a princess would help me as a goose girl. Did that mean some of the new skills I was learning now could help me when I returned to my old role again?

A picture of Alyssa formed in my mind. Undoubtedly it was so. And the more I thought about it, the more it made sense. As a princess, my role was to serve my people, and understanding their lives could only help me do that better.

"Get me out of this at once!" Sierra snapped. "And then go and check they're serving something I like for the midday meal. I've had a terrible day, and they owe me that much at least."

And that, right there—not her birth—was the reason Sierra would never be a true princess. She believed the kingdom owed her luxury and ease instead of realizing that she was the one who owed her people a lifetime of service.

I adjusted my position to stave off an oncoming cramp. I had been raised in luxury, and I now owed it to my people to use this strange situation to gain new skills and knowledge that would allow me to serve them better. I had thought I needed to prove myself by defeating Sierra and protecting my kingdom, but I had more to prove than that.

I just needed to get out of this chest first.

Fortunately, Sierra declared she would have a nap before the meal and ordered her maid to draw the blinds and close her bedroom door before leaving to check on the menu. As soon as I heard both doors close, I silently pushed up the lid of the chest.

After peering out into the empty room for a moment, I climbed carefully out and eased the lid back down again.

I had made it most of the way to the corridor door when I paused. The bag I had abandoned at Sierra's arrival still lay there where I had left it. On a whim, I snatched it up by the handles and slung it over my shoulder. She was the one who had claimed I was Sierra, her maid. No one could fault me for having my own possessions in my room. Let Sierra wonder how it had disappeared from her room and found its way to me. Already she seemed to be struggling with the role she had undertaken, and I wanted her to stay as on edge as possible.

Once again no one stopped me as I walked the corridors, passing quickly into the servants' part of the palace. When I reached my room, I shoved the bag under the bed, the only place big enough to hold it, and hurried to change dresses. The whole exercise had taken so long I was in danger of being late to the geese who were no doubt waiting anxiously for their afternoon's grazing.

CHAPTER 12

One particularly brisk morning, my failure to discover the handkerchief was on my mind as I approached the goose pen. In my abstraction, I nearly didn't notice a diminutive figure standing in front of the gate, arms crossed. The young boy glared at me fiercely, although I was sure we'd never met, and my initial failure to notice him only deepened his scowl.

"I suppose you must be *Elle*," he said, voice dripping with disdain.

"Yes, I am. But I'm afraid I don't know who you are."

"Don't know who I am?" The boy drew himself to his full height, visibly swelling with outrage. "I'm Colin."

"Oh. Well, it's nice to meet you, Colin. Can I help you with something?"

He stared at me as if I'd grown a second head.

"Help you with something? I'll have you know, you're the one helping me!"

A sudden suspicion filled my mind.

"Are you the goose boy? The usual one, I mean, who's been on leave visiting his family?"

"Aye, that's me. And if Betty hadn't been fool enough to get the measles and then give it to half the family, I wouldn't have had to go off in the first place." He paused to glare at me again. "And then I wouldn't be dealing with upstart maids who think they can come in and steal me job." He had worked himself into a crescendo of anger by his final words, and I hurriedly raised both hands in a placating gesture.

"No, no, I promise I'm not trying to steal your job. I'm sure you're far better at herding the geese than me."

"You can be sure of that," he muttered. "But the Poulterer is saying I have to work with you. Me! I haven't had anyone watching over me since I was a little 'un."

He still looked little to me—surely not more than ten at the most—but it didn't seem a wise idea to point that out.

"I'm fairly sure," I said instead, "that you're the one looking after me." I gave him an apologetic smile. "The truth is that they didn't know what to do with me and wanted to give me something quiet to do away from the bustle of the palace. I'm sure it is really Mrs. Pine who wants me to stay, not the Poulterer." I lowered my voice. "I'm afraid the Poulterer doesn't think much of me at all."

Colin's manner softened slightly. "Course he doesn't. He doesn't think much of anybody. Took me two years afore he stopped barking at me."

"A high honor," I said, with all sincerity. "I'm afraid the geese don't listen to me much either. I mostly have to let them pick their own grazing spots."

Colin shook his head in disgust, but he had considerably relaxed at these instances of my ineptitude.

"You've got to keep a firm hand with 'em," he told me in a wise tone. "They have to know who's in charge."

"Well I'm sure we'll have no difficulties with that now you're back," I said, causing Colin to abandon the last of his outraged air. I was only glad I had finally relaxed enough to start leaving the staff in the pen overnight again. I could imagine his reaction if he had found me wandering around with it.

He soon had the geese out of the pen in record time. He called to them as he walked, swinging the staff with an expert hand, and none of them protested as he led them toward a part of the park where I had not yet ventured. We stopped right on the edge of one of the small clusters of trees, Colin explaining that the shade they provided would be a necessity soon enough, as the weather warmed.

My heart sank at the image he presented. I sincerely hoped I wasn't still goose herding in summer. Who knew what damage Sierra would have done with her charade by then?

Colin chattered away about the family he had just left, seemingly unconcerned by my infrequent and confused contributions to the conversation. He apparently had a great many siblings, far more than I could keep track of. But I did manage to grasp that as well as the much-maligned Betty, who had brought the infection into the house, there was a younger brother who Colin held high hopes would soon join him to train as a herder.

His dark looks returned briefly during this segment of his spiel, so perhaps it was this brother's place he thought I was usurping more than his own. But as the day wore on, he turned his focus to teaching me the things I should know as a herder.

It took a great deal of restraint on my part to keep a grave and attentive expression since he wore a hat several sizes too big for him that was liable to fall off whenever he committed to a demonstration. It fell off three times in quick succession while he enthusiastically modeled the correct technique for wielding the staff, and I gathered my courage to say something.

"I think your hat might be a little large, Colin. Would you like me to talk to one of the maids and see if we can find you one that fits better?"

He immediately rounded on me, his expression filled with

horror. "Keep your hands off my hat!" Rescuing the fallen head-piece, he jammed it firmly back on his head.

"I have no wish to steal it, I promise. I was only trying to help."

He shook his head, clearly exasperated by my ignorance. "I worked for a whole year before I earned this hat." A note of pride entered his voice. "A proper herder's hat, from the hands of the Poulterer himself."

A status symbol then. I abandoned any hope of getting him to replace it with a more practical option. He was still shaking his head and muttering when the sound of hooves announced the arrival of Arvin.

"You're late," I called to the horse. "Did you oversleep?"

He pointedly ignored me, focusing his attention on Colin.

Why is there a child here? Again.

"This is Colin," I told him. "He's the true goose boy. Colin, this is Arvin. He likes to spend time with me and the geese during the day."

Arvin finally turned to me. *I do not like to spend time with geese. What do you take me for?*

"Now, *that* is a horse." Colin stared in wide-eyed, reverential wonder at Arvin. "Did you say he spends his days here? With us? He looks far too important."

Arvin whipped his head back around to stare at the boy.

Well, he neighed after a moment, *it seems there is occasionally some sense to be found among children after all. Perhaps his presence will not be so wearisome.*

I shook my head at both of them, wondering how long the apparent peace would last. But Colin's awe didn't abate, the poor boy running himself ragged finding patches of grass that might possibly tempt the horse and tirelessly rubbing him down with the brush I had borrowed from Harry. If Arvin had been a cat, I'm sure he would have been purring, although I knew he would declare himself far too dignified for such an activity if I suggested it.

With Colin's unflagging efforts with both the geese and Arvin, there was even less for me to do than usual, and an idea had begun to worm its way into my brain. Before I said anything about it, however, a young, piping voice called my name.

"Elle! Elle!" I turned to find the young prince and princess riding toward me.

They rode rather staid looking ponies, a fortunate thing since Princess Rose was bouncing in her saddle with excitement in exactly the sort of way Arvin had described. Prince Henry appeared to be putting effort into a good seat, looking very proper beside his younger sister.

A groom and three guards rode behind them, the guards looking alert and the groom long-suffering. Both children pulled up in front of us. Colin and the prince assessed each other with identical expressions—rank was only a small consideration when it came to two young boys weighing each other's relative attributes.

"Mama says you come from the new kingdoms," Rose said, her attention still on me. "Like Princess Giselle." She wrinkled her little nose. "But I don't think Giselle likes children. She always gives me short answers and then walks away."

Her brother broke off his staring match with Colin to admonish her.

"You shouldn't say things like that, Rose! She's our guest."

Rose just wrinkled her nose all the way into an angry pout. "But it's true! Mama and Papa say it's important to be truthful."

He frowned at her. "Yes, but that's not all Mama says. She's always telling you that it's important for a princess to be courteous and considerate to everyone." He glanced quickly at me, as if remembering his sister's words on the importance of truth, and added, "And princes, too, of course."

Rose gave an exaggerated sigh and rolled her eyes. "It's just that I wanted to hear about the twins." She turned back to me. "Have you met them?"

"She means our cousins," Henry explained. "Aunt Lily and Aunt Sophie live in the new kingdoms, and they both have twins."

"Their names are Hope and Owen, and Grace and Arthur, and they're two and a half, and I love them so much," Rose declared in a rush.

"Actually we've never met them," Henry said.

"I still love them," Rose declared defiantly. "They're my only cousins."

"You're such a—" But Henry cut himself off before uttering whatever insult he had intended to direct at his sister. Perhaps he had remembered the difficult requirement for a prince to always be courteous—even to a younger sister.

I hid a smile, thinking of the lessons of my own mother and how difficult they had sometimes been to remember at his age.

"Grandmama says we may visit, but not until next year, probably," Rose said despondently. "A year is a long time. And it may be even *longer*."

"Yes, it is a long time," I agreed, well remembering how long the years had seemed as a young child. "And it's hard to wait."

"So have you met them?" Rose asked, not to be diverted from her original purpose.

I bit my lip. I had. Several times, in fact. The four of them together were almost overwhelmingly cheeky and adorable. But how much could I admit in my guise as lady's maid? How much would the enchantment allow?

"I have seen them," I said after a moment. "Last year. They were walking and chattering away in baby talk. And they were very cute."

Rose giggled and clapped her hands.

"Can they say my name? Auntie Lily promised she would teach them all to say my name."

"I'm sorry, I don't know. But I'm sure if Princess Lily said she would, then she has."

Rose scrunched her face up in delight this time instead of annoyance. "Two of the nobles who live at the palace have babies, and they're *so cute!*"

I couldn't help but smile at her high-pitched interpretation of the usual adult response to babies. Did she really think them cute, or had she just learned that was the way you were supposed to talk about babies?

"Don't you have any other cousins here?" I asked. "Second cousins, perhaps?"

The prince sighed. "Rose is wrong, we do have other cousins. Mama's brothers have children, but they're all older and live very far away in the middle of a wood and don't like the city at all. Aunt Lily and Aunt Sophie were our only aunts here in Arcadie, but then they moved away. And Papa doesn't have any cousins."

That surprised me. My own palace seemed full of distant second and third cousins.

"Grandfather only had one sister, and she doesn't live in Arcadia," Henry explained. "Even Papa never knew her. I think she sailed somewhere." He looked at me brightly. "Maybe she went to the new kingdoms. Do you know her? Her name was…" He hesitated, as if trying to remember. "Princess Mina. My tutor made me memorize our whole family tree last year. It was awfully boring."

"If she sailed away somewhere before your father was born, she can't have come to my lands," I said. "The passage was blocked with storms until only five or six years ago. She must have sailed to Lanover or Northhelm perhaps."

"But then she would have visited," Henry objected.

"Maybe you should ask your father," I said quickly, rather afraid that "sailed away" was the euphemism he had been given for his great-aunt's death. Perhaps her ship had been lost at sea.

Their groom cleared his throat loudly, and the prince twitched, turning to his sister.

"Come on, Rose. We shouldn't be keeping the ponies standing so long."

Rose sighed but tugged at her rein to direct her pony's head around. As she rode back toward the groom and guards, she called a farewell over her shoulder. I waved at them both before glancing at Colin.

He watched them ride away with an expression I couldn't read. Was he like Sierra, wishing for a life that wasn't his?

"Do you ever wish you could trade places and be a prince for a while?" I asked.

He started and turned to me with a scoffing look. "Me? A prince? Hardly! My mam says they spend all their time at stuffy parties wearing uncomfortable clothes."

"Your mam is a wise woman."

If Sierra's mother had told her the same thing, I might not be in my current predicament. Although I reminded myself that Sierra clearly had some greater purpose than merely stealing my position, even if I hadn't worked out what it could be yet.

Colin snorted. "Besides, who'd want to be a noble when it means you might get poisoned?"

"Poisoned?" I stared at him. "What are you talking about?"

His eyes widened with a look almost like relish. "You mean you haven't heard?" There was no mistaking the glee in his voice at finding someone who hadn't heard whatever shocking news he was about to impart.

"That's why I came back early," he said. "Everything exciting is happening here. Plus, I'd had enough of nursing Betty."

"You mean your family is still sick?" I drew back instinctively, but he waved a dismissive hand.

"No need to fret. I had the spots years ago."

"Oh. Well, that's good," I said, a little doubtfully.

"You didn't hear me complaining like Betty, neither," he said, distracted momentarily by the memory of his irritating sister.

You know, Arvin said, ambling back over from where he had been nibbling at a patch of sweet grass Colin found for him, *I did hear a groom this morning saying something about poison. Sounded like a lot of nonsense to me.*

I ignored him, focusing on Colin. "Never mind your sister, what's this about poison?"

"Ah, yes," he said with relish. "Word spread as far as the city late last night, and I walked over to the palace before dawn. The story might not have reached the servants' wing by the evening meal, but didn't you have breakfast in the dining hall this morning? Everyone was full of talk of it. I thought for sure you'd have heard all about it already."

I grimaced. "I just grabbed a roll on my way through the kitchens." Of course something momentous would occur on the one morning I slept too late. "But please do hurry up and tell me what happened!"

He gave me a stern look for hurrying his story, but finally got to the point.

"Viscount Edgewaring has been murdered! With poison, the doctors say, although they don't know which type."

How unpleasantly dramatic, Arvin said, eyeing Colin with displeasure, as if he was at fault for the noble's death.

I blinked several times. "Viscount Edgewaring?" The name sounded vaguely familiar. "But who poisoned him—and why?"

"No one knows!" Colin sounded altogether too pleased by this information. A note of pride entered his voice. "We have very advanced doctors in Arcadie. We're known for it. They detected the poison right away, but it's some fancy one they don't recognize. So everyone thinks it must have been a rich noble. Who else could afford fancy poison?"

I shook my head, horrified, and by no means as convinced as Colin that the perpetrator must have been another Arcadian noble. "And this happened yesterday? How awful! His poor family!"

Colin looked unconcerned. "He was about a hundred years old, I reckon. And he didn't have much family. His only son died twenty years ago, my mam says. She says it's all very sad, but I saw him come through the palace yard a couple of times. He looked like an irritable old—"

I put up my hand to cut off whatever further insults were coming. "The poor man has died!"

What has that to do with anything? asked Arvin.

Colin seemed to agree with the horse. "Doesn't change what he was like while he was alive. Everyone has always felt sorry for Lord Thomas—he's his only grandson, and it can't have been much fun being raised by old Edgewaring. Although the old man has a whole host of nieces and nephews and great-nieces and great-nephews around the palace. He even has some in Lanover, they say."

He continued to chatter on about them all, but I couldn't follow the various connections. I did, however, pick up that while the viscount hadn't been a warm man, he had been held in at least a modicum of respect. According to Colin, no one had any idea why someone would want to kill him—and in such a dramatic fashion.

His mention of seeing the viscount in the yard had at least reminded me of where I had heard his name. My own brief encounter with him in the palace yard had done nothing to dispel Colin's notion that he had been a disagreeable old man. But he had been working in the palace for as long as most people could remember—why would anyone want to kill him now?

Unless...my heart sank. Unless the person responsible had only just arrived in Arcadia.

It grew more obvious by the day that whatever was going on in this kingdom was bigger than the theft of my identity. Alyssa had come to the servants when she wanted information, and I had now had ample opportunity to observe for myself that no one spread news as well as servants. When I first lost my title, I had thought all my power was stripped away, but I was learning to recognize a different sort of power. With no connections to the court here, I would have had little access to information as Princess Giselle. As a goose girl, I had the power to go unnoticed, and to talk freely to the servants.

Previously, the geese themselves had been a problem, keeping me tied to the park all day, but Colin's arrival changed all that. He clearly felt no need for my assistance—quite the opposite—so he had no reason to object if I occasionally disappeared.

I still wished the enchantment broken, of course—and as soon as possible. But if my godmother appeared right now and freed me from it, I wouldn't run straight to expose Sierra. I needed to find out what was going on first, and how far her scheming went. Exposing her now might allow anyone else involved to slither away undiscovered. I would have better luck investigating the strange occurrences while I could move around and ask questions unnoticed.

A certain face intruded on my thoughts, but I firmly told myself that my desire to linger a little longer as a some-time goose girl had nothing whatsoever to do with Philip.

CHAPTER 13

$\mathcal{E}$ager to test Colin, I waited until the geese got restless and then suggested he drive them home on his own.

"I'd like to go for a bit of a walk through the park," I said. "And it will be good exercise for Arvin." I knew I should ask the horse's opinion, but I couldn't easily do so in front of Colin.

The boy shrugged. "Do what you like. I don't need any help."

"Excellent. Well, I'll see you tomorrow, then."

Colin frowned, like he would have preferred not to see me again at all, but he glanced once at Arvin and didn't actually protest. I waved and took off, wanting to put some space between us before he changed his mind.

For some time I wandered, Arvin keeping pace in silence. The park was a great deal more peaceful without one hundred plus geese in attendance, and even the haughty horse seemed to be enjoying it.

We didn't pass anyone else out exercising, most people having already taken themselves home for the evening meal by this time of day. But the occasional sight of a distant trio of soldiers, still completing regular patrols of the palace grounds, kept any anxiety at bay, as did Arvin's warm presence at my side.

I stopped after a while for a break, letting my hand rest on the rough bark of an ancient oak while Arvin pushed between the trees, on the hunt for more sweet grass. Surveying the park, I let myself imagine what it would have been like to see it for the first time as Princess Giselle, riding Arvin perhaps.

I would be spending my time with Alyssa and her children, instead of Colin and the geese—and Philip. I shook my head, dispelling the vision. Sierra had intended to punish me, but I had already learned far more as a goose girl than she could have imagined.

Turning to call to Arvin, I caught movement in the corner of my eye. Spinning back, I located three figures walking swiftly across the park some distance from me. They moved away from the palace, not toward it like everyone else at this hour, but they wore nondescript clothing quite unlike the uniform of the guards.

One of them shifted, dropping back half a pace, revealing a clearer view of the man in the front. I hissed, my hands clenching into fists. One of his arms was slung across his chest in a sling.

My eyes flicked to the other two, focusing on the man who had dropped back. He walked awkwardly compared to the others, clearly favoring one leg.

"Arvin," I whispered loudly. "It's my attackers. Keep quiet."

To my surprise, the horse obeyed me, appearing beside me without a sound. I pointed across the park at the men.

"There. Those three. Do you see how one of them has a broken arm? And another has an injured leg. It has to be them." I hesitated, looking around for any sign of a patrol. None were in sight. "I want to follow them."

I expected Arvin to protest, seeing as he had assumed some sort of protective role over me, but instead he told me to mount up in a quiet whuff. Apparently he was as curious as I was. I didn't waste any time, digging my fingers into his mane and vaulting onto his back.

Arvin took off, more quietly than seemed possible. His smooth movements seemed designed not to draw attention as he moved from copse to copse. Goaded by their leader, the three men sped up. Were they aiming for the same gate they used last time? Surely they had heard they were all now guarded? It was clear from their tended wounds and new clothes that they had sought refuge with Sierra as I had guessed.

Darkness was starting to descend, both a boon and a hindrance. I strained my eyes to follow them in the dim light. They moved into a deeper shadow, and I looked ahead to where they would emerge again.

But they never did. I waited, my eyes flickering all around the space, but I could see no sign of them. I leaned down to whisper in Arvin's ear.

"They're gone! Can you see them?"

He shook his head, a quick negative, his ears pricking forward. Picking up our pace, we trotted over to where they had disappeared beside a stand of trees. One of the trees was a fig, its huge bulging roots showing above the ground, and its trunk splitting at once into several parts. I peered down behind every crevice and bend. There was no sign of them.

"Impossible." I slid down from Arvin's back. "There's nothing here. I thought for sure they were making for the wall."

Perhaps they meant to meet someone, Arvin neighed.

I frowned around. "If so, where is the other person? And where are they? Did they see us following and hide?"

I peered into a nearby patch of shrubbery, growing around the base of a tree. I walked over to investigate, unable to believe that three grown men could have secreted themselves among the dense branches.

Giselle! Arvin's loud whinny made me jerk around just as someone appeared from nowhere and grabbed me from behind.

I shrieked even more piercingly than Arvin, stomping down with both boots on the feet of my captor. He cursed and staggered backward, dragging me with him. Thinking longingly of my staff—now claimed by Colin—I drove my elbow back into the man's stomach.

He groaned, his grip loosening, and I tore myself free, only to have my arm grabbed by someone else. I tried to wrench it loose, but a third person grabbed my other arm, thrusting me sideways into the arms of my new captor who clapped a hand over my mouth.

"None of that now," he said. "Not like last time. You shouldn't have followed us, Princess."

A loud scream from Arvin made me grin behind his hand, despite my fear. He had clearly forgotten that, unlike last time, I wasn't alone.

The leader tossed a loop of rope over the horse's head and attempted to drag him away from me, the end of the rope looped multiple times around his good arm. At first Arvin dug his hooves into the grass, refusing to budge an inch. But just as the man leaned back with his full weight, he shifted, moving toward him. The man went down hard, helped by a kick from a sharp hoof.

My first captor hurried toward him, his gait even, which told me the identity of my current captor. As I fisted my hand, I pictured him as he had looked lying on the ground, with a knife protruding from his leg. As soon as I had the placement of his wound clear in my mind, I drove my fist backward into his thigh. The punch was awkward, my angle and momentum wrong, but my aim had been true. The man gasped and swayed, his hand dropping from my mouth.

But the leader on the ground recovered his breath and waved away the man coming to his assistance. Dodging another kick from Arvin, the final man ran back toward me. I had only made it two steps away from my captor and was trapped between them.

A final flash of the setting sun reflected off a length of steel which appeared between me and the approaching attacker. A body followed it in a perfect lunge, skewering the man's shoulder.

He yelled, his leader behind him on the ground giving an angry shout, and the man behind me cursing quietly.

"How dare you attack a lady!" the dark-haired stranger with the sword cried, rounding on me and the man behind me. "And she alone and weaponless."

Arvin gave a snort and stood on the hand of the downed leader. The man screamed, and the stranger flashed a grinning look at him.

"Apologies, not quite alone."

"Lark!" A distant voice called for me, and the newcomer raised his eyebrows.

"Not at all alone, it would seem. In fact, I fear my services are quite superfluous."

"No, indeed," I panted. "I thank you greatly."

The man behind me had slowly edged his way around us both, his eyes on the sword. He collected his bleeding companion, helping him stagger to his feet, and they both backed away toward their leader.

"Let that be a lesson to you," the stranger said sternly. "Help is always on hand for those who deserve it."

He kept his eyes on them but whispered loudly at me. "I do hope you're the deserving sort. You mustn't embarrass me now by turning out to be a thief or some such."

I giggled, my heightened emotions spilling out in the release the laughter offered.

"I'm the goose girl. Not a thief, I promise."

"Lark!" Philip's voice called again, nearer this time.

"If help is on the way, perhaps we should attempt to arrest these blackguards?" said the newcomer. "Three of us should be able to manage it."

"Over here, Philip," I yelled. Turning to Arvin, I added, "Can you find him?"

Arvin stilled for a moment, ears cocked, and then cantered away. I stared after him, soon seeing him return with Philip jogging beside him.

"Do hurry!" I called. "It's the men from before."

I turned back to the newcomer, who was peering toward Arvin and Philip just like I had been. When our eyes met, he smiled, and I noticed for the first time the piercing gray of his eyes and his attractive features. Then my gaze slid past him, and I gasped.

"Where are they? Where did they go? They were right there!"

The man swung around as well, his brow creasing as his eyes roved all around.

"Impossible," he said. "They could not have slunk into the darkness with such injuries. I'm sure the man on the ground had several broken ribs—if not worse—from the horse's kick."

"Quick! We must find them!" I turned again and collided with Philip who steadied me with strong hands on either arm.

"Are you hurt?" he asked. "I heard you and Arvin screaming. I came as fast as I could."

That was a bellow of anger, not a scream, Arvin said with dignity.

"There's no time for that," I said, my words pouring over each other. "We had the three attackers from last time at sword point. They were all injured, and now they're gone. We were standing right here, and they've disappeared. We have to spread out and search. Quickly."

Philip looked over my shoulder, frowning at the armed newcomer.

I glanced back at him as well. "He rescued me."

The man gave a shallow bow. "The lady and her horse had the matter well in hand when I arrived."

"Oh, never mind that! We must find them."

"Yes." Philip dropped his hands from my arms. "You're with

129

me. Arvin, you go with this gentleman. We'll cover more ground that way."

"We'll cover more ground if we all split up," I said.

"You're with me," Philip said firmly, and grabbed my wrist, tugging me into the deepening shadows.

I flashed an apologetic look at my rescuer who gave us an amused smile before starting in the opposite direction. Arvin looked after me for a moment, but Philip glanced back and nodded significantly toward the man's disappearing back. The horse nickered softly and trotted off after him.

We jogged, staying no more than two arms' lengths apart as we peered around trees and behind bushes. But we could find no sign of the missing attackers.

As the darkness grew deeper, we had to give up, returning to the place of the attack. Arvin and the newcomer beat us back, just.

"Did you find anything?" I asked, knowing already from their silence that they had not.

"Not a sign of anything," the man said.

Philip looked at him for a long moment and then turned to Arvin.

I did not let this man out of my sight. We discovered nothing.

Although Philip couldn't understand him, he seemed to recognize the import of the horse's tone. He growled quietly, under his breath.

My shoulders slumped. "I don't understand how they could have escaped. They really were right there." I frowned. "They disappeared the first time, too."

"The first time?" asked the newcomer, pulling out a cloth and wiping down his blade.

"I was following them," I explained. "And they disappeared. That's why I wasn't riding Arvin. I'd hopped down to try to see where they could have gone, and then they attacked."

"Well this time they have not merely hidden themselves

behind a bush, I'm afraid." The stranger slid his sword into the scabbard at his waist.

I frowned again but didn't dispute his words. They hadn't been behind the bushes the first time either, and given their second disappearance, I didn't think their first could be so easily explained. But neither did I want to start babbling of enchantments in front of Philip and a stranger.

"Thank you for coming to my rescue," I said instead, addressing them both.

The newcomer gave me a charming smile. "As I said, you were doing remarkably well on your own. And your horse was a great deal more assistance than mine."

Naturally, Arvin interjected.

"Your horse?" I followed the direction he pointed and saw a dainty mare calmly feeding among a distant copse of trees.

"She doesn't exactly have combat experience." He grimaced.

I glanced at Arvin, who was looking even more superior than usual. Some sort of explanation seemed to be required.

"He's a royal mount, so he's been well trained." I hoped Arvin would forgive me for describing him as *trained.*

"He belongs to Princess Giselle," Philip said.

"Princess Giselle?" The newcomer started and swept into a deep bow. "You're Princess Giselle? I've heard much talk of you on my journey here. I just didn't expect you to be…"

"So unimpressive?" I asked with a chuckle.

"Far from it!" he said quickly. "You are extremely impressive, I assure you. It is merely your wardrobe and location that took me by surprise."

"That's because this is Elle, the goose girl," Philip said stiffly, using my nickname for the first time. "She came here with the princess from Eldon, and she exercises her horse for her. I'm afraid I didn't catch your name."

"Oh! I'm sorry. It's Damon." He winced. "I'm making a mess of the whole thing. Well, it's very nice to meet you, Elle. And you...?" He turned to Philip.

"This is Philip," I said. "He's another one of the servants." I looked at him. "Although I don't know what he was doing all the way out here." My attackers had disappeared in one of the most remote corners of the park, only a short walk from the wall.

"Looking for you," he said. "Colin came back without you and said you were wandering around the park, so I set off to find you. And then I heard Arvin's and your screams. I would have been here sooner, but I wasn't riding a horse."

"I didn't mean to go so far," I said. "But then I saw my attackers and seized the chance to follow them. I wasn't alone," I added, hearing the defensiveness in my voice, "I had Arvin with me."

"That is at least something," Philip said dryly.

As we talked, we'd all walked over to collect Damon's mare. He made no move to mount up, however, looping her reins over one hand and walking on beside us.

"I'm glad I happened to be riding by and was able to be of some small assistance," he said. "It has somewhat salvaged my pride." He gave a small laugh. "I'm afraid I was letting my horse have her head and wander around the park while I tried to gather my courage."

"Courage?" I asked. "Whatever for?"

For the first time I closely examined his clothes. The elegant cut and expensive material suggested he was either a wealthy merchant's son, or else he had omitted a title when he introduced himself as Damon.

"I've never seen you at the palace before," Philip said. "You mentioned something about traveling to Arcadie?"

"Yes, I've come to visit family." He paused. "Well, in truth I've come to *meet* family, thus the need for courage. I would like to make a good impression, but I've arrived out of the blue, and I hope they won't be too shocked."

If his family lived at the palace, they weren't likely to be merchants. Many of the nobles—especially the younger ones—chose to keep rooms here in the spring and summer.

"Well, everyone is in an uproar today, from what I hear," I said. "So hopefully your arrival will be a pleasant diversion for them."

"An uproar?" He glanced behind us. "You're not talking about that attack?"

"No, nor the earlier one. One of the local nobles has been poisoned, apparently. But no one knows who did it."

"Poisoned! It seems I picked an inauspicious moment for my visit."

"Or a happy one," I said. "Hopefully your arrival can bring some comfort to your relations."

He looked a little doubtful but managed a smile.

"With those words of encouragement, I really should be going, or it will be much too late to present myself to them. I can see the palace up ahead, you'll be safe from here?"

"Arvin and I will look after her," Philip said, evenly.

"Of course." Damon smiled again and gave us both a half-bow, despite the clear disparity in our status.

As soon as Damon swung into the saddle and rode away, Philip stopped walking. I slowed and stopped as well, turning back to him with an inquiring look.

"What were you thinking?" he asked, his earlier calm gone.

"I thought it was safe enough with the patrols about." I bit my lip.

"And I'm sure it would have been if you hadn't gone looking for trouble in the furthest reaches of the park."

He is forgetting that I was with you, Arvin said. *Those men would not have succeeded in carrying you away.*

"Thank you for coming looking for me," I said to Philip, ignoring the horse. "I appreciate it."

He softened a little, gazing at me for a long moment before

looking in the direction of the now barely visible palace and sighing.

"As it turns out, it seems my assistance wasn't required anyway. I will be curious to hear who Damon's family turn out to be and how they react to his arrival. I would think him some impoverished distant relation, come to plead his connection with a wealthy family, but his clothes and horse suggest otherwise."

"It seems there are lots of mysteries in Arcadie at the moment," I said softly.

Philip frowned down at me. "And you seem determined to go investigating them." He rubbed his jaw. "You do seem to find yourself at the center of them in a way I don't understand."

He looked at me hopefully, but I stared back silently. And it wasn't just the enchantment keeping my lips closed. If he wanted to hear my secrets, he could start by sharing a few of his own.

As if reading my defiant look, his lips twitched.

"Yes, well…" He chuckled and held out a hand. "How about an agreement then? We will work together to uncover what we can of these strange doings. No more wandering off to investigate on your own."

I hesitated for only a second before grasping his hand and giving it a firm shake. We resumed our walk, arriving at the palace yard too quickly to allow any serious discussion of the theories we had each so far amassed.

Arvin surged ahead, his mind no doubt on the bucket of oats in his stall, and I called after him to take care as he nearly knocked down a young noble couple in his haste. The two walked arm in arm, their heads bent close together and their demeanors burdened. They didn't even appear to notice Arvin trotting past at speed.

I turned back to make an exasperated comment to Philip, only to find him gone. I stared around, but he had disappeared from sight at startling speed. I would have suspected him of being uncomfortable in the presence of nobles except that I had seen him entirely undaunted by royalty.

After standing awkwardly for a moment on my own, I headed for the servants' wing and my meal. I welcomed Philip's company in my quest to expose Sierra, but I also hoped that somewhere along the way, I would discover what secrets he was hiding.

PART II
THE PRINCE

CHAPTER 14

The next morning I hurried to the stables before breakfast to check on Arvin. I had been fretting all night after realizing I never checked him over after our fight. Would he have told me if he was injured in some way? Between my worry and the aftereffects of the fear and exertion of the evening, I had tossed and turned, getting up at first light.

Despite the early hour, the servants' wing and the palace yard bustled, and a number of grooms moved about the stables. I didn't spot Harry, but a couple of the faces were vaguely familiar. As I approached Arvin's stall, I could neither see nor hear any sign of him, and my heartbeat sped up as I pictured him taken off somewhere for treatment.

But when I finally reached his half-door, I immediately spotted his reassuring bulk further back in the large stall. I drew a shaky breath and gave myself stern instructions not to be so jumpy.

Slipping inside as quietly as possible, I tried to complete a full visual examination before he woke up. But as soon as I made it all the way up his right side to his head, he opened an eye.

Why are you creeping around my stall at the crack of dawn?

I jumped guiltily. "I just wanted to check you weren't hurt last night."

Of course I wasn't hurt. I would have informed you if I was. Clearly all these attacks have overset you. It's a very good thing the godmothers sent me to watch over you.

Something in his tone made it clear he hadn't been in favor of the plan at the beginning.

"Well, I just wanted to be sure," I said, shamelessly laying it on thick. "Since you're so brave, I thought you might not have mentioned it."

He snorted at that, clomping his hooves and snuffling around for his breakfast.

I am not swayed by your empty flattery. Where are my oats?

"I think I saw a bucket by the door. Hold on." I popped my head over the door. "Aha! Yes, there it is. Excuse me, could you please hand me that—"

I broke off as I looked up and realized the groom I was speaking to wasn't a groom at all.

"Oh! Damon! I didn't see you." I let myself out of the stall, self-consciously brushing some straw off my skirt now I could see his elegant outfit.

"Elle! What a delightful surprise." He gave me the same appealing smile I remembered from the evening before. "I had intended to make some inquiries as to your well-being, but how much nicer to be able to ask you in person. Are you well?"

"Yes, indeed. I'll confess I didn't sleep well, but that was probably to be expected. You're up early, did you have the same trouble?"

"I wanted to check on my lady before I'm expected at breakfast." He nodded several stalls down the row where the mare from last night stood with her head hanging over her door. "I'm not entirely sure how the day will go, so it seemed best to do it early."

"So you've met your family then? How did they receive you?"

"Better than I could have hoped—and better than I no doubt deserve," he said with a self-deprecating smile.

"But that's wonderful news," I said. "I'm so pleased for you."

"In truth, it's been a little overwhelming," he confessed. "Coming here early like this was a chance to grasp a moment of calm in the middle of it all."

"I think you'll find there's no getting away from it." Philip strolled up to join us, looking far better rested than I felt. "The whole palace is abuzz with talk of you, *Prince* Damon."

"Prince?" I squeaked, quickly clearing my throat and trying again. "You mean the family you came to meet is the king and queen? How is that possible? The children told me they had no…" My voice trailed off as I remembered exactly what they'd said. "Why didn't you say something last night?"

Damon gave an apologetic grimace. "My parents, Prince Friedrich of Rangmere and Princess Mina of Arcadia, were exiled from my father's kingdom of Rangmere before I was born." He shrugged. "A prince without a kingdom is no prince at all. I didn't feel the title was mine to claim unless King Henry was gracious enough to recognize me—and it."

"Very proper." I nodded. "But I still wish you'd told us."

"You will have to accept my nerves as an excuse." He gave me a slow grin. "And perhaps a bit of pride. I didn't want to admit my purpose here until I knew how I would be received."

I chuckled. "Well, we're all of us human. I suppose I shall have to accept your apology."

He didn't seem in the least bothered to be talking with a goose girl, despite his newly recognized title, and it made me like him even more than when he had come to my rescue.

Where are my oats? Arvin stuck his head out and glared at me.

"Sorry! I forgot." I looked quickly around and located the bucket, slipping back into the stall to put it in place for him.

"I checked both horses before retiring to my bed last night,"

Philip said. "Neither showed any sign of discomfort, and the mare was settling in well to her new stall."

"Thank you," I said as I slipped back out, once again ashamed for forgetting to do it myself. But I should have known I could always rely on Philip.

Arvin didn't turn to his oats, regarding the two men instead. *Did I hear someone say prince?*

"Arvin, this is Prince Damon—King Henry's long-lost nephew. Your Highness, you may remember Arvin from last night." Forgetting, I tried to say *my horse*, but the words wouldn't come. I quickly corrected myself. "Princess Giselle's horse." I smiled, trying to cover my strange pause. "We didn't exactly manage proper introductions yesterday in all the darkness and excitement."

"He's even more magnificent in daylight!" The prince looked him admiringly up and down. "Such perfect proportions! And such strength. And that is even if I had not seen him fight last night. I haven't had the pleasure of meeting Princess Giselle yet, but I shall have to ask her about his history."

He stepped forward and offered the horse a couple of sugar cubes from his pocket. "I don't suppose you think she might be induced to part with him? Although I fear even with my new rank, I would look outclassed upon his back."

I like him. Arvin visibly preened. *He has excellent taste.*

Ha! Not susceptible to flattery? First Colin and now Damon. Apparently it was only my flattery he was impervious to. But the prince's words alarmed me. I could only imagine Sierra would be all too willing to agree to sell "her" horse.

"Oh no," I said quickly. "I don't think you should suggest such a thing to her."

"Thank you for the warning. I would hate to unwittingly give offense."

Philip was looking at me strangely, but I determinedly kept my gaze away from his.

"Your parents didn't come with you?" I asked, eager to change the topic of conversation.

Damon's smile fell away. "I'm afraid they have both passed away."

"Oh!" My hand flew to my mouth. "I'm so sorry. How clumsy of me."

What I really wanted to ask was why his father had been banished and where they had been all this time, but I couldn't possibly ask such insensitive questions after my blunder.

"No, indeed, you couldn't have known," he said. "It is not a raw grief. My mother has been gone for three years now, and my father for two."

"I'm sure the king was grieved to hear of his sister's passing," Philip said quietly, and Damon nodded.

The whole palace must be buzzing with news that the vanished princess had a son, and that he had returned. How many of the courtiers and servants had known the king's sister before her marriage to one of the princes of their eastern neighbor, Rangmere? She must have been a similar age to the king, who was not old. Plus, she would have been an adult by the time she left Arcadia for her wedding. Surely many still remembered her.

"She would have been pleased to know her brother thought well of her despite her disappearance and all the years that have passed," Damon said. "She told me once when I was a lad that King Henry would have taken them in after Rangmere cast them out. But her brother had only just ascended to his throne, after the unexpected death of their father, and she did not wish to undermine his reign. Their presence would have placed Arcadia at enmity with the newly crowned King Josef of Rangmere. My Rangmeran uncle would not have appreciated his brother finding haven in the neighboring kingdom. He would have considered him a potential threat, hovering at his doorstep."

He grimaced. "I'm told Rangmere is a harder kingdom than Arcadia. They value strength over family."

"Aye, it was," Philip said. "But things are different there now. They have a queen on the throne, and she is bringing change, however slow."

The Rangmeran delegation which had visited Eldon had been full of praise for their young queen and her chosen king. They had told us of their new prosperity, Celine filling in the gaps by telling us of their past. Before Queen Ava won her throne, Rangmere had been a threat to all of the Four Kingdoms. A cold, hard land, as Damon described. Apparently they had even attempted an invasion of Arcadia before Max and Alyssa's marriage.

"Change, you say?" Damon raised his eyebrows. "It seems hard to believe after my father's stories." His face relaxed. "But perhaps in that case, I truly do have hope of rediscovering both my lost families. Max and his wife have been most welcoming and have already suggested I accompany them on a planned trip to Rangmeros in the summer in order to meet my cousin on my father's side." He nodded at Philip. "From what you say, they must be right in thinking I will find a welcome there where I did not expect one."

"So you will stay here through the spring?" I asked.

He nodded. "My uncle and aunt have been everything that is hospitable. Already a suite has been prepared for me, and Alyssa has begun planning I don't know how many parties and celebrations."

I laughed. "Welcome to the royal life. I'm afraid the balls never really end."

"Better you than me," said Philip.

Damon clapped him on the back. "Yes, but think of all the lovely women you could dance with."

"I like the women here just fine." Philip was looking in my direction as he said it, bringing a flush of color to my cheeks.

I stepped quickly back into the stall to check on Arvin who

had begun eating, hiding my face as I did so. I had already attended enough balls for a lifetime, but I couldn't help but enjoy the image of dancing at one with Philip. Not that he would ever wish for that, given his preference for the freedoms of a commoner.

"All too true," Damon said, and hearing the admiration in his tone, I was glad I had fled. "I must be off, though. I don't want to give offense by arriving late for the meal after all my family's kindness."

"No indeed." I popped my head over Arvin's rump. "I'm so glad it's all worked out for you. And thank you again for your assistance yesterday."

"It was truly my pleasure," he said. "And I trust you will not be so harassed again. I reported the matter to the king, and he intends to increase the patrols."

"Thank you," I repeated. "And I do hope the visit to Rangmere goes well, Your Highness."

"Oh no, this is not farewell," Damon said. "And you must call me Damon. You are my first friend in Arcadia." He nodded at Philip. "Both of you—and Arvin too." He smiled. "And I'm quite sure I shall find myself needing a break from it all again soon. You must promise me I can visit you and your geese."

I laughed. "With goodwill, as long as you prepare yourself for an unpleasant odor and a great deal of honking. You may find the court is more peaceful."

He grinned at me. "Some things are worth the sacrifice."

Before I could think of an appropriate response, he had given us a friendly nod and strode out of the stables. Silence fell.

"Well, he's interesting," said Philip at last, breaking it.

I like him, said Arvin. *Better than you.*

"Arvin!" I cried, swatting his side. Thank goodness Philip couldn't understand his insults. "You just like him because he complimented you so profusely."

And don't forget the sugar cubes, he said, entirely unashamed.

I rolled my eyes. "Well who was it who delayed his own sleep to check you were well last night?" I whispered. "That should count more than sugar."

Perhaps you should consume some more sugar cubes. You might change your mind.

"Ugh, you're impossible."

You find that surprising? I'm a talking horse, remember.

Philip, still standing outside the stall, cleared his throat. "I actually came looking for you when I didn't find you at breakfast."

"Oh goodness! Have I missed the meal?" I groaned, imagining being hungry until midday.

"I managed to steal this for you." He pulled a small package wrapped in clean white cloth from his pocket and handed it to me. Inside I found a large roll. "I'm afraid it was all chaos this morning, and they didn't have the packs ready with the midday meals."

"Perhaps I'd better save this until I get hungry, then." I grimaced, wrapping it back up. "What's happened in the kitchens?"

"They've got guards in there supervising everything that's happening, and the cook is enraged."

"Guards?" I stepped forward to the front of the stall. "Whatever for?"

"It turns out the viscount ate his midday meal here on the day of his death. And until the doctors can ascertain how the poison was administered, all food must be under guard. There are guards at the storerooms and accompanying all the serving maids as well. One of them had hysterics and had to be carried off to her room."

"Hysterics? Over an escort of guards?"

He grinned reluctantly. "The maid in question might have a particular taste for dramatics."

"No one else has died or come down ill, have they?" I asked.

He shook his head. "It was almost certainly a targeted attack, with the intended victim now deceased. But while they still have no suspect nor any idea of motive, they must be cautious. Someone out there has a deadly poison no one has ever heard of —one that the doctors have no antidote for."

I shivered. When he put it like that, I was glad to hear the guards would be watching our food supply.

"Thank you for thinking of me," I said. "I shall be doubly glad of that roll if no one thinks to bring me a midday meal."

"I'll bring it to you," he said quickly. "Although actually the food wasn't the main reason I was searching for you. We agreed that we would work together, and I wanted to let you know that I'm heading back to where we lost the men last night. Would you like to come?"

"That's a good idea," I said. "We may well find something we missed in the darkness. And I can help make sure we have the right spot. There was nothing particularly remarkable about it."

We walked together out of the stables, discussing how we might conduct such a search. I hadn't made it more than a few steps into the yard, however, before I heard hooves behind me. Had I remembered to latch the stall door? I couldn't remember now.

"I guess Arvin is going to help us look as well," I said. "Perhaps his horse senses will pick up something ours miss."

"He is more than welcome," Philip said. "I like how he sticks close to you. If he hadn't been there last night…"

I wasn't sure if I would have followed the men without Arvin with me, but I didn't want to say that and turn Philip against the horse, so I said nothing. We were about to turn the corner of the palace, heading toward the park behind it, when Arvin suddenly stopped.

When I turned back to him, I found him staring at something all the way across the yard, near the great gates to the city.

Get on my back.

"What?" I stared at him. "You never want me to ride you, and now is hardly the time for it. Not when we have Philip with us."

Mount up or I shall leave you behind, he neighed, his attention still across the yard.

I frowned and turned back to Philip. He had stopped several steps on and was looking quizzically back at us.

"I'm sorry, I don't think I'll be able to come with you," I said, wincing at my inability to explain my sudden change of mind. "I think...I think Arvin needs some exercise. He's very...unsettled."

Philip's eyes moved to the horse, who was standing stock still, facing the other direction.

Now, Giselle.

I grabbed his mane and swung onto his back. "I'm sorry," I said to Philip. "Please let me know what you find. I'll..." But my words were already lost as Arvin took off across the yard.

He ignored everyone in our path, people scattering left and right while I called apologies. When we reached the gate, he barely slowed, trotting out past a small line of carts bringing supplies into the palace. They appeared to be waiting their turn for a thorough search by the large team of guards manning the gates.

No one gave me a second look, however, and Arvin and I were soon trotting down Palace Way, the Nobles' Circle stretching beside us in both directions.

CHAPTER 15

"*A*rvin," I hissed. "What are we doing? Philip must think we've both lost our minds."

Shush. Don't distract me. You'll see.

We wound between carts and other riders, their numbers increasing as we passed out of the Nobles' Circle and into the Merchants' Circle. I would have liked to see the shops we passed, or explore one of the marketplaces, tucked away off this main road, but we moved too fast to take in much of our surroundings, my attention focused on apologizing to people Arvin nearly ran down.

"Slow down."

I can't, he said shortly. *We'll lose her.*

"Lose her? Lose who?" I scanned the streets ahead of us and after a moment picked out another rider whose movements matched ours.

The woman wore a riding habit that allowed her to ride astride, the material plain and sturdy. A matronly scarf covered her hair, although her bearing suggested she was still relatively young. Her horse was nothing remarkable, a little awkward in gait, but steady enough. In fact, nothing about her was remark-

149

able in any way. But the longer I watched, the more certain I became that we were following her.

Before much longer, she turned off the road into the large, enclosed yard of a prosperous looking inn. A bright sign proclaimed it to be the Blue Arrow. Arvin followed without pause, although it meant closing the distance between us and our quarry.

Only once the woman was well within the walls of the inn did she turn around, allowing me a glimpse of her face. I started, clutching at Arvin's mane to keep from sliding off in my shock. It was the princess.

"Harrison!" she exclaimed, tumbling off her horse and into the arms of a handsome man around her own age.

"Alyssa!" He embraced her back. "What are you wearing?"

I stared at them both in shock, trying to understand what I was seeing, until Alyssa spoke again.

"And how is Aunt Corilyn? Formidable as ever, despite everything?"

Harrison chuckled. "You know my mother too well to doubt it."

Her cousin. I examined him again with the knowledge of their relationship and could see some similarities. Mostly about the eyes.

"What are you doing here all alone and dressed like that?" he asked her.

She frowned. "Max is worried, and so are his parents. I am too, of course. It's been one thing after another, and now a murder in our own home. None of us are supposed to be leaving the palace, but I told Max I needed to get out, just for an hour or two to visit you. He made me promise to come in disguise."

Harrison raised his eyebrows. "I'm surprised he didn't send a squad of guards."

Alyssa sighed. "He would have liked to, of course, but that would have attracted all sorts of attention. And we decided no guards and a disguise were safer than giving myself away with just one or two."

Harrison, who had been gazing around the yard, stiffened, his eyes on me. "Alyssa, I think someone's recognized you."

I kicked myself for sitting there staring at them like an idiot. An obvious idiot.

"What? Who?" She swung around, her eyes alighting on me. "Oh, Elle!" She waved me forward to join them, and I reluctantly slid down and did so.

"Who is she?" Harrison's eyes moved to Arvin, trailing behind me, and he whistled. "Now, that is a fine horse."

I sighed internally. No wonder Arvin had such a big ego when he constantly elicited such reactions.

"Elle is our goose girl," Alyssa explained. "But she used to be Princess Giselle's personal maid."

Harrison, his attention caught, transferred his stare to me, and I couldn't blame him, given my strange history.

"But what is she doing here?" He fixed me with a piercing stare. "What are you doing here?"

"I'm guessing she was exercising Arvin," Alyssa said.

"In the city? Without a saddle?" Harrison's voice sounded disbelieving. "I thought you had a beautiful big park for that."

Alyssa smiled. "Apparently he doesn't like saddles. Or halters. And maybe she wanted a change. She spends every day in the park."

"I'm sorry," I said. "I tend to let him have his head, and he decided to come here."

"Perhaps he recognized my old girl from the stables." Alyssa patted the horse who still stood at her side. She smiled at me. "I'm starting to get the impression he is the true master, and you merely dance to his tune."

I gave a wry chuckle. "That sounds like a fairly accurate summation of our relationship, Your Highness."

Harrison hissed at my use of her title. "Watch yourself!"

"Sorry!" I whispered.

"We need to get out of the yard." Alyssa took command of the situation. "Harrison, you find someone to take care of the horses. Elle and I will wait for you in your sitting room."

Harrison looked at me uneasily. "You're bringing the goose girl with you?"

Alyssa shook her head at him. "You should know better than to think there's any use trying to hide the state of things from servants. And besides, I have a good feeling about her—and you know my instincts about people are rarely wrong."

Harrison took Alyssa's reins from her hands, muttering something from which I caught the words *pride* and *fall*, but he made no further actual protest. Alyssa grabbed me by the upper arm and hauled me after her through the tap room to a private sitting room at the back of the building. She let me go as soon as she had the door safely closed behind us.

"Do feel free to sit down. Harrison should only be a moment."

I remained standing, shifting uneasily from foot to foot. "I didn't mean to intrude, Your Highness. I can leave."

Alyssa shook her head. "I didn't want to admit it to Harrison, especially after I was so determined to get out of the palace, but I had the most horrid ride down here. I couldn't shake the feeling that someone was following me."

I grimaced, but she just grinned.

"Now I know it was only that strange horse of yours, I feel a great deal better, but I still don't relish the idea of a solitary ride back. And Harrison is too well known to accompany me. He would give me away. You, on the other hand, will be the perfect, inconspicuous companion."

The door opened, and Harrison appeared, slipping quickly inside.

"I feel as if I've suddenly become involved in some sort of espionage," he said, sounding less than thrilled at the prospect.

"Not at all," Alyssa assured him, unwinding the scarf from her head and freeing her golden-red curls. "I just want to find out what you're hearing here at the inn. What's the mood of the city?"

Harrison frowned and ran a hand through his hair. "In truth, it hasn't felt like this for a long time."

Alyssa sighed and sat on one of the small sofas, gesturing for us to do likewise. I imitated her, but Harrison strode to the small fireplace.

"I don't mean to say that people are unhappy with the throne. It's early days for that. They haven't yet forgotten the last twelve years of prosperity."

"But they will soon enough. If this goes on." Alyssa rubbed her head and glanced at me. "Is it the same in Eldon, Elle? Do the people have short memories?"

"I think everyone does when they're scared." I thought of Celine. "Although some things are hard to forget. Our people spent a long time under a curse, and they haven't yet forgotten their gratitude for being rescued."

"Celine!" Alyssa clapped her hands in apparent delight. "I heard about that." She leaned forward. "Is it true she can throw fire balls from her hands? I was hoping she would give us a demonstration."

I smiled. "Yes, it's true. We were fortunate she came to Eldon when she did."

And fortunate she fell in love with my brother. When she became our crown princess, she had bought the royal family a great deal of goodwill from a terrified populace. The people had found themselves suddenly released from a curse with few memories of the previous two years but overflowing gratitude for their savior.

But there was no Celine here to rescue Eldon this time. It was up to me to protect my kingdom. And yet I sat there, like a lump, unable to think of anything helpful to say.

"Fire balls wouldn't be much use against this enemy," Harrison said, clearly not sharing my confidence in Celine. "Not when you don't even know who the enemy is." He looked sharply at his cousin. "Unless you do?"

Her shoulders slumped. "Not the least idea. Viscount Edgewaring was…"

"A bore?" Harrison supplied. "With never a kind word to say? Heartless toward that poor boy left to his care?"

When Alyssa gave him a pointed look, he just grinned. "I'm only repeating the things we hear in the inn—as you requested."

Alyssa grimaced. "Well, yes, in truth he was all those things. But he didn't exactly have any enemies. The man spent his life with his head buried in endless paperwork. For all his personal faults, he was an excellent Lord Chamberlain. And he'd been in the position since before King Henry took the throne."

She threw up her hands. "The man was over eighty. If someone wanted him dead, why did they wait so long?" She glared at Harrison. "And don't you suggest young Thomas did it. You should see the poor boy, weighted down as he is now. He doesn't seem to relish being the new Viscount Edgewaring in the least."

Harrison shook his head. "No, no, those who dared suggest such a thing in the tap room were quickly shouted down on every side. The young lord is liked."

Alyssa smiled. "I'm glad to hear it. He'll make an excellent viscount once he adjusts to the idea. He was probably expecting his grandfather to live forever. And I suppose it must be a terrible shock to discover one of your relatives has been poisoned— however much you disliked them."

"He may fear being accused of doing it," I said.

"Oh, I should have thought of that." Alyssa looked horrified. "I'll talk to him as soon as I get back to the palace and reassure him. He was a good friend of Lily and Sophie's before they left, and I've known him myself for years. None of the royal family suspect him."

"Which leaves you where?" Harrison asked.

"Ugh. Nowhere." Alyssa threw herself against the back of the sofa. "As you see we have no information that is not being discussed right now through that door." She pointed toward the tap room before looking hopefully at her cousin. "I don't suppose you can think of anything else you've heard that might be relevant?"

Harrison reluctantly shook his head. "I wish I could say yes. I really do. But all I've heard is that same conversation a hundred times over. Along with a resurgence in talk about that missing squad and the attacks on the Eldonians." He looked quickly over at me. "Oh, wait! I suppose that's you. I should have connected it. That makes more sense as to why Alyssa wants you here. You're as much involved as either of us at this point."

I struggled to keep my face calm, not wanting to give away that I was a great deal more involved than they realized. Not that I knew how or why Sierra could be responsible for poisoning or missing soldiers. That she was responsible, I felt sure, but I couldn't accuse her while she wore my identity. Especially not when doing so might implicate me as well, given my supposed identity as her lady's maid.

I first needed to find out the full truth and discover a way to break the enchantment. Only then would I be able to tell them everything I knew about Sierra's involvement.

Alyssa stood up and began rewrapping the scarf around her hair.

"Elle and I should really be getting back to the palace before something else goes wrong. Everything's in complete chaos." She made a face. "It seems the Lord Chamberlain relied on his unfaltering mind to keep the many details of the castle's supply chains straight. We are trying to make sense of his system, but he's been running everything for decades, and no one else has the full picture. We're already missing shipments of several essentials, including flour."

I raised an eyebrow, forgetting for a moment that I was only supposed to be a maid and thinking like someone used to helping run a palace. "That will cause trouble—and soon—if you don't find those shipments."

Alyssa nodded, tying off the scarf. "For now I think the confusion caused by the guards' presence in the kitchens is distracting everyone enough that only the cook and some of her top servants know. And in the meantime, we're scrambling to find where the shipments have gone."

So the chaos of the kitchens was due to more than the presence of the guards. Was the cook encouraging the dramatic overreaction of her serving maids in order to keep the truth hidden? My respect for her was restored.

I looked speculatively at Alyssa. Did having guards on the food serve yet another purpose? If word of the food shortage got out, their mere presence would stop anyone losing their heads or attempting to raid the remaining food supplies.

"Remember you chose this life, cousin," Harrison said. "You could have had a nice, calm existence here with us, keeping our books."

Alyssa grinned at him. "You know perfectly well that Max, Harry, and Rose are worth every moment of stress. We'll find a way through this. We've seen our way through worse."

He rolled his eyes and ushered us both out of the room, hustling Alyssa toward the yard. I followed behind, my mind racing. I hoped Alyssa's optimism was founded, but my uneasiness had increased. I had been trying to think why Sierra would want to assassinate an elderly Arcadian noble, and I had missed the obvious reason—despite Nikki telling me of the viscount's long-standing role as Lord Chamberlain.

If Sierra and her unseen supporters wanted unrest in the Arcadian palace, his death was an excellent way to achieve it. But few people would think of something as ordinary as smooth-running supply chains. Yet the Lord Chamberlain's death had the potential to throw so many important, but often overlooked, elements of palace life into jeopardy. To think of such a thing showed a deviousness that surprised me from her. It shouldn't have, though. Not after the way she so deftly stole my identity.

It certainly seemed that causing upheaval and unrest in Arcadia was not a byproduct of Sierra's actions, but her goal. But how could she have known the way to accomplish it?

At the door to the tap room, Alyssa paused, resisting her cousin's attempts to tug her forward. Lingering just inside the hallway, she peered inside.

"Who are that group there?" She pointed at a group of men sitting around a couple of tables in the corner. "It looks like a whole squad, but something is wrong with their uniforms."

Harrison looked in the direction of her pointing finger. "Did I forget to mention them? They claim to be Prince Damon's honor guard. We've had a surge in customers come to get a look at them and discuss the miracle of the new prince turning up."

"But what are they doing here?" Alyssa asked.

"Apparently he didn't want to march up to the palace with soldiers in tow, so he sent them here to rent rooms until he had a chance to see what reception you all gave him. They weren't too happy about it, saying their place was at his side, but it seems he commands obedience."

"I suppose I'll get back and find he's asked the king over breakfast if he can bring them up to the palace," Alyssa said. "I should have known I would miss something interesting. But why do their uniforms look so Arcadian? They must have come from the island with him, mustn't they?"

"I heard one of the serving maids asking them about it after a couple of drinks last night," Harrison said. "They said they were designed by Princess Mina, so I suppose she was modeling them on her memory of the uniforms from her home."

He finally succeeded in pulling Alyssa forward, and I trailed behind, sneaking glances at the group of guards. Alyssa had said island. What island?

I had barely stepped outside when Arvin came clopping toward me, Alyssa's mount at his side. Harrison boosted me onto his back before I had time to tell him I didn't need the assistance, while the boy who had led up Alyssa's horse provided a step for her.

Before I knew what was happening, we were back out in the street, my mind racing frantically. I bent over to speak in Arvin's ear.

"Get as close to Alyssa as you can. I need to ask her something."

Arvin's only response was to flick his ears back, but he did as I requested. As soon as we crossed through to the relative quiet of the Nobles' Circle, I asked her the question burning in my mind.

"You said those guards came with Damon from the island? What island? Where has the prince been all these years?"

"I don't know if it has an official name," she replied. "It's not on any of our maps, and he merely called it *our island*, but it's apparently a long way from shore—straight out to sea. I suppose it's roughly halfway between our lands and yours. Just on this side of the impassable storms that used to constantly rage. Friedrich and Mina's ship encountered one of the storms, and they ended up washed ashore on the island. No one lived there, but Damon tells us it's large enough to accommodate a small community. They had the whole crew of the ship with them which included a number of women who had stayed faithful to Mina in her exile."

"So they stayed?" I asked, my voice coming out strangely. "They made a home on the island?"

"Yes. At first they thought of restocking and sailing back, apparently, but they had nowhere they could safely return. And life on the island was good. So they made their own community there. Damon was born there, and he said the first of the second-generation islanders have been born. But with his parents gone, Damon wanted to meet the family they'd told him so much about. So he risked repairing their old ship and sailing here. It should have occurred to me he would have others with him. He couldn't have sailed that ship alone."

Perhaps, I told myself, there were two uncharted islands in the middle of the ocean with populations cast adrift from the Four Kingdoms. Even in my head, I didn't sound convincing.

So Damon knows Sierra, Arvin said, not bothering with the mental escape I was attempting. *This morning he said he hadn't seen her yet. I wonder if they met at breakfast.*

Apparently the horse had been paying more attention in the stables than appearances suggested. He flicked his ears back toward me again, letting himself drift away from Alyssa.

"When he exposes her true identity, they'll assume I'm working with her," I whispered to him. "I still won't be able to tell them *I'm* Princess Giselle. They'll think she's some impostor and kick us both out of Arcadia. Or lock us up!"

They won't lock me up, Arvin said with far too much calm.

"That's not overly reassuring to me," I snapped before forcing myself to take a deep breath. None of this was Arvin's fault. "I need to find Damon."

CHAPTER 16

The guards at the gate signaled for us to stop, but as soon as their lieutenant got a proper look at Alyssa's face, he gestured us hurriedly through. Arvin trotted in beside her, neatly avoiding any explanation of what we'd been doing out in the city.

"We're lucky the princess decided she wanted to ride back with us," I muttered to Arvin.

Never attribute to luck what is actually skill, he said, making me snort despite my anxiety.

Harry appeared, taking Alyssa's mount without looking in the least surprised to see her in such unusual garb. She quickly pulled the scarf from her hair, resuming something of her normal appearance.

"Thank you, Harry," she said.

"And how is my namesake up in the nursery?" he asked with a wink.

Alyssa laughed. "Utterly delighted to now be old enough to leave the nursery."

I remembered that Prince Henry—clearly named for his grandfather, the king—was called Harry by his mother and sister.

Apparently it was a widespread custom, if even the grooms knew of it.

Alyssa said something else and started toward the stairs into the palace. Harry, shaking his head and smiling, led off her mare. The woodcutter-turned-princess certainly had the skill of making people like her. I'd rarely seen such an approachable royal. No wonder Celine had assured me the older woman would make me welcome.

Could I hope to one day be like her?

The royal breakfast must have been finished, because a tall, handsome man a dozen years my senior appeared at the top of the steps and swept Alyssa into an embrace. He rested his face for a moment in her hair, no doubt murmuring something I couldn't hear. It was the first time I had seen him this close, but he had to be her husband, Crown Prince Max. Had he been worrying about her the whole time she was gone? My heart melted a little.

"Mama! Mama!"

"There you are!"

The two eager voices broke the moment, and the pair pulled apart, smiling a greeting to their offspring. Out of the corner of my eye, I saw someone else standing as stationary as I was, watching the familial scene unfolding before us.

I slid down from Arvin's back. "You'll have to find your way back to your stall on your own. Find Harry, and I'm sure he'll wipe you down."

Charming, he snorted, but I ignored him, rushing up to Damon.

"Damon!" I gripped his arm. "I only just heard where you've been living all these years. Have you met Princess Giselle yet?"

He started, broken from his strange concentration, and gave me a confused look. "Elle! I wasn't expecting to see you here at this time of day. Are you looking for the princess? Apparently she has the morning meal on a tray in her rooms."

Fresh voices joined the scene, and we both swung around to

see King Henry, Queen Eleanor, and Sierra emerge to join the welcoming party. I looked from Sierra to Damon in time to see him stiffen and hiss.

It was his turn to grip my arm. "Who is that?"

"Princess Giselle." I watched a number of emotions flicker across his face.

"That is not Princess Giselle." He turned and gave me an intense stare. "What were you saying earlier? What exactly is going on here?"

I looked around, people bustling on every side of us. "We need to talk. But not here."

I began to drag him around the side of the palace, and to my surprise he didn't protest, although he did throw another look back at Sierra. When I looked back myself, I saw we had caught her attention across the span of the yard. She watched us with wide, shocked eyes.

Yes, I thought. *Be afraid, Sierra. Be afraid.*

Part of me wanted to let Damon go—to tell him to run and tell the truth to the Arcadian royals immediately. But if I did that, I would never have the chance to make things right here. I couldn't fail when I was still only at the beginning of unraveling the situation.

As soon as we reached the first copse of trees, I drew us under the leaves and stopped, turning to face Damon. He frowned at me.

"I know that girl. I grew up with her, years ago. She's most definitely not a princess. Her name is Sierra."

I put my hands on my hips and watched him, not speaking.

"I don't understand." He drew back a step. "She came here and claimed to be a princess, and you're her servant. What is she doing?"

I tried to shake my head, but my neck wouldn't twist. The sensation of paralysis sent a surge of terror through my body, and I stopped trying.

"Why aren't you saying anything?" he asked suspiciously.

Because I'm Princess Giselle, I tried to say, but of course nothing came out. I threw up my hands, keeping eye contact and willing him to understand.

He frowned, his expression more thoughtful than irritated.

"She's clearly here for nefarious reasons. Especially since things are going wrong in this kingdom." His eyes narrowed. "And you came with her. What do you know of what's going on here?"

I threw up my hands again.

"Are you bound in some way?" he asked, sudden enlightenment brightening his expression. "She's exiled you to herding geese, and you've twice been attacked there." He stepped forward again, looking protective now. "So you're obviously not a willing part of what she's doing."

I looked up at him with wide eyes, the only visible signal I could manage.

"I'll expose her immediately!" he exclaimed, half turning back toward the palace.

I gasped and grabbed at his arm, and he turned back, worry crossing his face.

"But what will happen to you if I do that? Will they believe that you stay silent of necessity and not your own will?" He bit his lip and looked down at me. "They are my family, I owe them my loyalty. Is it foolish I also feel loyalty to you?"

"Well, we did fight together," I said. "Brothers in arms?"

He shook his head, a smile playing across his lips. "Not brothers. I never had one, but I'm sure if I had, he would not have looked half so charming as you."

"I don't want to be locked up." I chose my words carefully so as not to trigger the enchantment. "Or thrown out, alone and with nothing. We just need a bit of time."

Damon's eyes lit up. "You're gathering evidence against her?"

I hesitated. *Gathering* might be a little generous since I had yet to actually find any, but the intent was right. I nodded.

"Do you know what she's plotting?" he asked.

"Not yet." I put as much conviction into my voice as I could. "But I will."

Damon looked down at my face for a long moment.

"Very well," he said at last. "I will give you some time. More than that. I will help you. Together we will find the truth and go to Their Majesties with it. It's probably for the best, anyway. If I went to them now, it would be my word against someone they believe to be a foreign princess with guards of her own to back her up. They have only met me yesterday, and I have yet to earn their trust."

He shook his head. "It is a good thing you stopped me, or it is perhaps I who would now be in a prison cell, not you. And while they sought confirmation of my claims—a task that would no doubt require travel to Lanover and back, at the very least— Sierra would be free to complete whatever plans she has unhindered. This way I will be able to stay close to her."

I exhaled a long breath, closing my eyes for a moment in relief. I was safe for now. And Damon was right. His assistance would be invaluable. He could watch the court and royal family while I worked to uncover Sierra's plans and the network of people who must be assisting her—the ones who might never be uncovered if we exposed Sierra too rashly.

"She will recognize me too, of course," he said. "But I don't suppose she'll say anything. The real Princess Giselle has no reason to know me."

He looked off into the distance. "What a remarkable thing. I never expected to meet someone from my childhood here."

I tried to ask a question about their history, but the enchantment deemed it too close to discussion of her identity, rendering me silent. He seemed to catch my struggle, however, guessing at my curiosity.

"When my parents were first shipwrecked on our island, all their focus was on survival. After the initial struggle to establish themselves, the settlers continued to recognize my parents as their leaders. But living in such close community and under such unusual pressures, it was inevitable that some among the group fell out with each other. Those who harbored various grievances against key members of the group decided to break away and form their own village on the other side of the island."

He pursed his lips. "Sierra was raised in my village, we even played together as children. But she was greedy and demanding and wouldn't do her share of the work. When she was caught stealing, she was told to leave. She went to the other village, and I only ever saw her in the distance after that. Until one day she disappeared completely. The whole second village did."

"Eldon," I said, understanding suddenly why the people our ship had discovered never mentioned a prince among them. Perhaps it had been their final spiteful act of rebellion—gaining a new start and freedom from the island without ever mentioning that a whole other village of people lived nearby in need of the same rescue.

Damon's brow creased. "Eldon? Oh! You mean a ship from Eldon discovered the island and took them away? I suppose there are lots of ships exploring the seas now that the storms have disappeared and the two sets of kingdoms have reconnected. That explains the connection with Princess Giselle." The creases deepened. "But it leaves a lot still unexplained."

He looked at me hopefully, but I could only shrug.

"I'm sorry," I said. "I wish I could…"

He took my hand and gave me an earnest look.

"Don't worry, Elle. We'll find a way to expose her without putting either of us at risk. We just need some actual evidence."

I nodded. "You should probably get back. They'll all be wondering where you are."

He looked torn, as if he didn't want to leave me, so I gave him a small push.

"I need to get to my geese anyway. I've been away too long."

"Very well," he said. "I'll see you soon."

He looked back twice as he hurried away, and it struck me that I was now investigating the disturbances in Arcadia with two men. I briefly considered telling them each about the other, but somehow I didn't think Philip would like being told I had made the same agreement with Damon.

And if you told them about each other, then Damon would tell Philip about Sierra, and he might think you're involved, a small voice said at the back of my mind. I pushed it away. Philip had secrets of his own, and he might not appreciate having them exposed to Damon either. I would stay silent for both our sakes.

Damon and I were investigating Sierra, and Philip and I were investigating the poisoning and the attacks. I would be the link between them. If either of them found out anything of relevance to the other, I would know. There was no reason to upset anyone by mentioning my dual role.

CHAPTER 17

Colin looked disgusted when I eventually found him, having wandered through the park for some time listening for the honking of the geese.

"I thought I got rid of you," he muttered.

"Not today." I plonked down in the grass. "Arvin needed me this morning."

Colin relaxed a little at the mention of the horse. "Well, I suppose that's all right." He looked eagerly in the direction I had come. "Will he be here soon?"

"I think he's back in his stable. Maybe he'll show up this afternoon."

After that, the goose boy threw me occasional dark looks and mutters for the rest of the morning. But when a midday meal failed to appear, he forgot entirely about my transgressions, all his ire directed toward the kitchen staff.

"Fluff for brains the lot of them," he assured me. "Don't they realize the guards are there to protect us all? It's like they want to be poisoned." His brow darkened. "Unless it's a guilty conscience they've got."

I looked at him sharply. "Do you think it's possible? That one of them was involved with the poisoning?"

He looked over at me and reluctantly shook his head, deflating somewhat. "Who in the kitchen would have it in for that old codger?"

"Maybe someone paid them to do it?" I suggested.

But he shook his head even more emphatically at that. "Cook runs a tight ship, and she wouldn't have anyone in there she couldn't trust. Watches over them with an eagle eye, she does. Jobs at the palace are highly prized, you know." He puffed out his chest proudly. "No one would risk losing their job and likely their head as well over such a thing."

I didn't actually think King Henry would chop off anyone's head, even if they were found to be involved, but I didn't mention that. I wasn't convinced that every single member of the palace staff was above suspicion regarding a bribe, but I was more swayed by his argument that the cook knew her people well and watched them closely. With everyone talking of nothing else, they'd have to be a cool player indeed not to give themselves away.

Just as we had both despaired entirely of any meal—my stomach reminding me angrily that it had been a long time since I consumed Philip's bread roll—the man himself appeared.

"Philip!" Colin leaped to his feet, rushing to snatch one of the food packages from his hand.

"You're welcome," Philip said with a humorous lilt to his voice.

He turned to me, a warm smile lighting his eyes as he held out the second pack. "And yours, Lark."

"My stomach and I thank you most gratefully." I took it from him. "It was starting to sound as if wild animals had taken over the forest with all the noise it was making. The geese would have been honking in fright at any moment."

He chuckled. "I'm glad I could rescue you today, even if you didn't need it last night."

I looked over at Colin who appeared engrossed in his food. Philip followed my gaze.

"Shall we go for a walk?" he asked.

I nodded, jumping up. "Colin, Philip, and I are going walking."

Colin grunted and didn't even look up from his food. I exchanged an amused grin with Philip as we made our escape.

"I can't believe Damon turned out to be a prince!" I exclaimed. "I'm sure King Henry must have been glad to meet him."

"It seems so indeed," Philip said evenly.

Thoughts of the returned prince reminded me of Philip's task that morning. So much had happened since then I had almost forgotten the way I had run off on him.

"I'm so sorry about this morning," I said. "Arvin was behaving strangely, and I could tell he wouldn't come calmly into the park with us." Not that it had required any great perception on my part considering he had told me so directly.

"Where did he want to go?" Philip asked, still in that even tone I didn't like.

I grasped at Alyssa's explanation. "He spotted another horse from the stables leaving the palace, and he wanted to follow." I hurried on, hoping my news would distract him from the strangeness of my departure. "It turned out it was the princess! She had ridden out in disguise to visit her cousin at the Blue Arrow."

Philip raised an eyebrow. "In disguise?"

"She said they thought guards would be too conspicuous. She decided a disguise would be safer."

"So that missing squad has them worried," he murmured quietly, as if to himself.

"The one from up north, you mean?" I asked.

He nodded.

I couldn't blame them. It must be uncomfortable indeed to

know that an enemy operated within your kingdom, unseen, unknown—but with the strength to disappear a whole squad, without leaving any sign of a skirmish. I had lived far too many uncomfortable days with that feeling, alone with Celine and Oliver in a sea of cold, enchanted people. I shivered. I could still call back the fear that had driven me up the mountain with them on their famous journey—I couldn't bear the thought of being left alone while my people turned to ice around me.

"Lark?" Philip's voice pulled me back from the memory. He sounded concerned. Had he spoken to me? If he had, I hadn't heard.

"Are you all right?" he asked.

I nodded. "Just remembering something I'd rather not. I have no desire to relive my own kingdom's dark time from four years ago."

"This isn't a curse," he said quickly. "Nothing like that will happen to us here."

I only just kept myself from retorting that I was already under another curse. I was as much bound now as I had been then. I shivered again. Although at least I had kept my mind this time.

I couldn't tell him about Sierra, but I could still tell him the conclusions I had reached at the Blue Arrow without mentioning her.

"I think the person who killed the viscount did it because of his role as Lord Chamberlain. Now the flour shipment hasn't arrived—that's part of the reason for the guards in the kitchens and storerooms. All the supply lines are falling apart. I think they killed him for the same reason they did everything else—to sow confusion and upheaval and a sense of danger."

Philip frowned off into the distance. "But why? What is their end goal?"

I deflated a little. "That I don't have a guess for." I bit my lip. "So what did you discover? Could you find the spot?"

He nodded. "There was no trouble with that, especially with

that distinctive fig tree. The ground was trampled and several of the bushes have snapped branches and missing leaves. But I couldn't find any trace of where they went."

He ran an irritated hand through his hair. "There were no tracks leading away, and I paced the whole area. It's too far from the wall for them to have gotten there without our noticing, especially given the shape they were in."

"No convenient drops of blood, then?" I asked, disappointed. "At least one of them was bleeding."

"Not a drop," he said. "Unless someone came back after we left and cleaned their tracks." He gave a frustrated growl. "I should have gone back with a torch while it was still fresh."

I shook my head, placing my hand on his arm. "You can't blame yourself. They were all injured. We have no reason to think one of them came back. We were all there and saw the way they were just gone." I hesitated. "I've wondered if perhaps they had an...enchantment."

Rather than scoffing, he looked down thoughtfully at where my hand rested on his arm. I quickly snatched it away.

"An enchantment is a distinct possibility. I don't know how else they could have managed it. But neither do I know how they could have gotten their hands on the sort of godmother object that would allow them to move unseen like that."

I had no answer, although I already knew Sierra had managed to acquire at least one such object. Damon had mentioned something about her being a thief. Was it possible one of his parents had possessed the object she had used against me, and she had stolen it from them? That would be a crime severe enough to make banishment from their village under-standable.

"Perhaps we'll have better luck at the viscount's mansion this evening," Philip said. When I gaped at him, he just grinned back at me. "Assuming you actually want to come this time."

"You want us to break into a noble's home?" I asked.

"Who said anything about breaking in?" He was still grinning as he flourished an ornate looking brass key.

"Where did you get that?" I tried to swipe it off him, as if I thought a proper examination would reveal it to be made of spun sugar, but he tucked it back in his pocket.

"Never mind that. Do you want to come?"

"Of course I want to come!"

"That's settled, then. Meet me in the stables as soon as it gets dark."

Stop your incessant movement, Arvin said. *It won't make him arrive any faster.*

"But where is he? It's dark outside. You don't think he went without me?"

I didn't know if horses could roll their eyes, but I could hear it in his voice. *Why would he have invited you if he intended to go without you?*

I grimaced. I knew I was being ridiculous, but I had worked myself up into a high state of nerves at the prospect of breaking and entering in a strange kingdom where I was already viewed with some suspicion. Even if it wasn't going to involve any actual breaking of anything. I hoped.

"You're going to wear a hole in the floor," a laughing voice said, and I was so relieved I nearly threw myself into Philip's arms.

Pulling myself up just in time, I glared at him instead.

"Where have you been? It's been dark for ages."

"I came as soon as I could." He glanced at Arvin inside his stall. "I'm afraid Arvin can't come on this adventure."

I have no desire to break into the house of a dead old man, Arvin said. *Even if he was poisoned. You children go ahead and have fun without me.*

"He doesn't want to come," I said to Philip. "He's quite comfortable in there for the night."

Adequately comfortable.

I turned back to Arvin with an unimpressed look which he seemed to interpret as confusion.

Adequately comfortable, not quite comfortable.

I threw my arms around his head. "You know you're a ridiculous horse, don't you?"

And you're a ridiculous human. But he actually sounded a little affectionate.

I gave him a kiss on his velvety nose and turned to Philip.

"Well then, let's do this before I lose my nerve."

Philip gallantly offered me his arm as if we were on our way to a ball. I slipped my hand around it and giggled, before clamping my free hand over my mouth. What was wrong with me tonight?

"The more I know you, the more I suspect losing your nerve is not something that is likely to happen," he said. "You were clearly wasted as a lady's maid."

His final sentence immediately killed the lingering amusement inside me. The closer I got to Philip, the more I hated not being able to be truthful with him. He thought he knew me, but he didn't know me at all. If I was here as a princess, he wouldn't be offering me his arm, or paying me compliments. We wouldn't have met at all, most likely.

I had enjoyed the taste of freedom that came with being a goose girl, and if I was honest, the freedom to be with Philip was what I valued the most. I had promised my parents I would give Percy a chance, and here I was, spending all my time with a strange servant who didn't even have a clear position.

My conversations with Damon and Alyssa had reminded me all too forcibly of my true identity. I could never turn my back on my kingdom, or on my family who I loved deeply. Which meant this game wasn't fair to Philip—or to my heart.

He looked down at me, a question in his eyes.

"Did I say something wrong?"

I shook my head.

We reached a small side gate where two guards stood at attention. My mind started racing. I hadn't even thought about the guards who stood between us and the city.

"Philip!" one of them called, with a grin. "Heading out to the night markets?"

I glanced up at Philip, who looked relaxed, smiling back at the guard. I had been distracted at the evening meal, eating alone—my mind consumed with thoughts of our planned misadventure and mourning for the absence of any bread. But I had noticed a certain extra buzz in the air and heard someone say something about a night market. Was there a reason Philip had suggested we go tonight of all nights?

"We've had a small stream of you lot," the other guard said. "Just make sure you're back by midnight like everyone else. Or you'll have to spend a cold night waiting for us to unlock the gate at sunrise."

"Have a good time," the friendly one said, with a significant look at our joined arms and a wink at Philip.

"Oh, we will." Philip put his arm around me, pulling me into his side.

Taken by surprise, I squeaked, then tucked myself into him to cover the mistake. The guard chuckled and held the gate open for us as if he were a footman at a grand ball.

Philip kept his arm around me until we heard the gate close behind us, his warmth enveloping me. Despite my earlier warnings to myself, I let my eyes close for one brief second as I imagined the charade was true, and we were just two servants off for a romantic walk to the night markets. But when the gate clanged behind us, and Philip's arm lingered around me, I made myself pull free. I wasn't a goose girl, not really, and we weren't going to the night markets.

"You should have told me the plan!" I said, rounding on him. "I nearly gave us away."

He looked entirely unrepentant. "You were perfect."

I glared at him a bit longer before giving up and shaking my head. "You're impossible." *And I liked your arm around me far too much. I'm going to have to be more careful.*

The only road I had yet seen in Arcadie was the broad Palace Way, but Philip led me through back streets instead. Here we saw only the rear of the nobles' vast city houses. High walls guarded some, but many others were open, their gardens running nearly to the edge of the road. Bright blooms filled many of them, and their perfume permeated the air, a pleasant change from an afternoon of goose stench.

In the semi-darkness, surrounded by flowers, with distant music from the night markets, and the warmth of Philip's arm lingering around my shoulders, it was hard to keep my mind strictly on the task at hand. I allowed myself to sneak a single side glance at Philip's strong profile. His hair was tousled, as always, the dark, disordered strands illuminated by the bright moonlight. He had a pleased expression on his face as if he was enjoying the adventure. Not once had he shown any nerves at our planned criminal activity.

As if he felt the weight of my eyes, he turned his head and grinned at me. I told myself to look away, but his eyes captured me.

"You're not regretting coming are you, Lark?" There was amusement in his voice.

I pulled my gaze away. "Never!"

"That's my girl," he said softly, pulling my eyes back to his again. But the emotion in his face sent mine running again, focusing on the ground beneath my feet instead.

"Here we are, this is the one," he said in a bracing voice that gave me the courage to look back up again.

Thankfully this was one of the mansions without a wall, so we were able to step straight off the road and into the grounds. Unlike most of the other houses there were no fancy bushes, shaped into animals or spirals, and no intricate arrangements of flowers and trees. A rather sad gazebo stood in the center of a lawn, and a few flowerbeds grew in a riot of mixed color. Otherwise it was all gravel paths and tall, box hedges.

"The viscount wasn't much for throwing parties," Philip said.

"And I'm guessing he didn't believe in wasting time shaping bushes into mythical creatures like elephants," I said. "From what I hear, he didn't seem the type."

Philip chuckled. "You've clearly got a sense for him. I believe the flowers were planted by his daughter-in-law in the few years she spent here, and he only kept them for the sake of his grandson."

"It must have been a lonely life for him here." I looked around sadly, trying to imagine a young boy in this place with only an elderly grandfather who didn't believe in flowers.

"I believe he spent a large part of his time living with various more distant relations," Philip said, but he didn't sound like he wanted to talk about it.

"Which door does the key fit?" I asked.

"The front one, of course." He led me around the house and approached the front door, set well back from the distant Palace Way.

He approached as if it were his own home, his confidence not faltering for a moment. Without knocking, he inserted the key, opened the creaking door, and ushered me inside.

CHAPTER 18

We entered into a grand hall, all echoing marble and decorative vases on plinths. I blinked at them, wondering if they predated the recently deceased occupant. They looked old enough.

Slow footsteps sounded, and I clutched at Philip's arm. He didn't flinch, however, merely turning to meet the approaching servant. The old woman frowned at us both.

"Sorry to disturb you so late," Philip said. "But we just need to do a final sweep."

"At this time of night?" The woman—who must be the house-keeper—sighed. "And the house barely quiet from the last lot. I suppose you can find your own way, then?"

"Yes, indeed," Philip said. "We don't want to disturb you in the least. We shan't need to come near the kitchen."

"Well, that's a mercy at least," she muttered. "Make sure you lock the door again on the way out. And make sure you tell that pushy captain that I want my key back when you've all finished. I can't present the house to the new viscount with one of the keys missing."

Philip gave her a half-bow. "Of course not. No one would dream of such a thing."

"Hmmm, we'll see about that." She turned and started back toward the depths of the house, muttering inaudibly to herself.

"You took that key from a guard captain?" I hissed. "Please, please tell me it wasn't Captain Markus!"

"Fine, I won't then." Philip gave me the same carefree grin.

I groaned. "He's the captain of the king's guard! You're going to get us both arrested."

"But would it be fun if there wasn't any risk?" He collected a burning lantern from beside the door and headed through a large arch.

I threw up my hands. "Men!"

Following behind I wondered how long it would be before I became the old woman shuffling along and muttering to myself about pesky youths. The image made me chuckle, and I had to clamp a hand over my mouth before it turned into full laughter.

Philip smiled over his shoulder at me. "See. I told you this was fun."

Shaking my head, I caught up and peered around us. "This place doesn't have much of a lived-in feel. Surely the viscount's servants all reside here still?"

"He lived here year-round, but apparently he only kept a skeleton staff. I have it on good authority he used the formal dining room as his study, though."

We turned to the left through another arch and both came to a standstill. My mouth dropped open.

"How many nights did you say we were going to be here?" I asked, my voice weak.

The vast room had clearly been designed for hosting meals for fifty or more. I had only ever seen a table that large in the formal dining room of my family's palace back in Eldon. But this one looked nothing like ours.

The entire length of the table was blanketed with haphazard

piles of paper, most of them covered in tight, cramped handwriting. Gazing around the space, I saw that the sideboard carried a similar load, and that many pieces of paper had fluttered down to rest on the floor in strange locations.

"I can suddenly see what Alyssa was talking about," I whispered. "This is madness. Why haven't they boxed it up and taken it to the palace?"

"My guess is they think there's some system to it, even if it's not immediately obvious. They're hoping to crack it. Displacing it all would likely make that impossible. And there are so many papers here it would take months to read through them—even for a team."

I wandered over and looked at the top page on one of the stacks. It contained a list of delivery dates for orders that were labeled using a series of letters and numbers that meant nothing to me.

"This page is full of deliveries from eight years ago." I glanced at the sheet beneath it. "And this one is deliveries from twelve years ago. Are you sure he had a system?"

"He must have," Philip said. "Or how else would he find anything? He was famous for always being able to deliver any detail the king requested, no matter how obscure. It was why he kept such an important post for so long and despite his age."

We moved up the table, being careful not to displace anything as we skimmed the top pages of many of the piles. I didn't see anything more interesting than the first page I had read.

"I must admit, after all the buildup, this is strangely flat," I said. "We're not going to find anything here."

"Not in this room, no. But we should look at his personal rooms."

"Do you know where they are?"

"No, but I can guess."

He confidently led us back into the entrance hall and up the grand staircase to the gallery above. Turning right, he stopped at the first door and pushed it open. When we both leaned inside and saw a large sitting room with enough personal items scattered around to show it had been in recent use, he gave a flourishing bow.

"Impressive!" I led the way inside.

But looking around the abandoned room, my mood dropped. I had pitied his grandson, but now I pitied the viscount himself. For all his unpleasant manner, he had spent his life serving his kingdom, and he had deserved a better end.

Philip moved efficiently around the space, disturbing as little as possible, as if he too had been touched by a certain reverence. I glanced through into the connected bedroom, but there was nothing inside beyond a large four poster bed with a small table beside it, holding a half-burned candle and an empty glass.

When I turned back to the sitting room, Philip was opening the drawers of the desk.

"Surely he didn't keep any papers in there," I said. "Surely there can't be *more* papers."

Peering over his shoulder, I watched him open each empty drawer. When he found nothing, he returned to the top drawer, reaching inside with his hand and feeling along the top. His fingers must have found some sort of latch in there because with a loud click, a hidden compartment of the drawer opened, revealing a large, slim book.

"How did you know to do that?" I asked, remembering the similar compartment I had found as a child in one of the drawers of my father's desk. He had laughed and called me his clever girl, telling me that some very special—expensive—desks were made with such hidden places. I didn't feel so clever now. I should have thought of checking myself.

"Just a guess," he said, his attention on the book which he had laid on the desk. Flipping through the pages, he revealed a sparsely filled diary with appointments marked carefully down against dates and times.

When we found the day of the viscount's death, we both leaned forward, our faces almost touching as we read the words. I leaned back first, frowning.

"So he spent the whole day at the palace. No wonder the king and queen are concerned. Especially since I'm guessing the rest of his servants are like the one we saw—the kind who've spent their whole life in his service and aren't likely to be involved in something like this. So the poisoning almost certainly happened at the palace."

"The servants were all cleared of involvement yesterday," Philip said. "There aren't many of them, and not a one who hasn't spent at least six decades in this house working for the viscount. The new viscount vouched for them all."

He turned the next few pages, looking for an upcoming appointment that might have been moved earlier and not noted down, but his dissatisfied expression told me he didn't find anything.

"I was hoping to find evidence he had someone here that day," he said. "It would simplify things."

"What do we do with the diary now?" I asked. "Surely we should hand it over to the proper investigators?"

Philip closed the hidden compartment and placed the book in the top drawer.

"We'll leave it here. I'm sure they'll send a junior guard to do a second look at some point, and he can take credit for finding it. There's nothing in here anyway."

"So, what now?" I asked.

He sighed and stretched, rubbing his neck. A faint creaking noise made him freeze, one hand still behind his head.

I ran for the door, tripping over a spindly table on the way and just catching it before it hit the ground. I leaned my head against the door for a second, catching my breath and trying to quiet my thudding heart. Placing one hand flat against the door, I carefully opened the latch and eased the door ajar.

Voices filled the hall below, and boots stomped toward the stairs, echoing off the marble. I eased the door back closed, whirling around and standing with my back against it, wide eyes staring at Philip.

"Guards. And they're coming upstairs," I whispered.

In three strides, he cleared the desk, heading for the door into the viscount's bedroom. Pausing, he gestured for me to join him. I hesitated for a moment, remembering how empty the room had been, but stomping boots behind me sent me flying across to him.

I whisked myself through the doorway, and he followed, closing the door behind us. We both looked frantically around the room. Could we fit under the bed?

Philip moved toward it, while I was still eyeing it doubtfully. Most of its height was made up by a double mattress, meaning the frame itself sat low to the ground. I might squeeze under there, but could he?

The outer door to the sitting room opened, and the voices invaded the viscount's rooms. I hurried to the bed, reaching it just as Philip swung himself up on top of the coverlet. I scrambled up beside him, barely making it out of the way before he whisked closed the four poster's curtains.

I tried to quieten my breathing which sounded ragged and loud in the confined space. The top of the bed opened to the ceiling, but with the room so dim, hardly any light made it through. I could barely make out the dark lump of Philip beside me, crouched on the mattress.

I hadn't dared move from my hands and knees, afraid of making any noise that might escape through the bedroom wall. Were the guards looking for us? If so, I couldn't imagine we'd be safe behind a curtain. Or were they sent for the second look that Philip had predicted? If they already knew the bedroom was empty, we might still have a chance of remaining undiscovered.

The air around me felt stifling, and I wished for light, even though I knew we were safer without it. But we had both abandoned the lantern when we ran to hide.

Wait.

"The lantern!" I breathed at Philip, as quietly as possible. "We left it behind."

The mattress dipped slightly as he moved, easing toward the edge of the bed. Did he think we would have to run? We would need to fight our way out in that case, and it had sounded like at least five guards. Guards who were just doing their jobs.

"The new lord needs to hire some younger servants," a loud voice said through the closed door. "These ancients have left a burning lantern up here." A derisive snort followed. "Although I don't know why they'd need one since they've hardly done much cleaning."

"They were told not to touch this room," said an authoritative voice in cold tones. "It is likely our own comrades who left the lantern here earlier today. We should be grateful they appear to have been less than careful and thorough—perhaps we will manage to find something after all."

"Yes, indeed," a third voice said. "I heard the captain saying he refused to appear before the king empty-handed in the morning. If we're to search until we find something, I'd rather not be searching all night."

I closed my eyes, relief sinking through every part of me. They didn't suspect our presence. My eyes shot open again as footsteps neared the bedroom door.

"Do we need to search through here?" the third voice asked.

"That's just the bedroom," the derisive voice said. "Empty as the inside of Reg's head." He guffawed at his own joke.

The footsteps paused.

"You might as well take a look," the authoritative voice said. "I'll check the desk."

The footsteps resumed.

A warm hand closed over mine, squeezing gently. I made

myself breathe, two long, slow inhales. If he just glanced inside, we might still be safe.

The doorknob rattled, turning slightly, and Philip's hand squeezed mine more tightly.

"Wait! There's something here." At the words, the doorknob settled, the door remaining closed.

"They missed something in the desk?" The derisive voice sounded condescending. "It must have been an incompetent team here earlier."

"It's his diary," the authoritative voice said. "We should get this straight back to the palace."

A jumble of voices sounded over each other, getting quieter as the speakers filed out of the sitting room. For a long moment we both remained frozen in place. Now that the immediate danger had passed, I could feel Philip's hand burning into mine. It was too dark to see him, but every part of me was aware of his presence beside me in the darkness.

"Lark," he breathed, his weight shifting toward me.

I held my breath, my heart beating as fast as it had moments before when the guards nearly discovered us. I was in a new kind of danger now—one to my heart.

For a single breath, we both stayed there, anchored in the dark together, shut off from the world. Then Philip gave the softest of sighs and leaped from the bed, pulling the curtain aside for me. Gesturing for me to stay in place, he crossed over to listen against the door. After a moment, he opened it, peering into the room beyond.

"It's clear," he said to me quietly.

"We can't leave the house until they're completely gone, though," I whispered. "I hope they all mean to return to the palace immediately."

"Let's not wait in here," Philip said. "In case it occurs to them that if someone overlooked the diary, they might have overlooked something else as well." I could hear his opinion of their efforts in his voice.

I clambered down off the bed, and we slipped together into the sitting room and across to the door into the corridor. Philip opened it this time, checking the corridor before leading the way out.

We made it several steps along the gallery, when a woman's voice sounded over the hubbub.

"What? More of you? This is disgraceful! Don't you lot know it's the middle of the night? Two of you was bad enough, but I won't have a squad tromping through the house at such a disrespectful hour."

The authoritative voice cut across her outraged exclamations, latching onto her mention of Philip and me. The two of us froze, exchanging looks.

"We are the only guards sent here tonight," the authoritative voice said. "Those people were intruders."

"Intruders?" The woman sounded astonished. "But he had the key. And politer than you lot they were, too. They're still here, somewhere."

"Still here?" A stream of orders followed, but I couldn't hear them through the blood pounding in my ears.

Philip snatched up my hand, and we ran. Dashing down the gallery, we didn't slow until we reached less decorative doors at the far end. He pulled open the first one, closing it again after only a second's glance beyond. I wrenched open the second door and had barely recognized the stairs behind it before Philip was crowding in behind me.

Together we raced down the servants' stairs, moving so fast I stumbled twice and would have fallen if Philip's hand hadn't moved at lightning speed to steady me. The bottom of the stairs spat us out in a narrow, unadorned hallway, an open door giving a glimpse of the bright kitchen.

Philip looked calculatingly at it and then down at me. I

chewed on my lip, glancing back at the bottom of the steps before nodding my head. We couldn't afford to go stumbling around the house looking for a way out.

We burst into the kitchen, my gaze scanning the open space. A single, half-drunk cup of tea sat on the table, a chair askew beside it. No one was in sight.

My anxiety eased slightly only to increase again as Philip paused to unlatch the outside door. Was that footsteps I heard? Perhaps the housekeeper returning to her interrupted drink.

The door swung open, and we spilled out into the garden, Philip gently closing it behind him. I leaned over, pulling in panting breaths.

"What do we do now?" I gasped, looking over at him.

He wore an exhilarated grin that sent my heart rate straight back up.

"Now we run." He seized my hand and towed me into the gardens.

CHAPTER 19

*O*ur feet scrunched against gravel, but more box hedges soon sheltered us from view. I kept glancing over my shoulder, so it took me a moment to realize Philip wasn't leading me back the way we'd come. Instead, we ran toward Palace Way.

"What are you doing?" I hissed.

"Going to the night markets."

"What?" I slowed, pulling back against him.

"We can't go back so soon, especially not now they know there were intruders at the house. If we run straight back to the palace, we'll give ourselves away—even if they don't catch us on the road. The guards from the gate think we're enjoying an evening at the night markets." He smiled enticingly. "So, let's enjoy an evening at the night markets."

"Alternatively," I said, falling into step beside him as he tugged me out onto the road, "we could go back now, and I could slap you dramatically right as we walk through the gate."

He laughed. "I vote for the night markets."

I gave an exaggerated sigh. "Fine, if we must. But I think I could be a good actress if I had prior warning."

"I'll bear that in mind."

We soon joined others moving in the same direction, and I could see the logic of Philip's plan. Alone in the back streets, we would have stood out. Here on Palace Way, there was already no way to distinguish us from the other market goers. And my nervous glances over my shoulder still gave no sign of pursuers. The guards must still be searching the house for us.

My heart slowed, some of my nervous energy draining away, but it didn't subside completely as we plunged into the crowded market. The music swirling between the people was compelling without being overpowering, and the scent of delicious sizzling meat and spices teased my nose.

Torches and lanterns burned all around the large open space full of stalls and people. From the clothing, I guessed they were largely servants and laborers whose days were spent working, meaning they couldn't attend the regular markets. But a few of the outfits suggested the festive atmosphere had drawn some wealthier residents as well.

We wandered among the stalls, admiring the wares, and stopping to watch several performers. We came back twice to the man who swallowed fire, my amazement managing to drown out my lingering fear.

"How utterly horrid." I stared transfixed at him.

Philip laughed and threw a small coin to the boy who was walking among the crowd collecting money for the fire breather.

"When I was a boy," Philip said, "I horrified my parents by telling them I wanted to become a fire breather when I was grown. My father nearly banned me from ever attending any markets or festivals again, but my grandmother talked him out of it. She told him banning me was the surest way to send me off in pursuit of my dream at the earliest opportunity." He chuckled. "In my family, my grandmother's word is law, so it's fortunate she's so wise."

"I like the sound of her," I said.

"I hope I can introduce you to her someday," he said, his voice light. "I'm sure she would like you."

I turned away, pained once again by my deception, and admired a stall of expensive jewelry. The brooches and bracelets gleamed in the light of the flames around us.

"I'll buy you one of those one day, too," Philip said quietly, his breath tickling the back of my neck.

I shivered and had to steel myself not to lean back against him.

"They're beautiful," I whispered, "but I don't need one."

"Who buys such things because they're needed?"

I tried to say I didn't want one either, but I couldn't make the words come out. I had been overtaken by a sudden, burning desire to possess such a gift from this man—the sort of gift that came with love attached and whispered compliments and walks in the moonlight.

I spun around, gasping at the closeness of his face. "I think we've been here long enough. It should be safe to return." My voice was as steady as I could make it.

"Yes," he said, not breaking my gaze. "I think it should be safe enough."

For a long moment, neither of us moved, and I tried to remember how to breathe. Then he took my hand, threading it back through his arm, and guided me back to the road.

For the second night in a row, I struggled to sleep—although for entirely different reasons. I replayed the night with Philip over and over in my mind and admitted to myself that if he had tried to kiss me there in the market, I wouldn't have stopped him.

But I had to be stronger. He had said he had no interest in balls and the expectations of nobility, and I had no place among his clearly loving family. I could picture them easily, the smiles and laughter as they gathered, overflowing whatever modest house they had chosen as their meeting place, all of them deferring to the matriarch. I wanted so desperately to be part of that picture.

But for how long? How long before I chafed at such a life and longed for my own home and family across the ocean? I was enjoying life as a goose girl far more than I would have dreamed possible, but I couldn't deny my identity forever, or the other parts of my true self.

We could never work, and I knew it. I was keeping secrets from Philip, though they weren't of my own choosing, and I had to keep my distance.

It was a long night, and if tears were shed, my pillow had no way to betray me.

In the morning, I couldn't face the dining hall, so I went to Arvin instead. He was already awake and eating his bucket of oats, so I tucked myself into the far corner of his stall and told him all about what we had found at the viscount's home and our narrow escape.

Paperwork! The obsession of you humans for scratching things on pieces of paper never ceases to astound me.

I rolled my eyes. "Don't pretend you don't know the value of reading and writing. You're far too intelligent for that. And think how much worse it would be if the viscount had kept everything in his mind and not written anything down!"

Arvin snorted, apparently unimpressed by my argument, and was about to lower his muzzle back into his bucket when he froze. His ears pricked back just as I also heard voices.

"Hey, you! Stable boy. Fetch us horses." The speaker sounded arrogant but young, almost certainly a noble youth.

When there was no response, he repeated his words more stridently.

"You mean me?" asked a familiar, disbelieving voice. "I'm not a stable boy."

My heart sank, and I scrambled to my feet.

"What are you doing in the stables, then?" the first voice asked. "Stop your games and fetch us horses. Or I shall have you punished."

"You aren't in charge of me," Colin said, his voice just outside Arvin's stall now.

"I am if I say I am," the older boy replied, a nasty edge to his tone.

Arvin turned to face the front of his stall, his oats abandoned. I slipped forward to stand at his head, neither of us noticed by the group of boys who stood a short distance away. The noble youth had a companion with him, another noble from his clothes, although the second boy looked uneasy, glancing around the large building.

I followed his gaze and caught a flicker of movement. Was that Harry? But any hope that he might step forward and help Colin was dashed when he took one look at the unfolding drama and escaped out a side door. Which meant if the conflict escalated, it would be up to me to step in.

Walk away, Colin, I pleaded silently. The last thing either of us needed was a fight with some unknown noble in the middle of the chaos already unfolding.

The noble boy stepped forward threateningly. "I said, prepare me a horse."

"And I said, I'm not a stable boy," Colin said. "Not only do I not work for you, but the grooms would have my hide if I touched any of their stuff."

The noble stepped closer again, lowering his voice. "I don't care if you're a stable boy or not, *fetch me a horse.*"

I'll fetch him a horse. Arvin surged forward, and I only just managed to throw my arms around his neck and weigh him down.

Out in the open it wouldn't have worked, but penned in by

the stall and its closed door, my force made him stop. I could feel him quivering with rage beneath my arms.

Let me go this instant, and open that door. I'll show them some manners.

"No," I whispered firmly, fear lending me unnatural strength. "You go out there, hooves and teeth flying, and you're just as liable to hurt Colin as those other boys."

I didn't add my greater fear. For all his bluster, the damage a young noble boy could do to a servant of the king was limited. The monarchs took their responsibility to those who worked for them seriously. A mere horse, on the other hand, and one whose owner was eager to see him killed...

If a noble reported Arvin had attacked him, Sierra would leap to have him put down.

Movement outside the stall distracted me from my single-minded purpose. The noble boy closed the distance and picked Colin up by the front of his shirt, pulling him off the ground.

Colin yelped and swung at the boy. He missed him, but the attempt enraged the noble.

"Why, you little—" He slammed Colin's back against the wall, knocking the wind from him.

Arvin screamed, surging against me, and my own feet left the ground as he slammed against the stall door. The noble didn't seem to notice, all his attention on Colin, but his companion looked our way, his eyes widening when he saw me there, witness to the interaction.

He grabbed at his friend's sleeve, but the other boy shook him off with an irritated sound. Glancing around, the angry noble spotted a large bucket of dirty water and strode toward it, dragging Colin behind him.

I sucked in a breath. With Arvin leaning heavily against the stall door, there was no way I could get it open and get out without also letting the horse out. But I couldn't stay here and let that boy dunk Colin's head in the water.

Colin, his breath returned, also seemed to realize the noble's intention. He struggled, but the other boy had a firm grip.

My hand reached for the latch. "You leave this to me," I said to Arvin as firmly as I could. "Stay here!"

But just as I was about to throw the door open and send us both tumbling out to confront Colin's attacker, new footsteps sounded. Someone hurried toward us, and even the noble boy paused to see who had arrived.

For a moment I almost didn't recognize Philip, although he wore one of his usual nondescript outfits. Harry followed behind him, the groom keeping several strides back as if he didn't wish to be involved. Arvin instantly went still and stopped fighting me.

"What is going on here?" Philip asked in a voice laden with anger and authority.

"Nothing to do with you," the noble youth said defiantly, but he didn't sound quite so confident anymore.

"So that is not a servant of the king being detained from the king's work?" Philip asked, his low volume somehow suggesting danger.

The youth said nothing this time, looking back at his captive with an uncertain expression.

"Let him go," his friend hissed, and the youth reluctantly dropped Colin, stepping back and straightening his jacket in a failed attempt at nonchalance.

Philip stepped close, lowering his voice even further, although I was close enough to hear his words.

"You come here throwing your weight around again—or if anything happens to this boy here—I'll go straight to your father and ensure *you're* the one to get a whipping."

It didn't seem to occur to anyone present that he might not have the status to follow through with this threat. And I couldn't blame them. He radiated authority and danger.

The boy's face paled, and when his friend grabbed his arm and towed him out of the stables, he didn't resist.

Colin scrambled to his feet, not bothering to dust himself off. To my surprise, he gave Philip a broad smile.

"That was the best thing I've seen in a twelve-month. Did you see him scamper off?"

Philip cast his eyes upward. "What are you doing getting into a scuffle with a noble, Colin?"

"It wasn't me." Colin leaned over and began collecting something off the ground. "Harry would have thrashed me worse than that 'un if I'd done as he asked and started mucking about with a saddle and such like."

Harry, coming forward, grinned. "Aye, that I would."

Colin grinned back at him, remarkably unperturbed by the entire incident. He stepped toward Arvin and me, holding out his hand and displaying what he had been collecting from the ground.

Arvin whuffed with approval at the offering of sugar cubes, apparently not in the least minding that they had been scattered over the ground, one looking half-crushed by a boot. So that was what Colin had been doing in the stables. It was a kinder gesture than I had seen him display toward any humans, and demonstrated why he made such a good herder. He truly cared for the animals.

While Arvin was distracted eating the sugar, I slipped out of the stall, latching it firmly behind me.

"Lark! I didn't realize you were here." Philip's expression was hard to read, and I rushed to explain myself.

"I was shut inside the stall with Arvin when they all arrived. I'm afraid I was caught between helping Colin and trying to prevent Arvin trampling everyone involved." I grimaced. "You came along at just the right moment. Thank you."

Philip shrugged as if it were nothing, some discomfort still lurking in his eyes at my presence. Did he think less of me for not stepping in myself?

"I'm just glad I found you so quickly," Harry said to Philip. "I shudder to think of the havoc that blasted animal would have wrought."

He resents my superiority to his own horses, Arvin whinnied.

I directed a quelling look at him. "You keep quiet! If you hadn't lost your head, I could have easily dealt with the situation."

I have never lost my head in my life, Arvin said with dignity.

"I'd have liked to see it," Colin announced. "Arvin would have sent that fool running with some hoof prints on his fine jacket." He began to chortle to himself at the vision.

Philip shook his head, an expression of long-suffering on his face. "Get off to your geese, boy, or I won't come running so quickly next time."

"I'm going, I'm going." Colin gave Arvin's nose a pat and began to walk out of the stable. He paused to look back at me. "Well? Are you coming? You are still a goose girl, aren't you?"

With a single regretful look at Philip, I rushed after him. With so much going on, I sometimes forgot about the geese entirely, but without them I had no reason to be here, and the palace had no reason to feed, house, or clothe me. Talking to Philip would have to wait.

CHAPTER 20

a serving maid brought our food packs at midday, complaining loudly of the smell, the mud, and the goose droppings. I looked for Philip all afternoon, but he never came. I told myself it was a good thing—I had just resolved I needed to keep my distance, after all—but the day dragged intolerably without his presence.

At the evening meal, Philip joined me with his usual smile, but Nikki sat down across from us a moment later, so we didn't manage any private conversation. Other servants soon flocked to join us, and in their presence my mood lifted. Despite my initial issues, I had become part of the servants' community after all. Any fears that I was no better than Sierra's false image of a princess had long since melted away.

Someone called for music as soon as most people had finished eating, and a cheer went up. Nikki left us for a while to circulate the room, coming back as the musicians were tuning their instruments. She was clearly bursting with news.

"The guards are to be gone from the kitchens tomorrow!"

Philip straightened. "They've found the poisoner?"

She deflated slightly. "No. Unfortunately not. But the doctors have determined that the poison wasn't ingested. It was inhaled. So the kitchens are free again."

"That's good news enough for me," a footman further down the table said.

"But haven't you heard?" asked a serving maid sitting across from him. "There's still no flour. That's why we haven't had rolls for days."

A loud groan rang around the table. Philip opened his mouth to speak just as a scullery maid burst into the dining hall, still wearing her apron.

"The flour's arrived!" she yelled, and an even louder cheer broke out.

One of the fiddlers struck up a bright, celebratory tune, and the other musicians scrambled to join in. Cheery laughter bounced around the room at the prospect of no more guards upsetting the kitchen staff *and* fresh bread again. Before I knew what was happening, the gardeners had started stacking the tables against the walls, and some of the footmen were grabbing maids and dragging them into the middle of the room.

"Oooh," Nikki cried, "it's been too long since we had an impromptu dance."

She threw an inviting glance at Philip, apparently undeterred by his being a decade younger than her. When he didn't take her bait, she accepted the offered hand of a footman and disappeared among the dancers.

Philip helped the gardener who approached our table to lift it and place it on top of one of the others already pushed against the wall. I trailed behind, unsure what to do with myself. The boisterous dancing was unlike the choreographed movements I was used to, and I didn't recognize the tunes.

But when Philip turned and held out his hand, my own hand reached out of its own accord and took his, even while my brain tried to tell me I needed to refuse. I did pull back against him when he tried to tug me onto the makeshift dance floor, though.

"I don't know these songs," I said, glad that my foreign status gave me an excuse.

"Don't worry," he said. "Just follow my lead."

As a princess, I had danced with a great many people, old and young. I had learned the art of gracefully leading without appearing to do so to ensure my more inept partners didn't make fools of us both. With Philip, I had no such issues. After the first minute, I let myself relax, following his strong, confident lead.

As he swung me around, I realized the key was to keep moving, circling and swinging in time to the music, hands tightly gripped to keep us from losing each other in the mass of swirling people. I smiled up at him—I couldn't help it given the music, and the dancing, and the laughing people around us—and he tightened his grip on my hands, swinging me in a little closer to him.

"You're doing excellently," he said.

"I'm a fast learner." I laughed up at him, telling myself I was flushed from the exertion not his nearness.

He grinned and swung me through a more complicated maneuver, finishing with a flourish as the song ended. All around us the cry went up for more, and the musicians launched straight into another dance tune. I wondered briefly if dancers were required to find new partners for every dance, but Philip's grip didn't loosen. I let him pull me into a new rhythm, losing myself in the moment.

But when that song ended, a laughing maid stole him away. He gave me an apologetic grimace as he was carried off through the crowd, and I laughed and gestured for him to go. With the connection of our hands broken, however, my reckless good humor abated. I had utterly failed at my previous night's resolution, and I no longer felt in the mood for dancing.

Slipping through the crowd, I escaped the room, pausing a short way down the dark corridor. Music and merriment spilled out of the dining hall, echoing through the empty space. Already I felt cut off from it, utterly alone. For all my dreams of belonging, this wasn't truly my home, and Philip wasn't my future. I stood there for an unknown length of time, my thoughts and emotions too chaotic to arrange themselves into neat sentences, even in my mind.

"Elle? Is that you?" a voice asked, breaking the solitude.

I started and peered into the dimly lit hallway. "Damon? What are you doing down here?"

He stepped up beside me, a smile on his face. "I heard a great commotion and came down to see if the kitchens had caught fire. But it seems there was a happier reason for the noise."

I managed a smile despite the great weariness that had claimed me. "There is flour again, you see. And that is a definite cause for celebration."

Damon chuckled. "I did not expect my meager efforts to be quite so warmly appreciated."

I looked up at him. "Your efforts?"

"I asked the king this morning if I could be of any assistance, given everything going on." He shook his head with a rueful smile. "I must admit I was picturing something that involved riding a horse and carrying a sword. But he said if I wanted to help, I could make sure the palace was restocked with flour by sundown."

"So they didn't find the viscount's missing shipment," I murmured.

He gave me a slightly bemused look but didn't question my knowledge.

"No, I'm afraid not. It's entirely disappeared. But after a day spent in the merchants' district, I was able to put my sword and my men to some small use by guarding the wagon as it was loaded with sacks of flour and driven direct to the royal kitchens."

"There you go," I said with a grin. "Some small glory and action for you after all."

"Alas!" He chuckled. "We were not besieged by villainous thieves. It was an entirely uneventful journey."

"Oh well." I patted his arm in a comforting way. "There is always next time."

He looked down at my hand. "That's a very catchy tune they're playing. But I suppose my new rank precludes me from joining such merriment now."

He sounded sad, but I couldn't deny it.

"Unfortunately you would only ruin their fun by going in." An image of Philip, laughing in the middle of the dancers, filled my mind, making my eyes sting with unshed tears. Philip was right. For all the privileges of a royal life, there were limitations, too.

"It's hard to resist dancing to it, even out here," Damon said, the invitation in his words and face unmistakable.

But fatigue still pulled at me, and I couldn't face accepting.

"It's a lively tune, indeed. But I'm afraid I, for one, hear the siren call of sleep more strongly." My two disturbed nights in a row were catching up with me.

Damon instantly stepped back and gave a small bow.

"Then, please, don't let me keep you from your bed."

I smiled at him gratefully. "Thank you for the flour."

"You are more than welcome, I can assure you," he said, as if he had gone and fetched it just for me.

I shook my head at the fanciful notion, no doubt produced by lack of sleep, and hurried off to my room with a farewell wave. And this time, when my head hit the pillow, my body overwhelmed my mind and carried me straight into sleep.

The next morning I turned up at the goose pen before Colin, not wanting to be late yet again. He grunted a sour greeting at me when he arrived, but since he also glared at the geese, his staff, and the sun in the sky, I decided I wasn't the cause of his ire.

Most likely he had stayed up far too late at the unplanned celebration.

For a brief moment I was tempted to ask him how late Philip had stayed and who he had danced with, but I managed to refrain. Philip was free to dance as late as he liked and with whatever partners he chose.

When we reached a suitable grazing position, the boy promptly lay down flat on his back and put his beloved hat over his eyes. Within minutes, his snores competed with the rustling and honks of the geese. I stared at him in utter bemusement, trying to remember if I had been able to sleep as easily at his age.

When he awoke an hour later, he bounded up, once more full of energy, and began to chatter about the treats the cook had promised she would make with the newly arrived flour. Since none of these treats were before us now, it was a rather painful topic of conversation, and when I spotted someone approaching across the grass, I leaped up, glad of the diversion. I had expected Philip, but as the man drew closer, I realized it was Damon.

I told Colin I'd be back soon and hurried to meet the prince.

"Elle! I was hoping I would find you," he said as soon as I reached him.

"You're not needed to fetch more vital supplies?" I asked with a smile.

"It's funny you should mention that…" He looked uncomfortable.

"Oh no!" I cried. "Please don't tell me we're out of sugar now. I've just spent the last hour listening to all the desserts the cook has promised to make for tonight. I could not bear the disappointment."

He chuckled. "No, indeed, your sweets are safe. It just seems I proved myself overly helpful yesterday." He gave me a mock stern look. "Which should be a lesson to us all to underperform whenever possible."

I rolled my eyes. "You're not fooling me. You don't seem the type to have ever underperformed in your life. But do tell me what new task you've been given."

"It's a little more than a single task, I'm afraid." He took a deep breath. "King Henry has declared the role of Lord Chamberlain must be filled as soon as possible, and apparently being a close relation qualifies me for the honor."

I clapped my hands. "Congratulations! And it is not only because of being the king's nephew. You've also showed yourself capable. The king must have been testing you yesterday, and you passed."

"Thank you." He shook his head. "I would no doubt be lapping up the congratulations and basking in my new importance if the king hadn't seen fit to warn me exactly what sort of task I'm facing."

My eyes widened as I remembered the viscount's dining room.

"I decided I could afford a short walk in the beautiful outdoors since I may not see it again for several months," he said in long-suffering tones. "Apparently the previous owner of my title left six decades of paperwork behind him. Not exactly the adventures I had in mind when I offered to help. This is what comes of seeking to be useful."

"You are to be commended," I told him.

"I thought I had better come and wish you a temporary farewell," he said. "In case you began to fear that I, too, had been poisoned upon assuming my new role. So, never fear. I might wither of boredom, but I can't imagine anyone will think me valuable enough to murder for at least a year or two."

I shivered. "Don't joke about it."

He instantly looked contrite. "No, indeed. I'm sorry. It's no laughing matter. I'm merely attempting to console myself at the prospect before me."

I forced a smile. "And why should you not laugh while you still can? This is an excellent opportunity for us. If the viscount kept such detailed records, you might be able to uncover some clue as to why he was killed. I still cannot understand how any of this connects."

His expression immediately turned serious. "Don't worry, I haven't forgotten that we need evidence. In truth, I'm delighted to have such an opportunity to look for it. I actually came this morning to let you know I'll be searching for it."

"I wish I could help," I said.

"I'm apparently allowed to hire staff, and I would request you as an assistant, except I fear provoking Sierra," he said. "We are the two who know the truth about her, and if she feared we were locked away, conspiring against her, I don't know what she might be roused to do."

"No, it's best I stay here," I agreed. "At least for now."

"And I cannot linger longer, I'm afraid." He looked genuinely regretful. "But I will visit again when I can."

Taking my hand, he bowed over it, leaving a soft kiss on my knuckles before disappearing back toward the palace. I watched him go, my hand tingling strangely. What had he meant by that?

My mind wanted to contrast the gesture with Philip's warm grip the night before, but I forced it back to Damon. He was a prince, though he hadn't been raised as one. If my parents had known of his existence before my departure, they would have asked me to give him a chance even above Percy. And if I succeeded at breaking the enchantment, then my own rank would be restored. Damon seemed to enjoy my company—what sort of intentions might he form toward me if he knew I was a princess not a goose girl?

My mind shied away from that train of thought, and I turned hurriedly back to Colin. But a shift of movement in the corner of my vision made me spin back around.

Sierra, mounted on a placid looking gelding, stood just inside a copse, some distance away. Her eyes remained trained on me as she prodded her mount into movement, eating up the distance between us. When she reached me, she signaled for her horse to stop, her eyes flashing down at me with dangerous fire.

"Why can I not be rid of you?" she hissed.

"It's not for lack of trying." I glared at her. "But I'm not so easily disposed of."

"If you know what's good for you, you'll stay away from Damon," she snapped. "Or I'll make sure the next attempt doesn't fail." She leaned forward across her horse, her eyes boring into me. "No matter what it takes."

I opened my mouth to make a defiant retort only to close it again. Damon's earlier words could not have been more immediately justified. I didn't intend to cut off contact with Damon, but openly declaring my defiance seemed foolhardy in the extreme. A flash of white gripped in her fist caught my eye. So she did keep the handkerchief with her as I had suspected.

I gulped, realizing I needed to pick my words carefully.

"I won't go looking for him," I said. Hopefully I wouldn't need to. He had said he would come to me.

Sierra narrowed her eyes, but apparently she trusted in the power of the handkerchief to reveal the truth of someone's words. Which must mean it still worked. How much assistance had it given her? I ground my teeth, carefully keeping the boiling emotions from my face.

"See that you don't!" she spat at me, and wheeled her horse around, pushing him into a canter.

When I turned back to the geese, Colin was watching me with narrowed eyes and a creased brow. I hurried back before he could complain that I wasn't at my post.

CHAPTER 21

*T*wo weeks passed without sight of Damon. I could feel his presence around me, however, as the normal rhythms of the palace resumed, the supply runs facing no further disruptions. Twice I heard his name on the lips of nobles riding past, their tones full of praise.

Each time a group rode past, Colin told me their names and titles, plus whatever tidbit of their history caught his fancy. He had clearly listened to years of gossip about the inhabitants of the palace.

One morning a young couple rode past who I hadn't seen in the park before. The young woman called a laughing challenge over her shoulder at the young man, and both of their horses leaped forward. I nearly didn't recognize them as the couple Arvin had nearly knocked over in the palace yard. Their demeanors couldn't have been more different from that occasion.

Idly, I remembered how Philip had disappeared at the sight of them.

"Who are they?" I asked Colin, pointing at their rapidly disappearing figures.

"What?" He stared at me. "You don't know the new viscount?"

I stared after them, wishing I'd had a better look. "That was Thomas? The new Viscount Edgewaring?"

"Course it was." Colin shook his head at my ignorance. "And Lady Georgiana. They've been betrothed for two years. Everyone says their wedding will happen as soon as the mourning period is over."

Alyssa must have spoken to the young lord as she had intended, then. Certainly they both seemed freed from the heavy weight they had been carrying when I last saw them.

I had intended to ask him more about the couple, but Philip's arrival distracted me. He came every midday now, though we were once again able to collect our packs of food after breakfast.

He claimed he came to fulfill a promise to teach Colin to juggle, and he always brought his three juggling sacks with him. When I laughingly accused him of using them to bribe Colin, he was all innocence, but his eyes twinkled at me.

After his lesson, Colin always begged a chance to practice with the sacks, and Philip used the opportunity to steal me away. But no matter how many times we searched the place where my attackers had disappeared, we could find no sign of their means of escape. And when we meandered without purpose, discussing the pieces of information we had both collected from the other servants or from Philip's undisclosed daily activities, we couldn't bring the various problems of the kingdom together into a cohesive whole.

Perhaps we would have more success if I could talk openly, but the enchantment showed no sign of waning. I thought often of that glimpse of my handkerchief in Sierra's hand. It wasn't a surprise to know she carried it with her, and I had started having daydreams of finding her alone in the park again and forcing it from her before anyone could discover us and intervene. But I only saw her in the distance, and always with Percy and attendant guards.

I felt useless, my resolution that I would prove myself by

finding a way to defeat Sierra seeming nothing more than fool-ishness now. Despite my nineteen years, I kept imagining myself as a child pretending to be a capable adult while all the true adults smiled indulgently. Except this was no game, and it was my kingdom that stood to suffer when Sierra's final plan was unleashed.

I had actually accumulated some wages by now, a fact that made me surprisingly proud. With a churning in my gut, I even contemplated taking it and running for Lanover. I could let Celine and Oliver save Eldon, as they had done before.

But everything in me rebelled at the idea, and every day, I lingered. If I truly believed I had the qualities of a princess Sierra lacked, then I would prove it by finding a way to protect my kingdom from the political disaster she was ensnaring us in.

I was getting less and less sleep, the nights absorbed in useless, circular thoughts as I tried to work out what I had missed. There must be some clue somewhere that would make sense of Sierra's schemes.

One midday walk, at the end of the two weeks, Philip ran a hand through his hair and sighed.

"Everything seems to be returning to calm. Perhaps whatever these attacks were, they're over now." But he sounded more frus-trated than convinced.

I looked away, trying to hide my tension. Unlike Damon, Philip still didn't know of my personal connection to this, beyond the two attacks. He didn't know that, for me, there could be no return to normal until I found a way to expose Sierra.

"I'm sorry," Philip said, apparently picking up on some part of my emotions. "I didn't mean to suggest your attackers should go unpunished."

He tried to clasp my hand, but I whisked it away, pretending not to have noticed his attempt. He gave a soft sigh and didn't try again. It was his first attempt at physical contact since we had danced together, and I was proud of myself for sticking to my resolutions this time. I just wished my success didn't leave me feeling weary and empty inside.

Each day I had watched for Damon, but he never came. Had he forgotten me in his new role? Surely the daily sight of Sierra would remind him. Perhaps he didn't mean to keep his promises.

That night, I returned to my cupboard immediately after the evening meal, my steps heavier than usual and my mind weary. I pushed open the door and stepped into the tiny space only to collide with another person.

I screamed, but a hand clamped over my mouth, strong arms encircling me. For a moment I thrashed, my mind panicking. Then my captor's words made it through the haze of fear.

"Elle! It's me, Damon! Calm down."

I stilled, the tension leaking out and normal thought resuming. I could feel his broad chest pressed against my back, and his arms wrapped around me were strangely comforting. An exhausted part of me wanted to sink back into them and let someone else carry my burdens for a while.

But true sanity returned a moment later, and I pulled myself away just as he let go. I slowly turned to face him.

"You're not going to scream or try to bite me or something, are you?" Amusement lurked in his face.

I rolled my eyes. "You deserve such treatment for hiding in my room. But no."

"It's not my fault that your room appears to be a cleaning cupboard." He looked around the tiny space. "I was expecting a bit more room in here."

"Ha! That's what I said." I sat beside my pillow and gestured for him to take a seat at the foot of the bed. "But what are you doing here at all?"

"I thought it might be a good idea to meet somewhere a little more private," he said. "Because of Sierra."

Given what had occurred last time we spoke, I couldn't fault his wisdom.

"I would have invited you to my rooms, but that seemed fraught on multiple levels," he added. "I don't think anyone saw me arrive here, and you can check the corridor before I leave."

"Have you found something, then?" Sudden excitement flooded me, sweeping away my previous malaise.

Damon nodded. "It took me longer than I'd hoped due to the chaos of the viscount's papers, but I stumbled on a collection of records quite unlike the others."

"What did they say?" Eagerness made my voice quiver. Finally we had some evidence.

I realized I was leaning further and further toward him and straightened before I toppled over.

"The old Lord Chamberlain was a highly factual man," Damon said. "And he wouldn't allow conjecture to find its way among proper records. So he kept a separate group of papers where he recorded every little suspicion or hint that he was still working to substantiate. He had accounts of misdemeanors of various merchants, nobles, and even craftsmen and laborers. When he discovered something untoward within the course of his work, he would carefully build a complete picture and then present it to the relevant authorities."

"Sierra," I breathed.

Damon nodded. "The picture was not as complete as old Edgewaring would have liked, and he never got the chance to finish it and present it to the king."

"Because she found out and poisoned him," I finished for him. "We should go to the king immediately!"

Damon shook his head. "I'm still checking and sorting. There may be more. I need to have it all in order first. I just didn't want to leave you waiting any longer."

I frowned. "Don't make the same mistake as the viscount! We have to warn the Arcadians!"

"Of course we must, and I don't suggest we delay long." He hesitated. "It's just that Sierra is not the only thing Edgewaring wrote about. I think he had found some hints of who is behind Sierra."

"What?" I slammed a hand over my mouth, lowering my voice. "Who?"

He watched me closely. "If Sierra sailed away from our island in an Eldonian ship, can you tell me how she might have ended up in contact with my father's kingdom—with Rangmere?"

"Rangmere?" I stared at him. "What could Rangmere possibly..." My eyes widened. "Wait! Last year a Rangmeran delegation visited Eldon. They spent weeks with the royal family and moved freely through the palace and the city."

Damon drew a deep breath. "That is a helpful piece of information to present to the king. But this isn't like the accusation against Sierra. This is a very serious matter, and we need to have everything as clear and ordered as we can make it."

"Gracious, yes." I felt the blood draining from my cheeks. "Princess Alyssa and Prince Max are close to Queen Ava from what I hear. They would take an accusation against her very seriously indeed."

"I'm not accusing the queen," Damon said quickly. "There's no evidence of such a thing in the papers. It may well be rogue forces within her kingdom. But it seems that someone in Rangmere wishes to destabilize Arcadia. The viscount made a number of notes referencing that it wasn't the first time."

I nodded slowly. "Twelve years ago. Before Max and Alyssa were married. I've heard stories about it."

"The viscount suspected that Sierra wasn't who she claimed and that her crimes here were intended to undermine relations between Arcadia and Eldon, as well as Arcadia and Lanover."

"Celine and Oliver," I breathed. "If Arcadia and Eldon are at enmity, Lanover will have to side with their princess."

"And Northhelm would side with Lanover and Eldon as well, would it not?" Damon sounded grave. "They also have a Lanoverian princess married to their crown prince."

"Arcadia is the only kingdom not to have any such ties with Lanover—and therefore Eldon," I said, the scope of the plot breaking over me. "This kingdom could find itself standing alone."

"But not if we reveal what's really going on and that Sierra isn't really a princess of Eldon. Then it will be Sierra and Rangmere that stand alone," Damon said. "Or at least whatever rogue elements in Rangmere are behind this."

"You have to get that evidence." I slid down the bed and gripped his arm, my knuckles white with my force. "As fast as possible."

A strange expression crossed his face as he looked down into mine, and his eyes dropped to my lips. For a moment I froze, unsure of the emotions that gripped me. Then I shook myself free and slid away again.

"Go now!" I urged, trying to cover up my confusion. "There's no time to be lost."

"Of course!" He stood, and if there was a flicker of disappointment on his face, he didn't speak it.

I stuck my head out into the corridor but saw no movement. Ushering him out, I gave him a shove.

"Go! Go! We'll speak again soon."

He opened his mouth, only to shake his head and close it again, striding off down the corridor. I watched for only a moment before turning back to my door. My eyes slid over a statue on the far wall, making me jerk to a halt and slowly spin back around. There were no statues in this corridor.

My eyes found Philip. He stood utterly still, his face pale, and his fists clenched at his sides. His eyes were focused on Damon's retreating back, but as the prince disappeared from sight, they turned slowly to me.

"I didn't realize you and the prince were so close," he said, something of the danger I had heard in his voice in the stables returning.

"What?" I squeaked. "No! We just needed somewhere private to talk."

Philip took a step toward me, his hand reaching out before he pulled it abruptly back. "I didn't mean to suggest…" His tone now held a hint of contrition. "I just meant that I didn't realize you trusted him enough to allow him in your room."

I chuckled. "Well, I didn't exactly *allow* him in."

"What?" Philip's hands balled back into fists, and I quickly held mine out in a placating gesture.

"No, no, never mind. You're right, I didn't tell you that Damon and I are working together, and I should have."

He frowned. "Working together?"

"The same as we are." I gestured between us, and a shadow passed over his face.

Footsteps at the other end of the corridor made us both look up. I drew a step closer to him.

"We can't talk here," I whispered. "But the prince has found something. Something big. He's gathering evidence now, and then we're going to present it to the king."

The servant passed us, and I fell silent. He gave us a curious glance but didn't stop. I opened my mouth, but the voice of another servant, calling to someone out of sight, interrupted me.

"Tomorrow," I said quickly. "In the park. I'll explain it then."

Philip looked reluctant, but as the two new servants approached, he nodded once.

"Very well. I'll see you tomorrow."

CHAPTER 22

"So, you see," I finished. "It looks like Rangmere is behind everything. They want to destabilize Arcadia just like they attempted twelve years ago. They must be planning a coup or an invasion or something."

Philip's frown had deepened throughout my explanation. Because of what I was saying, or because he didn't believe me? I was conscious the tale was less convincing when I wasn't able to include anything about Sierra's involvement.

I had been thinking through the revelations all night and had concluded she must mean to flee soon. I was fortunate she hadn't attempted to do it already because she no doubt intended that I would not survive her departure. When she disappeared, leaving behind evidence of her robberies and murders, Arcadia would turn in wrath to Eldon, never knowing Sierra wasn't who she claimed.

My family—including Celine, and all of her family, most of whom I'd met—would be enraged, not only at my disappearance but at the accusations against me. They would never believe it. And Arcadia and Eldon would never realize they weren't referring to the same person.

No wonder Sierra had instructed her men to kill me. I was no doubt only alive because for now she needed to maintain her charade. She couldn't move against me openly. Not yet.

I shivered. What final crime did she have planned? It would have to be something bigger and more grievous than any so far. Perhaps the rest had merely been warmups, rehearsals for the final performance.

Philip, unaware of my frantic thoughts, glanced back toward Colin, checking the boy was still out of earshot. When Philip had arrived, I had dragged him only a short way away before spilling out everything the enchantment would let me say.

"Twelve years ago, King Josef was on the throne," he said at last. "But now Queen Ava sits in Rangmeros. I can't believe she would be working against Arcadia now. She has a busy enough job keeping her own kingdom in line."

"Exactly!" I pounced on his admission. "Her ascension to the throne was unexpected, wasn't it? Surely it's possible there could still be some rogue group—or even a single noble if he had resources enough—rebelling against her leadership. Maybe they wish to expand their power into Arcadia now that Rangmere is turned against them? Or maybe they think to goad her into a war she doesn't want? Damon didn't say it was the queen herself."

Philip ran a hand through his hair. "I suppose it's possible."

I looked him in the eye, gripping both his wrists. "Philip. I know you haven't told me everything. I know you've been keeping secrets from me." I felt guilty even saying it, given my own secrets, but I had to try. "What exactly is your role here at the palace? What do you do all day when you aren't with me?"

He looked down into my face, his eyes widening slightly. When he didn't reply straight away, I rushed on.

"I know I can't make you tell me the truth. But if you have some influence, some knowledge, or some ability to help with this, then now is the moment to use it. We need every bit of evidence and every ally we can get to convince the king of what is happening in Arcadia."

He groaned, his arms twisting so that now it was his hands gripping my forearms. "You have no idea how much I want to tell you the truth, Lark. But I made promises...and I'm afraid. Afraid that you'll—"

But whatever he was afraid I would do was cut off as Colin raced toward us, calling excitedly. Philip dropped my arms, stepping back from me, although not quickly enough to avoid a suspicious glance from the goose boy.

The news he had hurried over to share took precedence, however, and he blurted it out. "The king has called for a grand celebration! Not just a ball for the nobles, but a party for all the servants as well. A grand festival!"

"What?" My mind struggled to disengage from my conversation with Philip and take in what Colin was saying.

"We're going to get a whole day off and a giant party with food, and music, and performers and everything!"

"When?" I asked.

"Only two days!" Colin crowed. "And it isn't even a normal day off. This is the best!"

"It's been quiet for a couple of weeks," Philip murmured. "It seems the king wants to reassure the palace that there isn't anything to worry about."

"But there is." I gulped.

Whose idea was the party? If Sierra wanted a grand finale—a spectacular, visible blow to the rulers of Arcadia—what better time could there be?

Colin chattered on, his excitement endless. Whoever had brought him the news of the celebration had said the fire eater would be there. Colin was too young to be allowed out to the night markets, and apparently seeing the performer would be the culmination of a lifelong ambition.

Philip and I had no more opportunity to talk alone, but I

caught his eye as he left, mouthing the word *please*. He hesitated, looking torn, before nodding once and striding off. I spent the rest of the afternoon wondering what his nod had meant.

I looked, but he wasn't at the evening meal. When he wasn't at breakfast the next morning either, I grew nervous. All morning, I could barely absorb any of Colin's chatter. Thankfully Arvin joined us, and the horse received most of the boy's attention.

Stop fretting, he told me when Colin went to fetch a goose who had attempted to wander away from the group. *It will not make him appear any faster. Besides, we do not need his assistance. The prince will help us to reveal the impostor.*

"Us? Are you going to be talking to the king with Damon and me?" I smiled at the mental image although I was still a little disgusted with his insistence on placing more trust in Damon than Philip, just because the prince showered him with compliments and respect.

Of course. He sounded astonished. *You are my charge, and this could be a dangerous moment for you.*

I was oddly touched. "I appreciate the thought. But how would you protect me? You're a horse, not an army."

So little imagination. He sighed. *It must be quite sad to live with such limited capacity.*

"And yet, somehow I manage."

It is frequently a matter of some wonder to me. Especially when you insist on going around with that disheveled man.

I put my hands on my hips. "Arvin! Philip is kind and thoughtful—to both of us, I might add. And he's brave and more than competent. Do I have to remind you how he saved Colin from that awful noble boy?"

Arvin sniffed. *Colin wouldn't have needed Philip to save him if you hadn't insisted on getting in my way.*

I glared at him but decided that his use of Philip's name was a small sign of concession on his part.

Colin returned, and our conversation died. Midday came and went, and Philip didn't appear. I tried to remember the last time he hadn't joined us for lunch. Was it something I had said? Or was it Damon? I kept remembering Philip's face when I found him outside my room. Had he been coming to talk to me? What had he wanted to say? And did it have to do with whatever he was afraid of—the fear that had to do with me?

Colin seemed disgusted with my low mood, so at odds with his feverish enthusiasm, but I couldn't muster even the appearance of excitement. Instead I spent the day alternating between thinking of Philip and planning how I might free myself from the enchantment.

I had to get that handkerchief, and tomorrow might be my only chance. Sierra would have to attend the ball, and I had no doubt she would have the handkerchief on her person. If I could get near her, I would find a way to snatch it. And as soon as I had it back, I would run to the nearest candelabra and burn it.

It wasn't exactly a plan. More a vague idea. But it was my only opportunity, and I was determined not to waste it.

As soon as I got back to my cupboard that night, I drew out a bag from beneath the bed. It was the one I had stashed there after returning from my investigation of Sierra's suite so long ago. I had examined its contents back in her room and remembered no more than that it held only her dresses and personal care items. With no desire to wear or even touch anything that belonged to Sierra, I hadn't looked at it since. But now I needed something to wear that could get me close enough to her to try for the handkerchief, and I didn't know where else to look.

Digging through the bag, I had already despaired of finding anything nice enough for the occasion when my hand brushed against something soft. Tossing dresses over my shoulder, I exposed what lay at the bottom of the bag, covered in a protective layer of plain cotton. Sierra's unexpected arrival at her suite must have interrupted me before I discovered there was something hiding at the bottom.

Carefully drawing out the dress, I held up a beautiful creation of filmy green. The top two lawyers were made with a delicate, transparent material, creating an effect that was both soft and full. Laced at the back with a black velvet ribbon, the dress would sweep the floor.

"Unbelievable," I muttered.

I already knew the dress would fit perfectly. I remembered the fittings, and how much I had looked forward to wearing it. But the gown had disappeared, lost somewhere between the seamstress and my wardrobe. Now I knew the truth. Sierra had taken it. But why?

Damon had said she was a thief, and here was the proof. But it was such a pointless thing to take, especially in light of her subsequent assumption of my identity. I was forcibly struck by the impression that she was a child, playing dress ups as she dreamed of being a princess.

Back in Eldon, I had asked her what gift she would like for Midwinter. If she had said a beautiful dress, I would have bought one for her. Why had she stolen mine instead? I pushed the thought aside. I had no way to know. And it worked to my advantage now.

I carefully folded the dress back up, rewrapping it in its protective layer. I didn't want to risk it somehow being dirtied or torn before tomorrow. A knock sounded on my door as I was stuffing the discarded dresses back into the voluminous bag.

I abandoned the task and flung the door open, Philip's name already on my lips. But I cut myself off when I saw who was standing there.

"Oh, Damon, it's you."

He gave me a quizzical look. "Were you expecting someone else?"

"No. I wasn't expecting anyone."

He looked like he wanted to come in, but I stayed in the doorway. "Have you found what we need?"

"As much as there is to find. I don't think there's any value in waiting longer."

"We have to talk to the king at the celebrations tomorrow," I said. "I have a feeling Sierra is planning something terrible for tomorrow night. At the ball."

Damon looked thoughtful. "It makes sense. In a horrible sort of way." He frowned. "The king has public audiences all morning. He'll be attending various celebrations in the city and the palace. But by afternoon he should be with the nobles. The ball is to last all afternoon and evening, with plenty of food provided."

"That's perfect," I said. "We want *the princess* to be there." It hurt to talk about her that way, especially when Damon knew the truth, but it was the only way the enchantment would let me say what I wanted to say. "I need to talk to her first."

Damon's face lit up. "You're coming to the ball? We'll go together. We'll expose Sierra and reveal the truth before she has a chance to do anything."

I nodded. "Exactly."

PART III
THE BALL

CHAPTER 23

$\mathcal{T}$he king had granted the day off for everyone who could possibly be spared. And all those performing essential functions, such as the kitchen staff, rushed to complete their duties as quickly as possible. But none of the servants minded the simple breakfast provided or how speedily it was cleared away. Everyone was saving room for the feast to come.

Extra help had been brought in the day before, enticed with promises of participation in the festivities of today, and the kitchens had rung with noise and hubbub from sunrise to sunset. A vast array of delicacies had been prepared. The queen had reportedly spent two hours in consultation with the cook to develop a list of foods that could all be prepared in advance. The kitchen staff were to be released to join the party after breakfast was cleared away.

I slept in, enjoying the rare luxury, and spent the rest of the morning in the servants' bath house. No one else wanted to waste time there on such a glorious day, so I was able to commandeer a tub long enough for a proper soak.

But I was starting to feel a little sick by the time I made my way back to my room to prepare for the ball. Perhaps the roiling in my stomach came from too little food. I entered through the door that led into the kitchens, figuring that leftovers from breakfast might remain there, given the staff's early release.

It was strange to find the giant room empty, the fires banked and several of the large stoves sitting entirely cold. Had I ever seen a deserted kitchen? I couldn't remember it. Kitchens were a central hub that always bustled with enthusiasm and delicious smells.

Some of those smells remained, and I tracked one down, finding a number of sweet rolls in a covered basket. I had just finished one and was licking my fingers when someone made a small noise behind me. I spun around.

"Philip!" I nearly tripped over myself rushing to greet him. "Where have you been? I was worried!"

"For me?" He sounded surprised. "I'm sorry, I didn't mean to distress you. I had people I needed to consult."

"About tonight?" My stomach dropped out, and I wished I hadn't been quite so greedy with the sweet roll.

He nodded, but he seemed distracted. "I've been looking for you all over."

"I've just come from the bath house," I said apologetically, thinking a little guiltily of how long I had stayed there. "I didn't realize anyone wanted me."

He gave a small shake of his head at that, a bemused look in his eyes.

"Do you really doubt it?"

My brows drew together. What were we talking about?

"Why were you looking for me?" I asked.

Worry filled his face. "I found Colin talking to the Poulterer. And afterward I made him tell me what they were talking about."

"The Poulterer?" That was the last answer I had expected. A conversation between Colin and the Poulterer couldn't possibly have the significance to fill Philip's face with such concern.

"Was he complaining about me?" I asked.

Philip nodded. "He said you're always disappearing and leaving him to do all the work."

I grimaced. It was a legitimate complaint, although I hadn't thought he minded particularly. He had done the job alone before my arrival.

"And he also mentioned how many visitors you have." Now Philip was the one to look guilty although he shot me a strange look when he added, "He said you have all sorts of noble visitors."

"That's a bit of a stretch." I rolled my eyes. Although now I came to think of it, I had been visited by Princess Alyssa and her children, Prince Damon, and Sierra. But they'd hardly been daily visitors.

"He was babbling about a brother," Philip said. "And something about an assistant."

"Ooh, that makes sense then. He wants his brother to become his assistant and get trained to have his own herd or flock one day. He's probably trying to get me ousted so his brother can take my place."

"The Poulterer told him that it was never his choice to have you there," Philip said. "He said Mrs. Pine had told him you were to be kept occupied and out of the way. As a gesture to the foreign princess. But he did promise to talk to her about it again."

"Well, it won't matter after tonight," I said. "One way or the other, I think my herding days are over."

"What does that mean?" Philip drew closer. "You don't think you'll be blamed for what's happened? It's not your fault your delegation was chosen as a target by these enemies of the kingdom."

I noted he didn't name them as Rangmerans. Did he still doubt Damon's evidence?

"Or that there's something strange about your princess," he muttered.

I looked up at him, hope in my heart. He knew there was

something strange about Sierra? What did he know? What did he suspect?

He gazed down at me, his expression changing at the sight of my bright eyes and flushed face. Stepping forward, he closed the space between us.

"Lark," he said, his voice heavy.

All thought of Sierra fled my mind. I wasn't ready for this. I tried to move backward, to give myself room to breathe, but my feet didn't move.

"You asked me to tell you the truth," he said. "And I want to tell you everything. But there's something I need to know first."

I bit my lip. I didn't think I wanted to hear what came next, but neither could I bring myself to flee this conversation.

When I still said nothing, he continued. "You came here with a mistress who abandoned you to herd geese. I know you love her horse, but you don't seem to bear any great loyalty to her."

"What mistress?" I asked. "I work for the king of Arcadia now."

"So you would consider staying?" he asked, too eagerly. "In the Four Kingdoms, I mean? You don't intend to leave with her when she departs?"

"I have no intention of traveling further with her," I said truthfully. But honesty compelled me to add, "But neither do I intend to stay here. Not for much longer anyway."

He reached out and gripped my arms. "What if you had a reason to stay?"

I swallowed. It was an enticing vision. I had let myself dwell in it before. But those daydreams meant I already knew the answer.

"I have to return to my family." I paused, struggling against the emotion in his gaze. "Even if I wanted to stay, I owe it to them. It is beautiful here, but Eldon is my home."

"Lark." He pulled me closer. Now there was no space between us at all. "What about me? Could I convince you? I can't bear for you to leave me behind forever." The anguish in his voice tore at my heart and brought tears to my eyes.

"You're so beautiful," he whispered, tracing the curve of my cheek with gentle fingers. The pressure was enough to tip a tear out of my eye, spilling down my cheek. He wiped it away.

"And you're brave. You're fierce, and resourceful. And you never complain. I love that about you. Despite becoming a goose girl overnight. And you have an impossible, crazy horse." He gave a rough chuckle. "Don't tell me he's not yours. It's clear he is, by heart if not law."

"Oh, Philip!" I cried. "Don't do this to me."

He froze, his eyes drinking in every tiny expression on my face.

"So you do care," he whispered.

"Of course I do! How could I not? But it's impossible, it's all impossible." I drew a shaking breath. "You're not the only one with secrets."

For all my desperation to prove myself, it was Damon who had found the evidence we needed to expose Sierra. At the end of the day, I had done little beyond herding geese. I couldn't fail my family on top of it. Not without at least trying. Not without keeping my promise to give an alliance a chance. No matter what my heart said.

"I don't care about your secrets, Lark," he said. "I'm used to secrets."

"Not these ones," I said in a small, miserable voice.

"I don't care," he said firmly. "I love you."

I sucked in my breath, looking back up into his eyes. But that was a mistake. As soon as our eyes met, he lowered his face to mine, and I was powerless to resist the overwhelming surge of my emotions.

His arms slid around me, pulling me against him, and his lips pressed down hard on mine. My heart lifted, driving me to slip my own arms around him and lean into his embrace. In this moment it was my heart in control and not the memory of my duty.

He wrapped his arms more tightly around me still, lifting me up off the ground, and lengthening the kiss. I let my hands steal up to feel the softness of his riotous hair just as I had been longing to do for weeks. My soft sigh of joy broke the kiss, and he lowered my feet gently back to the ground, keeping his arms around me.

I nearly raised my lips to his again before my mind reasserted itself. With a pained cry, I pulled free. He let me go, but his hands and eyes reached for me.

"I can't," I said. "I can't."

"If you think I'm letting you go after that, Lark, you don't know me very well at all."

I stared at him, anguished. He had no idea how loving me would completely upend his life. And I couldn't return to my family a complete failure in every respect. I just couldn't.

"Please," I said. "Please. I...need some time. Can you give me some time?"

"Of course I can," he said promptly. "All the time you need. I want to give you everything, Lark." His voice dropped. "I'll wait for you as long as you need."

I wiped the tears from my eyes and felt the gentle pressure of lips on my forehead. When my vision cleared enough to see, he was gone.

I drew in deep, shuddering breaths. None of this was fair to him. And hurting him, hurt me. But if everything went to plan tonight, at least tomorrow I could talk to him openly and honestly. I could tell him why we couldn't be together. And then he would feel differently. He had no interest in the restrictions that came with the life of royalty and nobility.

I stood there for a long time, struggling to return to the moment and remember what I needed to be doing. A ball. There was a ball, and I needed to dress for it.

I was still standing there, though, when I heard voices. They were rough voices, and an instant fear response shot through me. On an instinctive level I recognized them, even while my brain was struggling to catch up.

My body urged me to move, urged me to hide, and I looked frantically around the kitchen. The voices moved closer. An iron stove beside me stood cold and empty and, without thinking, I pulled open the door, climbed in and shut it behind me.

The space inside was large enough for me, but only just. I had to curl around in an awkward position, although I didn't have long to get comfortable before the voices sounded so close that I froze, hardly daring to breathe. Of all the foolish places to hide! Hadn't there been a pantry somewhere nearby I could have stashed myself in?

The voices stopped.

"I swear this is the only empty place in the whole palace," growled one.

"It's strange to be in an empty kitchen," said another. I recognized him as the one who told me my friends were still alive.

"Never mind that. Is it past midday yet? She said not to go to her suite until after midday."

"Good thing the guards didn't search her room on any of the previous occasions," one of them grunted. "If they'd found us and our injuries, we'd have been in trouble."

"The royals are finally getting suspicious. That's why it's time to move," said the one who seemed to be the leader. "We stash this vile stuff there for the prince and princess, and then we need to be on the road. We're going to run out of time if we don't move soon."

"I think it's just gone midday now," the one who had injured his leg said.

"Well, maybe we give it another five minutes to be sure. Can anyone see any food?"

They spread out, upending the kitchen in their search for

food. One of them found the basket of sweet rolls and called the others over, and the talking was replaced with noisy munching and burps of satisfaction.

The aches of my awkward position had disappeared, replaced with a strange sensation of cold that brought my senses jangling into full awareness. None of the confusion of earlier remained, my mind utterly focused.

The vile stuff, they had said. Poison?

And *the prince and princess*. Now that I heard it, it seemed an obvious choice. What bigger crime against a kingdom could there be than killing their crown prince and princess? What would rouse a king and queen to greater anger? The sort of anger that would lead them to throw away generations of alliance with those who sided with the murderer.

I considered leaping from the stove now and trying to wrest the vial from the men by force, but a moment's consideration revealed the flaws in that plan. I would have to wait until they'd gone and then go to the ball as planned. I would tell Damon what I had overheard, and we would make sure Alyssa and Max didn't go anywhere near Sierra—or anyone else, if we couldn't find that vial.

Impatience filled me as the men ate and ate. Would they never leave? Finally one of them grunted and said it had been long enough. I strained my ears, listening as they clomped their way out of the kitchen, heading for the guest suites upstairs. With so many festivities underway in the palace, they were likely to reach their destination unchallenged.

I debated running after them, in the hope I could find someone along the way who could help me stop them. But the doctors had declared the poison was inhaled. What if it came to a fight, and the vial was crushed? I might end up killing whoever was helping me, and myself along with them.

No, I needed to get to the royals. They were the only ones in danger. I would go straight to Alyssa. She would listen to me.

Half falling out of the stove, I scrambled to my feet. But the sight of my arms made me pause. My short stay in the stove had entirely undone my long soak in the bath. I was covered in dust and soot.

I turned and ran for the bath house, this time planning the fastest possible wash. Once I was clean, I would throw my dress on, leaving my hair in its usual braid down my back. There was no time for anything more fancy now.

CHAPTER 24

I expected to find it strange to attend a ball after so many weeks as a goose girl, but putting the gown on was like standing in the guest suite upstairs. Nineteen years of my life hadn't disappeared—it was waiting to resurface at the smallest reminder of my old self. I was Princess Giselle, not Elle the goose girl, and balls were familiar territory.

I avoided the crowded yard outside where nobles poured into the palace for the party. Especially since servants also overflowed into the space from their own festivities in the park. Instead, I hurried through the mostly deserted corridors, only occasionally passing a small group of nobles making their way to the enormous throne room from their suites inside the palace.

They gave me strange looks, either because of my odd haste or because they didn't recognize me. I ignored them all after a brief glance confirmed they were neither Sierra nor Princess Alyssa.

The event bordered on informality—at least for a royal ball—and I burst into the room without being announced, my dress gaining me the entree I needed. Looking around frantically, I could see nothing but a sea of people.

Most ballrooms opened onto a small platform with shallow steps descending down to the ballroom floor—providing a stage for the announced arrivals. But this event was being hosted in the throne room—the largest of the palace's rooms. Here, the raised platform was at the far end of the room, holding the thrones. They stood empty, the monarchs presumably mingling with their guests, but I could hardly climb up there to get a higher vantage point over the crowd.

Should I have waited for Damon as we had originally planned? I shook my head. No. His extra height would give him a small advantage, but I couldn't afford to lose time waiting for him.

I pushed through the people, as the first strains of music began. All around me, people either pushed toward the edges of the room or formed into partners, moving inward ready to dance. Caught, I was carried with those surging away from the center. I let them carry me backward until the movement slowed and then wormed my way forward. Surely the royals would open the dancing? This might be my chance to find Alyssa.

The occasional protest sounded as I pushed my way through the crowd, but I ignored them, finding myself a place in the front row of watchers. But while my eager eyes picked out King Henry leading Queen Eleanor onto the floor, I could see no sign of either Alyssa or Max. Where were they?

My eyes fell on Sierra, just joining the dance with Percy. Should I abandon my search for Alyssa and go for the handkerchief instead? But the dance floor didn't seem the ideal location to confront my maid. In this crowd, if I could brush up against her before she saw me coming, I would have a better chance of success. I'd have to wait until she went for refreshments, or something.

Standing on tiptoes, I scanned the edges of the room, returning to my original search. But I had no hope of distinguishing every individual in the enormous room.

The first scraping note of a violin sounded, and in the second's pause before the rest of the instruments joined, I heard a high-pitched, childish giggle. Whipping around, I stared at the throne. There! It was Rose, peeking from behind the ornate chair. I stepped out into the edge of the space cleared for dancing and rushed down the room, bumping against dancers as I went. A disapproving murmur followed my progress, but I didn't slow.

When I reached the bottom of the dais, I fixed gazes with Rose and beckoned the girl forward. She cast a wary glance at the dancers before skipping forward to join me.

"Elle," she said, not seeming in the least surprised to see me. "Did you bring your horse?"

I nearly laughed at the memory of Arvin assuring me he would attend with me. It was impossible to imagine the horse squeezed into the ballroom.

I shook my head. "Not today. But I'm looking for your mama. Do you know where Princess Alyssa is?"

"Mama's not here," Rose said, matter-of-factly. "She and Papa had to go out today." She wrinkled her nose. "I thought she would be back for the start of the party, but Grandmama says she won't be back until the evening."

"Out?"

"They took the carriage somewhere early this morning." Rose pouted. "I had to get ready for the party with only nanny to help me." She gave a twirl, causing her rose-colored brocade dress to spin around her. "Aren't I beautiful?"

"Very," I assured her, my mind already elsewhere.

Were Max and Alyssa investigating some clue on behalf of the king and queen? The monarchs might want their people to believe the troubles were behind them, but surely they didn't believe it themselves?

What had Sierra's men said? Something about needing to be on the road and running out of time. I had been wasting my time washing and dressing and coming to a ball, when the real danger was on the road.

Sierra's minions had a head start on me, but they didn't have Arvin.

I groaned. He had told me I would want him here with me, and he was right. I didn't have any time to waste.

"Where were they going, Rose?" I asked urgently. "Which direction?"

She shrugged. "I don't know."

I sighed, picked up my skirts, and ran. I crashed through the middle of the dancers in my haste to reach the door. Hopefully one of the grooms would be able to tell me which road the prince and princess had taken.

On the far side of the dance floor, I nearly bounced off Percy as he swung Sierra around. My maid saw me and hissed, her eyes widening with anger as she looked me up and down. She and Percy faltered, dropping out of the movements of the dance. I hesitated, once more torn by her nearness.

Before I could decide either way, however, a group of newcomers appeared in the door of the ballroom. Unlike the glittering gowns and dashing outfits of the revelers, these men wore guard uniforms, and their faces suggested they were on duty.

Those nearest the door fell back, making room for them to enter. They looked toward the dancers, and I froze. Had Damon somehow got word to the king? Were they here to arrest Sierra? If so, this might be my only chance to get the handkerchief.

I turned and stepped toward her, her wide eyes flashing between the guards and me.

"Halt!" one of them cried, and rough hands grabbed at me.

"Elle of the geese, you are under arrest," the voice continued.

What? Me? I couldn't see the faces of the guards, but I could see the surprise on Sierra's face change into smug satisfaction. The music continued to play, but whispers spread outward from our position. The king and queen appeared, having skillfully maneuvered their way across the dance floor.

"I'm so sorry, Your Majesty," Sierra simpered. "I have no idea how she acquired that dress or what can have possessed her to appear here. I knew nothing of her intentions."

"Her presence here is immaterial," King Henry said, his stern gaze on me. "But Mrs. Pine has just brought to my attention some disturbing irregularities in the behavior and company kept by your former maid. Irregularities that call into question her presence at the center of three separate attacks. Indeed, I do not wish to cause you or your kingdom offense, Princess, but with this new information, I cannot overlook the possibility that she is working with whatever forces seek to attack my kingdom."

"No, indeed, Your Majesty!" she said. "It is a betrayal of me as much as of you. You have my full support."

The king inclined his head in her direction before directing an unimpressed look at the guards behind me. "I am only disappointed that such a scene needed to be made."

"I apologize, Your Majesty," said a crisp voice behind me. "But we were unable to track her down before her unexpected arrival here. And your orders were that she be apprehended as soon as possible."

The king sighed. "No, you did right."

"I had nothing to do with those attacks, Your Majesty." I could hear the desperation in my voice. "In fact, I came here to warn you. Prince Max and Princess Alyssa are in danger. There is a conspiracy against their lives tonight!"

"Is that a threat?" Anger radiated off the king.

"No!" I cried. "It's a warning. I'm trying to warn them."

"The throne does not take kindly to threats," he snapped, "in any guise." He looked over my shoulder. "Take her away and lock her up."

"Wait!" I cried, desperation making me change tactic. "I didn't act alone." The guard and the king both froze.

"It was her!" I nodded my head toward Sierra. "She ordered me to do all of it. It was her plan!" If they were going to lock me up, then maybe I could incapacitate Sierra with me.

"How dare you!" Sierra stepped forward and slapped me across the face.

Growling, I wrenched my arms free of the guard's hold, his grip having loosened at Sierra's unexpected attack. I launched myself at her, my clawing fingers scrabbling at her sleeves. It couldn't be coincidence that she had made the unusual choice to wear a long-sleeved gown to a ball.

She gasped and tried to push me away, but the tips of my fingers brushed against soft material. I drove my hand forward and pulled out the handkerchief with a triumphant yell. Moving faster than I ever had before, I thrust it down the front of my dress and stepped backward away from her.

Sierra let out a piercing shriek and threw herself at me, punching and kicking as she spluttered incoherently and pulled at my dress.

"Stop!" roared the king, and he must have made some signal I couldn't see because the guards surged forward, recapturing my arms but also grasping Sierra.

She continued to strain toward me, shouting curses, and another guard had to step forward to assist the one already holding her.

"Never in my life have I witnessed such behavior," exclaimed the king.

"It's all lies, Your Majesty!" Sierra cried, seeming to regain some semblance of sense.

I kept my mouth shut, hoping she had done enough to negate any need for further accusations.

"She is your maid, and you brought her here," said King Henry. "I hope most sincerely you are innocent in this, but I have never witnessed a princess behave such, and at such a moment. I can take no chances, and neither can I investigate this matter fully in the middle of a ball. You will both be locked up until I can get to the bottom of what is going on here."

The guards nodded at the king and pulled us roughly through the crowd. Still the music played and on the other side of the room, dancing continued, but the crowd around us watched with avid interest as we were hauled away.

As soon as we were out in the relatively empty corridor, Sierra lunged for me again.

"None of that now." One of the guards pulled her forward some way ahead of me. "Try to remember your dignity. No one's going to hurt you. His Majesty's prison cells might not be luxurious accommodation, but you won't find any rats or rotting food."

Sierra shuddered and finally stopped fighting, merely casting a deadly glare at me over her shoulder. My heart raced so hard, I feared I might collapse and have to be dragged the rest of the way unconscious. Those men were still out there, on their way to intercept Alyssa and Max.

But I had succeeded in getting the handkerchief! If only there had been a candle nearby and time enough to burn it.

Did my possessing it break the enchantment? Could that be enough? I tried to declare myself the true princess, but no words emerged.

Instead of being taken to stairs that would lead us downward into the bowels of the castle, the guards dragged us out the open doors of the palace and into the yard. Latecomers to the ball watched us with astonished gazes as we were escorted toward the barracks.

"You have to listen to me," I said desperately to the guard pushing me along. "Princess Alyssa is in danger! And Prince Max. Someone has to warn them."

"Their Highnesses have guards of their own," the man said.

"But guards can't fight against a poison that floats through the air," I said. "Surely you can see that."

The man faltered slightly before picking up his pace. "That's not for the likes of me. You've had your say to the king, and my orders are to see you safely locked up, which is what I'm going to do."

I groaned in frustration, but until I could destroy that handkerchief, I could think of nothing more to say that might convince him.

The large, square shape of the barracks loomed out of the darkness, outlined by the many bonfires burning in the park. A small, single-story wing jutted off to one side of the building, and our guards dragged us toward it.

The one leading the way rapped on a plain wooden door, and it was pulled open from inside.

"You found her?" a voice asked.

Sierra was thrust into the building, and an exclamation of surprise floated out.

"You've got the princess, fools! That's not the goose girl."

"King's orders," said the guard holding me as he pushed me through the door after her. "We're to lock them both up."

The man standing guard inside whistled and scratched his head.

"In league together, are they? Why, that's a whole conspiracy!"

"I'm not working with her," Sierra spat. "It's all a mistake."

"Aye, well, that will be for the king to sort out. Tomorrow." The guard who had been holding her let go, but the door had closed behind us, and we were surrounded by guards now.

She turned on me, a gleam in her eye, but the man caught her again by one arm.

"Oh no, you don't. We're not starting that back up. You can just cool off in here." He thrust her through an open door, slamming it closed behind her.

I had time to see a large grate in the upper part of the door before I was thrust through a matching doorway next to it. I staggered, nearly losing my feet, and by the time I had my balance, the door had slammed closed behind me. I rushed forward to the grate in time to see the guards leaving through a door opposite the one we had entered. They must be passing through to their barracks.

Four remained behind, their backs to the opposite wall, and their eyes on our doors. I drew away from the grate and examined the rest of the room.

The guard had spoken accurately when he described our accommodation. While the cell contained no adornment or excessive comfort, it did hold a simple pallet, laid directly on the ground, and a basin full of clear water. A window in the opposite wall gave a glimpse of the outside world, bars preventing any potential escape.

"I'm going to kill you!" said a voice through the wall.

I walked over, placing my forehead against the wood. "I already worked that much out. All those attacks were something of a clue."

"You'll see," Sierra hissed, her voice full of rage. "Don't think Damon will—"

Damon! I jerked away from the wall. How could I have forgotten Damon?

Ignoring the rest of Sierra's words, I rushed back to the door and pressed my face against the grate.

"Excuse me!" I called. "Excuse me."

"Pipe down," one of the guards called back.

"Please!" I called louder. "If you don't believe me, send someone to find Prince Damon. Tell him I need to speak to him. Tell him the prince and princess are in danger."

A loud scoff told me Sierra had also approached the door, but she didn't attempt to override my request.

The guards looked at each other uneasily, communicating silently. I held my breath until one of them shrugged and crossed over to knock at the internal door. It opened, and he held a whispered conversation with someone on the other side before returning to his post.

I let out a long breath and stumbled back into the room, collapsing down to sit on the pallet. I had done everything I could.

After another steadying breath, I pulled out the handkerchief that had once been my most prized possession. Now to work out how to destroy it.

CHAPTER 25

*S*ome time later, I was still sitting on the pallet, staring at the piece of material in frustration. Burning it would have been simple, but the only light in my cell came through the external window and the grate of the door.

I had hoped ripping it might be enough, but it had a thick decorative border that resisted every effort to tear it. My mother had woven one of my hairs into the border to extend the enchantment to me, and I suspected she wasn't the only one to have done so. How many generations had added to the border of the small scrap, unintentionally strengthening it?

I groaned. What good was recovering the handkerchief if I couldn't destroy it? I threw it across the room, but it only made it halfway, fluttering gently down to rest on the floor.

"Ugh!" I stood up and kicked the pallet, a better outlet for my irritation, before retrieving the object and returning it to my dress.

If Damon managed to convince the king and have me released, I would go straight to one of the lanterns outside my cell and burn it. I just had to hold on until then.

"Lark! Lark!" The piercing whisper sent me hurrying to the external window.

Philip stood outside, his face stark in the moonlight.

"What's going on? I couldn't find you anywhere at the party." His face twisted. "I thought you must be with Damon, but then the rumor came around that you'd been arrested. I didn't believe it could be true, but..." He trailed off given the obvious truth of the report.

"I think the Poulterer must have gone to Mrs. Pine more quickly than we were expecting," I said. "And she thought my behavior suspicious enough to report to the king, who evidently agreed with her." I tugged at my braid, remembering how easily I had dismissed Colin's reports against me. I hadn't dreamed they might lead to this.

"This is madness." Philip kept his voice to a strained whisper, gripping the bars and staring in at me.

"I'll go to the king myself and tell him he's wrong. I'll remind him I saw you fighting for your life with my own eyes. We have to convince him there is no truth to this."

"Don't be ridiculous!" I hissed. "What credibility do you have in the eyes of the king? You'll just convince him that you're involved as well."

His eyes shifted slightly. "I may only be a servant, but I can be extremely convincing. I love you, Lark! I won't leave you to spend the night in a prison cell."

A strange sensation washed over me. A vague uneasiness, like a churning in my stomach except I could feel it in my mind not my body. I jerked back, staring at him.

I recognized that feeling. I had felt it at home while I experimented with the handkerchief's powers.

When I held the object in my hand, any untruthful words seemed to shine in my mind, picked out as if repeated in fire across my inner eye. But I didn't hold it in my hand now. Instead it rested against my skin, beneath my dress. Connected to it in such a way, it would only give me a general sense of unease when a lie was spoken.

Philip had said he loved me, and the handkerchief declared it a lie. But it couldn't be. Everything he had said and done for me flashed before my eyes. In the space of seconds, I relived every emotion we had shared. I had been a fool, secure in his affection, and now that it was in doubt, I saw my own heart clearly.

I loved him, and I could not bear the idea that it had all been a deception. I loved my family and my kingdom, and I would spend my life serving them, but I would go to any lengths to find a way to do it with this man at my side.

Except now it turned out he didn't love me after all. When he found out the truth of my rank, he would probably feel obligated to obey any orders I might give or pleas I might make. But I couldn't bear to entrap him in such a way.

I gasped, feeling wetness on my cheeks, although I hadn't noticed the tears building.

Philip cursed, pressing as close against the bars as he could. "Don't cry, Lark. Please don't cry! I'll get you out of there. I swear it."

A loud whinny sounded behind him, and a large head thrust him to one side.

I will kick down this wall, Arvin said, indignation lacing his words. *I will show them you are not to be caged.*

I chuckled shakily. "Even you could not kick down a stone wall, Arvin." The sight of him brought back a flood of memories, centering around a ballroom and a deadly threat.

I kicked myself. Here I was, worrying about my heart, when even now, good people might be dying. I looked at my horse and then at Philip. He clearly didn't doubt me for a second, despite my arrest. But what about me? Did I trust him? He might not love me, but could I trust him to help me with this?

I didn't have to reach for the answer, it was already there. If his love for me was a lie, it must be a lie he was telling himself as well. I could not believe he would allow harm to come to anyone, let alone the crown prince and princess.

"Never mind me," I said, pressing forward to the window again. "I overheard the men who attacked me. They have the poison that was used to kill the viscount. And their target is Princess Alyssa and Prince Max."

"But they aren't even here." Philip frowned. "Harry harnessed a carriage for them early this morning. They haven't returned yet."

"I know." Now I was the one gripping the bars. "They're on the road, on their way home, and Sierra's men have gone to intercept them. Do you know which road they've taken?"

Philip shook his head. "Harry will know, though."

"You have to take Arvin and go," I said. "He's fast. Faster than any other horse. Together you can catch up to them. I know you can."

A suppressed scream of outrage sounded from the next cell, telling me that Sierra was listening to our conversation. I couldn't have asked for clearer confirmation.

I turned to Arvin. "Please let him ride you. Just this once. Lives depend on it."

Do you really think you have to ask?

I gave a gasping sob of relief, wishing I could throw my arms around his neck in thanks.

"But what about you?" Philip asked, clearly torn.

"Don't worry about me. I'm safe enough here. Stopping those men is what matters."

Arvin stepped back, tossing his head and neighing loudly. But Philip lingered a moment longer, wrapping his hands around mine where they gripped the bars.

"Hold on, Lark," he said. "I'll save the prince and princess, and then I'm coming back for you."

He looked so honorable and brave in the moonlight that I couldn't resist surging forward and pressing my lips against his through the bars. Arvin neighed again, and Philip groaned and pulled away.

Only as he was riding off did I realize that I had felt no further warning from the handkerchief. He had said he would save them, and he had meant it. My trust hadn't been misplaced.

I stood there for a long time, listening to Sierra cursing and kicking things. A clang and a splash told me her basin had caught one of the kicks.

"Settle down in there, you two," yelled one of the guards.

When Sierra gave no sign of quieting, his boots sounded as he crossed over to her cell. Before he could berate her further, however, the external door burst open.

I rushed to my grate to see Damon enter the room, dressed in his ballroom finery, his eyes blazing.

"What is the meaning of this?" he said.

The guard faltered and returned to his post.

"We're just following orders, Your Highness," one of them said.

"Damon!" I cried, just as Sierra's voice also called his name through her grate.

He glanced at her but strode quickly to me.

"I was waiting for you, but you didn't come. When a guard arrived to tell me you had been arrested and were asking for me..." He broke off and threw another furious look at the poor guards.

"The king got the idea I was involved in it all," I said breathlessly. "We shouldn't have waited to tell him the truth." I thought guiltily of the handkerchief against my skin. If I hadn't been so determined to retrieve it, I would have insisted we talk to the king before the ball. "At least I made sure I wasn't the only one arrested."

"Sierra's men are still free, though," Damon said. "We must not waste any time."

I nodded but didn't want to explain Philip's mission where the guards could hear us. "The king needs to know the truth as soon as possible. They need to search—" My words cut off as I tried to say *Sierra's room*. I wasn't free yet.

Damon drew even closer, his voice dropping.

"Elle, when I heard you were arrested…" He paused and drew a breath. "It made me realize my true feelings for you. I love you. I don't care about your rank. I want you to be mine."

His intense eyes beseeched me, his handsome face filled with earnest emotion. But my mind roiled, my natural shock strengthened by the unnatural sensation. Could this really be happening? Could I really be receiving a second false declaration of love in one night? What was happening?

"I *need* you to be mine," he said. "Please, promise me that you'll marry me. I'll order you released, and then we'll go to the king together. Once we expose the plot against Arcadia, I'll tell him of our betrothal."

A yell echoed from the cell next door, the rage in this cry making her earlier one pale. All of Sierra's plans were crumbling around her. But my confused attention remained on Damon.

The sensation from the handkerchief had disappeared as abruptly as it had appeared—gone as he delivered the second part of his speech. I blinked, trying to make sense of it and separate my real emotions from the influence of the object.

Those words at least were true. His proposal was real. But my heart, full of Philip's kiss, recoiled at the idea.

An image of my mother's face filled my mind, sending my heart into further turmoil. She had made me promise to give an alliance a chance, and here was a proposal my parents would approve. If I had no hope of being with the man I loved, could I refuse the man they would choose so lightly?

But what of the handkerchief's warning? Something of his initial words had been untrue. Which part? If only I had been holding the material in my hand.

"Damon, I—" I tried to form an answer while my mind still whirled.

"I'm sorry," he said quickly. "I've taken you by surprise. Just promise you'll think about it. Tell me I have a chance at least."

I gulped. "I'll think about it."

Later. When I was out of prison, and no one's life was in danger. Surely I would be able to think more clearly then.

Damon whirled on the guards, and for the first time I noticed that his own guards—the ones I had seen in the Blue Arrow—had crowded into the prison with him.

"Release her at once!" He bristled with imperious fury.

Two of the guards exchanged uneasy glances. "She's here under the king's orders, Your Highness."

Damon drew himself up, his eyes flashing dangerously. "And I speak with the king's authority. If you value the well-being of the royal family, you will not stand in my way."

The guards glanced between him and the men he had brought with him, their eyes finally resting on my cell.

"Very well, then, Your Highness," one of them said at last. "If Your Highness is taking responsibility for her—"

"Of course I'm taking responsibility for her," Damon snapped. "Now hurry up."

The guard stepped forward, fumbling with his key ring. He must have looked through every key twice over before he managed to select the right one, inserting it into my door.

As soon as it was unlocked, Damon yanked it open and pulled me into his arms. I rested there a moment, my forehead against his chest, trying to make sense of the chaos of the last few minutes.

I had no time for reflection, however. He immediately let me go, grabbing my hand instead and tugging me toward the door. As we passed Sierra's cell, I saw her pale face at the grate.

"Damon, you can't do this!" she screamed. "You can't leave me here! Damon! Damon!" She wailed, the heartrending cry of someone who had just had everything in life taken from her.

I tried to close my ears and shut it out. She had brought everything on herself. I would not take responsibility for her pain.

"Ignore her," Damon said as we hurried out into the fresh air. "She's just jealous. She could never be the princess you are. Blood cannot be bought."

The image of the little girl playing dress ups flashed across my mind, but it shattered as I nearly stumbled over a paving stone. Damon moved so quickly I could hardly keep up, stumbling behind him. I wanted to ask him to slow, but I knew how important it was that we move quickly.

It made it hard to think, though.

My thoughts still swirled wildly within my head, one no sooner alighting than it took off again, to mix with the others in half-formed sentences and barely realized emotions. Something beat against my mind. If I could just be still for a moment, it would have a chance to form into coherence.

The sick feeling had returned, although this time it was anchored deep in my stomach. Something was wrong. I knew it.

Damon pulled me up the stairs and through the entrance hall. For the second time that afternoon, I burst into the ballroom at a half-run.

The crowded room, swirling with dancers, was like a visual image of my overcrowded mind. And yet, for some reason, the familiar environment made everything in my head slow and stop. For one brief moment, it all appeared, still and clear, the relevant pieces glowing brightly in my consciousness.

CHAPTER 26

I came to an abrupt stop, my connection with Damon breaking as he surged ahead. He lurched to a halt and turned, confusion on his face.

"We have to find the king!" he said.

I didn't move, and he hurried back to me.

"You said I was a princess."

"You are." He frowned. "You will be."

I shook my head. "No. *You said blood can't be bought.* How do you know?"

"Sierra," he said. "I went to her before the ball. We were childhood friends, I thought maybe I could talk to her. But she…" He sighed and shook his head. "But everything makes sense now—I should have guessed, really. After this is over, I want to hear everything that happened—everything she did to you."

Oh. I relaxed. Yes, Sierra knew the truth. But my mind had started swirling again. Something wasn't right.

"We need to gather the royal family," Damon said. "Make sure they're all safe. You find the king and queen. I'll find the children. Meet at the dais. There's a private room behind it. They'll be safe there."

He didn't give me a chance to respond, diving into the crowd and leaving me standing alone.

The children? For a moment I couldn't think who he meant, but then my thoughts caught up. Henry and Rose, of course. The young prince and princess.

Everything around me froze, the music fading away as blood pounded through my head.

The prince and princess. Henry and Rose were a prince and princess, not just their parents. How could I have made such rash conclusions in the kitchen? How could I have been such a fool?

The words of the men resurfaced with more clarity than I had realized my memory of them possessed.

She said not to go to her suite until after midday. We stash this vile stuff there for the prince and princess, and then we need to be on the road. We're going to run out of time if we don't move soon.

Why would they leave a vial of the poison in Sierra's room if they were going to deliver it themselves to Max and Alyssa on the road? I should have realized immediately which prince and princess they meant, and who it was that would be delivering the poison. But they had mentioned the road—it had seemed like a confirmation of my assumptions.

My mouth went dry. Unless both were true. Sierra wasn't just targeting Max and Alyssa but their entire family.

I tried to calm my panic. Philip and Arvin had gone after Max and Alyssa, and Sierra was imprisoned. She couldn't hurt the children from there. And when we told the king the truth, he would have her searched. When they found the vial on her person, it would prove everything.

But to kill such small children? How could she? Their deaths weren't necessary. The deaths of their parents would be a big enough blow to the king and queen—to the whole kingdom.

The ball continued around me while I stood there, still frozen, unhearing, unseeing. The death of Prince Max's whole family was more than a statement or a threat. His younger sisters were both far away, a queen and a crown princess of their own kingdoms. The death of Max's family would be a decimation of the royal line—a destruction of every heir to the throne.

The ball returned, sound and movement roaring back around me. All the heirs except one. One who was newly arrived in the kingdom. The thoughts that had beaten, half-formed against my consciousness, paraded now through my mind in perfect clarity.

The heartbroken wail of Sierra—Damon's childhood friend— as he declared his love for me and left her behind in a cell.

Her words in our carriage so long ago, declaring that the enchantment bound both of us from revealing the truth of our tangled identities.

And the swirling warning of the handkerchief when he told me he loved me and when he said he had learned the truth from her—both times with a face of perfect sincerity. I had never seen such an accomplished actor, but the enchanted object did not lie.

Damon, who had been there when Sierra's injured men left the shelter of her suite to venture into the park. Damon, who had been the one to sift through the viscount's papers and discover the evidence against both Sierra and Rangmere. Evidence I had yet to see.

And Damon who was even now searching for the children.

My stomach surged so violently I nearly wretched. Rose was here, I knew that much, which must mean her brother was also. Did Damon intend to claim he found them moments too late? Just in time to avenge their deaths, perhaps, but tragically not in time to save them?

Determination surged through me. No. I would not let that happen. He would not kill those children. I had managed to get everything else wrong, but this was my moment—my true chance to prove myself. I would save those children, whatever the cost.

I surged into the crowd, wishing desperately I had some sort of weapon, beyond the knife in my boot. I would dearly appreciate my staff right now. Even just to clear a path through the celebrating throng.

I made for the throne, hoping against hope Rose would still be there. Damon had a head start, but he didn't know where to find her. I pushed blindly past people, not bothering to apologize or slow.

But my eyes caught on one familiar face in the otherwise unfamiliar crowd. Percy. And he wore his scabbard strapped to his belt. I could have kissed him.

"Percy!" I screamed over the music. "Thank goodness. Quick! We have to protect the children."

He stared at me as if I had lost my mind. "Do I know you?" He peered closer. "Wait...aren't you the goose girl? Didn't you just get arrested?"

"Argh! Never mind that!" I grabbed his arm and tried to tug him with me. "Come on, Perce! It's me!" My panic rendered me incoherent enough that the enchantment allowed the unhelpful exclamation to slip through.

I tried again. "Princess Rose is in danger. We have to protect her!"

Percy still looked confused, but that got through to him. He glanced around.

"Where is she? What danger?"

"It's Damon." I was almost moaning now in my panic and haste. I tugged again, and this time he came with me.

"The prince?"

"He means to poison them and blame..." I quickly changed words, "Eldon. Maybe he even means to implicate you?" The thought burst over me. "It would be a neat trick, and you have been close with...we can't let that happen."

"Implicate me?" Percy still looked bemused and unsure, but a little bit of anger had seeped in now too. He no longer resisted my efforts to pull him along.

"I saw Rose last at the throne. Have you seen her since?"

He shook his head. "No, but I did see Prince Henry heading in that direction. Perhaps he was looking for her."

We finally burst through the last of the crowd, almost stumbling over the first step of the dais.

"Come on, Rose," a young voice said. "You can't hide back here until Mama and Papa get here. They wouldn't like it."

"Oh yes, I can," her piping voice replied.

Trembles shook me. We had made it. They were still alive. But as I turned back to Percy, my eyes met Damon's through the crowd.

He was only a short distance away from us, separated by a few remaining clumps of people. His eyes flicked to Percy, whose sword was now drawn, then to the children, half-hidden by the throne, and then back to me. In that moment enough passed between us that he knew. And I knew. We both knew that the other knew.

There was no more pretense between us, and death filled his eyes. If I knew, then I had to die alongside the children, and Percy with me. He surged forward, pushing people out of his way.

"Percy!" I screamed, pointing at Damon. "Hold him off!"

I leaped around the thrones, grasping Henry and Rose by an arm each.

"Hurry," I cried. "You're in danger. Come with me."

"Elle?" Henry pulled back against me, fear in his eyes. "What's going on?"

I didn't bother taking the time to explain, instead dragging them forcibly toward the wall. Damon had said there was a private room here...There! I saw the door. Dropping Rose's arm, I whipped it open and grabbed her again just as she threw herself at her brother in terror.

Sticking my head inside, I scanned the room. Damon had been the one to mention it, so I had to be sure he didn't have any guards stashed here. But it was empty. The room had been part of his original plan, the one where the king and queen and I all stayed ignorant of the truth.

I thrust both children inside and slammed the door behind us. The prince stepped forward, trembling but standing tall, sweeping his younger sister behind him.

"What is this? What are you doing to us? I demand you let us go."

"I'm just trying to protect you." My eyes skimmed over the room, looking for something I could use to barricade the door. There was nothing but two sofas, both too heavy for me to move on my own.

I knelt down and looked Henry in the eyes.

"I know Damon is your cousin, but he is a bad man. He wants to hurt you. Both of you." Henry drew back, and Rose started to wail. "Prince Percy and I will protect you. We will try to keep him back. But you have to stay in this room."

Henry swallowed and nodded. "Mama and Papa?" he asked, quick in spite of his fear. "Are they in danger too?"

"I sent friends to help them," I said, unable to give any more certain promise. "But I need you to be strong for your sister now. Hide, if you can. Under one of the sofas maybe? Don't open that door!"

I wished I could stay to comfort and reassure them, but I had left Percy to face Damon alone. I had to help him.

Slipping out the door, I closed it, placing my back against it while I surveyed the scene. Screams had broken out, and people scattered in all directions, pressing back from the violently dueling men. This could still go in Damon's favor. If he managed to kill Percy, he could blame the children's deaths on him. Whether I would feature as innocent victim or villainous accomplice I wasn't sure. But that I had to die was certain.

I followed the flash of the blades, my bottom lip between my teeth. Damon was skilled, but Percy was holding his own. I couldn't see any way to help the Talinosian prince without putting him at risk.

Several guards pushed through the crowd, and I turned to them in relief. But their uniforms made me pause. Half of them were Damon's men.

Damon risked a single glance sideways, catching sight of his men. He gave a jerk of his head toward the door behind the dais, and two of them started toward me.

I ripped the dagger from my boot.

"Treachery!" I screamed. "Guards, to me!"

The Arcadian guards turned toward me, confusion across their faces. Several of them also started in my direction.

"She's escaped!" one of Damon's guards cried, pointing at me.

The Arcadian guards slowed. How many of them had witnessed my arrest? How many of them recognized me?

The first attacker reached me, driving his sword toward my heart. I dropped to the ground, stabbing my knife through his foot. He screamed and staggered, dropping his own weapon.

I snatched it up, scrambling back to my feet and re-taking my place in front of the door. I had a longer weapon now, but the new attacker rushing for me had two more men closing fast behind him. I cast a desperate glance at the Arcadian guards, but they still hung back, their eyes jumping between me and the duel. They were clearly far too confused to know what to do.

I barely turned aside the first thrust, falling back so I stood flush against the wood of the door. I had nowhere left to retreat.

Over my attackers' shoulders, I saw the flash of the duel. In the middle of battle, flushed with exertion, Percy's and my eyes met. Sudden recognition, like lightning, flashed through his gaze.

"Giselle?" he cried.

He faltered, Damon gaining the advantage just as my own attackers closed the last of the distance between us. With a surge of despair, I knew we were both about to fall. Damon would win.

A wild, inhuman scream rang through the crowded ballroom.

Even Damon and his men faltered, everyone swinging toward the door. The crowd surged and parted with further, more human, screams to reveal Arvin, rearing. Philip sat astride his back, somehow keeping his seat, although his hair was more disheveled than ever.

Arvin crashed back to the ground, galloping forward through the cleared pathway. Damon swung around, desperation on his face as he lunged at Percy, but Percy had used the distraction to leap up the steps onto the dais, gaining the upper ground.

Two of my attackers turned to flee, but the third pressed forward, thrusting his sword toward me. I deflected it again and again as he tried to drive me sideways away from the door. I knew what he wanted. If he could get inside that room, he could claim he found the children in there, killed by my hand. I would not allow that to happen.

As I deflected again, his blade flashed back and around in a feint. I desperately tried to push my sword to block him, but I couldn't move fast enough. Pain ripped up my arm.

"Lark!" Philip appeared behind us, having somehow acquired a sword.

My attacker pivoted to meet him. I swayed, dizzy with pain and scared. Servants didn't know how to wield swords, and the weapons were dangerous in the hands of a novice. What was Philip doing? He was going to get himself killed.

But before I could call a warning, he made a perfect lunge, his sword moving faster than I could follow, twisting up and around and sending the sword of the guard flying. The man went white and held up both hands in surrender, but Philip's sword was already driving toward his throat.

Somehow, impossibly, Philip pulled out of the lunge, his sword halting, the tip quivering a mere inch from the man's throat. He held the position, his voice ringing with authority.

"Arrest this man."

This time the Arcadian guards didn't hesitate to obey.

"Alyssa?" I asked Philip. "And Max?"

He pointed silently toward the dais.

Percy no longer stood alone. Max stood beside him, sword drawn and blazing anger in his eyes. Damon fell back before them, his confidence finally faltering.

Alyssa stood shoulder to shoulder with her husband, despite not having a weapon in her hands. But as soon as Damon retreated, she turned, her questioning eyes finding me, still against the wall. Moving so quickly she almost tripped over the dais steps, she flew to me.

"My children." Fear filled her face. "Where are my children?"

I stepped away from the door. "Safe. They're safe."

She flung open the door and disappeared inside. For a second there was silence and then a boy's voice cried, "Mama." Scrambling sounds followed, like children crawling out from under a sofa, and childish sobs from Rose.

I closed my eyes. They were alive. The children were alive and so were Alyssa and her husband. And so was I. When it most mattered, I had succeeded. I had proven the most important quality of any princess—her willingness to sacrifice herself for others. But I felt no great swell of accomplishment. If I hadn't made so many mistakes, it might never have come so close to disaster.

CHAPTER 27

*A*rms wrapped around me, and a voice murmured in my ear. Philip's familiar presence brought me back to the moment. My eyes flew open.

"Damon! It was all Damon. Where is he?"

He's trying to run. Arvin sounded strangely matter-of-fact about it. *You seem to be injured.*

"Never mind that," I said. "It's only a shallow cut."

Philip swung around, still cradling me with one arm, careful not to touch the gash which still seeped blood. Together we looked for the prince in the chaos of the shattered ball. Many people had fled the room, but many more still remained, pressed against the walls.

The enemy guard who had surrendered to Philip knelt beside the dais, one of his companions beside him, and a row of Arcadian guards in front of them. But the others still fought in the distant doorway, their swords clashing with the weapons of another contingent of Arcadian guards.

I had a single glimpse of Damon before he drove his sword into a guard, leaping over the man as he fell and running out the door. Philip let go of me, retrieving his sword from where he had

259

apparently discarded it on the ground, and ran across the throne room.

More guards poured into the room from somewhere. The king appeared and directed them toward the struggle at the doorway. He and the queen hurried in our direction, however, their concerned eyes on their son who still stood on the dais. But Max didn't wait for them. He was looking around wildly, so I caught his eye and pointed through the doorway behind us.

He took the steps in a single leap, pausing beside me to clap me on the shoulder. Gratitude filled his eyes as they rested on me for a moment, and then he disappeared into the room beyond.

"You should go too," I said to Arvin. "You might help distract the children. They liked you."

It is true that it is difficult to be fearful or downcast in my presence, the horse said. *Please endeavor not to collect any more wounds in my absence.* He trotted off toward the doorway, everyone giving him a wary berth.

King Henry and Queen Eleanor reached us, the queen following immediately after her son. The king paused, however, to give me a puzzled look. But he had seen his son's gesture, and apparently that was enough to prevent him ordering my immediate re-arrest.

"It was Damon the whole time, Your Majesty," I said. "He was behind everything. I'm sorry I didn't realize it sooner. But they're all safe." I pointed at the doorway. "Back there."

The king looked toward the door but turned to his guards.

"Bring those men," he ordered, pointing at the two kneeling by the dais.

He didn't wait to see if he was obeyed, hurrying away toward the entrance to the throne room. I followed behind. I needed to find Philip.

The fighting had finished by the time we reached the doorway. Two injured Arcadian guards were being assisted by several of their fellows, cursing creatively until they caught sight of their king and fell silent. A third casualty, wearing Damon's uniform, lay still and unmoving on the ground. Damon himself and the rest of his men were gone.

King Henry paused for a brief word with the injured guards before continuing through to the large entryway. There was still no sign of Damon or his men, so the king didn't stop, and I stayed at his heels.

We paused in the doorway of the palace, gazing down into the yard. People filled it in every direction. Nobles, having fled from the ball, crowded together in clumps. A whole crowd of servants massed on the side near the stables and the servants' wing, apparently having come running from their own festivities at the rumor of battle.

Philip stood in front of the open gates, a small number of guards beside him. They faced Damon and his men, the only barrier between them and escape.

"Close the gates!" shouted the king. "Close the gates!"

The gatekeeper, stirred to action by his king's voice, sprang forward. Several servants raced to help him, the heavy gates swinging slowly closed.

I could hear Damon's curses from all the way across the yard. He looked disheveled and dirty, his elegant clothes torn. How had I been so taken in by him?

I expected him to make a desperate lunge for the closing gap between the gates, but he took off across the yard, aiming for the opposite side of the palace to the gathered servants. His men were only steps behind him. Philip and the guards were taken by surprise, however, giving Damon precious seconds of advantage.

Without thinking, I jumped down the stairs and ran to intercept him. But, as I neared the place where I could block his passage, I remembered I no longer held a weapon.

Damon didn't even see me, his entire focus on escaping around the palace, although I didn't know where he thought he could go after that. I could hear the king behind me, issuing a stream of orders, and more guards were arriving in the yard at every moment, recalled from their participation in the servants' festivities.

Damon put on a spurt of speed, leaping ahead of me. But a man rounded the corner just as he did so, the sword in his hand indicating he was a guard, despite the lack of uniform. The prince, more focused on speed than defense, cursed and tried to swerve around him.

The guard, caught by surprise, made a wild lunge. Damon's swerve nearly carried him past the attack, but the sword caught on his leg, cutting a deep gash. But no blood spurted out. The cloth had been torn apart, and I could clearly see as his skin closed back over. The prince barely faltered, continuing on his dash for the park.

I stopped, my mouth dropping open. Impossible. The guard also faltered, his sword hanging loose at his side as he stared after the fleeing Damon. The prince's men streamed past us both, intent on their leader.

I turned to look at the guard. "Did you see that?"

He nodded slowly, holding up his sword. We both saw the red at its tip. We hadn't imagined the injury. More guards hurried past us, these ones a mix of uniformed and non-uniformed Arcadians, and the guard shook himself and joined them.

Philip appeared beside me and gently took my arm in his. At the soft touch, stinging pain rushed to the forefront of my mind, no longer driven back by the intensity of the moment.

"We need to get that injury treated," he said.

The king appeared beside us. "You may return with me to the throne room. I don't understand what's happened, but I sent for a doctor to check over my family. I'm sure they can tend to your wound as well. I want a full accounting of what transpired here."

I nodded, swaying a little on my feet now the excitement had passed. Philip slipped his arm around my shoulders to support me.

"What about Damon?" he asked.

"Where can he go?" The king looked grim. "My guards will catch him and his men." A guard I recognized stepped up beside the king, who turned to speak to him. "Markus, make sure he's found. I want him brought in alive."

"Yes, Your Majesty." The captain saluted before sprinting after his men.

"You two are coming with me." The order was clear in his tone this time.

"Of course, Your Majesty," Philip said. And then more quietly, "Come on, Lark. Not much further."

I hadn't realized I was swaying again, exhaustion and pain overwhelming me. Pulling myself straighter, I nodded.

The three of us hurried back through the ballroom, heading for the back room where we had left the other royals. We had nearly made it to the dais when one of the remaining nobles stepped forward. I had been ignoring the frantic hubbub of the room, but the young man addressed us directly.

"Philip? What are you doing here?"

I tried to remember where I had seen him before. After a frantic moment of mental searching, the answer surfaced. Thomas. The new Viscount Edgewaring.

How did he know Philip?

The king glanced back at us, raising a single eyebrow. "You'd better come along as well, Thomas. You have as much right as anybody to know what has been going on in this kingdom."

The young viscount fell in behind us readily enough, despite the surprise on his face.

"What's going on, Philip?" he asked. "I didn't expect to see you here."

"It's a very long story," Philip said. "And I don't know it all myself. Best to wait and hear it all in order, I suspect."

Thomas raised his eyebrows but didn't question us further.

Inside the private room, Alyssa and the queen sat on one of

the sofas. Rose nestled on her mother's lap, her arms around her neck. Arvin stood beside them, the young prince patting his mane, though I suspected the boy was receiving comfort rather than giving it.

Percy also stood, his sword still in his hand, and his eyes on the door, Max beside him talking to him in low tones.

To my surprise, however, they weren't the only people in the room. Sierra stood in one corner, flanked by two guards who each kept a grip on one of her arms. Apparently a doctor wasn't the only person the king had ordered to be brought to this room.

She looked nothing like the last time I had seen her in the prison. All the fight had left her, and she slumped listlessly between her guards.

"Excellent," the king said when he saw her. "Everyone is here, then."

His wife crossed to him, and he embraced her briefly, whispering something I couldn't hear.

"Markus is tracking down Damon and his men now," the king said to everyone. "I expect they'll be back soon enough. I just hope none of the servants are injured in the struggle. This wasn't what I had in mind when I thought to provide my people with some festivities."

"As I recall," Queen Eleanor said with a hard look at Sierra, "hosting festivities wasn't your idea in the first place."

The king's eyes narrowed. "True enough. I think, Princess Giselle, it is past time for you to tell us precisely what is going on here, and what is your connection to my nephew."

Sierra looked up but didn't speak. Instead her eyes traveled to me, the dull look in them shocking after her previous sparks. I shook off Philip's arm and stepped forward. Now that it came to it, I felt a strange reluctance to burn the handkerchief. I glanced back at him. There were so many questions I wanted to ask him while I held it properly in my hand.

But the time for secrets had passed. We needed openness now, and only the destruction of the handkerchief would allow that. Philip's trust in me had never wavered, and he had succeeded tonight more completely than I could have dreamed. It was time for me to trust in him.

"Actually," I said, "Princess Giselle can't tell you what's going on until I do this."

Everyone's eyes followed me as I crossed to an elegant candelabra on the mantel. Pulling out the handkerchief, I held it to one of the candles. It resisted the flames for a moment before the fire jumped across, racing along the material. I dropped it into the empty fireplace, watching as the bright orange and red consumed the small item.

Slowly I walked back to Philip's side. The door opened quietly, and a young man appeared, unobtrusive but confident, a large bag in his hand. He glanced around the room before pinning his focus on my arm.

"Ah, Aldric," said Max. "It would appear the young lady needs your assistance."

The doctor crossed over to me, placing his bag on the ground and rummaging inside before producing a roll of bandage. I looked across at the king.

"Aldric has our complete trust," he said. "You need not hesitate in his presence. What exactly is your connection to the princess? It is clear things are not as they have appeared."

"I *am* the princess," I said simply.

"The princess?" Philip's shocked voice was the first to respond, and I carefully kept my eyes averted from him.

"I am Princess Giselle of Eldon, and that—" I pointed at the girl between the guards, "is my maid, Sierra. I would like to begin by giving Eldon's most profuse apologies. We had no knowledge of the plans against you and did not play a willing part in either the deception practiced on you or the crimes committed against you."

"I don't care who are," Alyssa said in an impassioned

voice. "You protected my children. You will always be a friend of Arcadia."

"I fear I made a great many mistakes," I said in a heavy voice. "Mistakes that aided in us arriving at such a dire situation. My own foolish desires to prove myself made me all too susceptible to the lies Damon told."

"You are not the only one he deceived," Queen Eleanor said gently, sorrow in her voice.

"I still don't understand." The king glanced toward the fire-place. "What did that handkerchief have to do with this?"

"It's a long story, but I will tell it as best I can." I tried to ignore the man now bandaging my arm. "There are many parts that even I don't fully understand."

I told of the ship from Eldon which had been exploring the seas after the disappearance of the High King's storms and the small island they discovered on their journey. When I spoke of the people who had chosen to leave its remote shores in favor of positions in Eldon, a number of murmurs broke out over this connection between Sierra and Damon. But the king waved everyone to silence and gestured for me to continue.

I told of Celine's illness on the boat and the unexpected damage it had sustained, causing only a small group of us to set ashore for Arcadie. I related the attack on the road as I had first perceived it and then as I now realized it had actually happened. And then Sierra's betrayal on the road to Arcadie. I explained her efforts to thrust me out of sight in the position of goose girl, and her subsequent attempt to have me killed. I explained how Philip and I were attempting to investigate the strange happenings in Arcadia and about our first meeting with Damon.

"It feels so foolish that it never occurred to me those men were out there to meet Damon," I said.

"I never fully trusted him," Philip said, glancing sideways at me. "But I'll admit even I didn't go so far as to suspect him of being the architect behind it all."

I detailed my subsequent encounters with Damon, and the story he had fed me about his history with Sierra. "I have no idea which parts of it were true—if any." And then I finished by skimming over my arrest and the things that finally made me realize what I should have seen much earlier.

"The true heroes are Philip and Percy," I said. "I don't know how Philip managed to save Princess Alyssa and Prince Max and still make it back to save us. And if Percy hadn't taken a chance and believed me when I waylaid him in the ballroom, I never could have held off Damon and his men long enough for you all to arrive."

"Alyssa had a feeling something was wrong and insisted we turn back early," Max said. "Which meant we were closer to the palace than expected when Philip came riding for us. He only just caught us as the men arrived."

I finally looked at Philip, going pale at the thought of him confronting the men with their vial of poison. But this time he was the one carefully avoiding looking in my direction.

"It was nothing so very heroic," he assured us. "I have never in my life encountered a horse that runs like Arvin can run. I spent the whole time hanging on for dear life and hoping I didn't make a fool of myself by flying straight off into the dirt."

My riders do not fall off unless I wish them to.

I glared at the horse. "I fell off once, not long after you arrived!"

I sensed you needed a little humility, he said, without the faintest trace of guilt.

"There is something more than unusual about that horse," Philip said. "Can you actually understand him?"

"Understand him? Do you mean he can *talk*?" Prince Henry stared at Arvin with increased admiration.

I bit my lip. "Yes," I said reluctantly. "Though no one knows it but my family. He was a gift from my godmother and comes from the High King's Palace of Light. Sierra thought it was the handkerchief that gave me the ability to hear him and was most put out when it didn't confer the ability to her. That's why she tried to have him killed."

Arvin snorted. *I am not controlled by a mere handkerchief, I assure you.*

A chorus of amazed exclamations broke out across the room. I stared around at everyone. "Did you all hear that?"

Every head nodded.

"Arvin!" I glared at the horse. "Do you mean you could have spoken to whoever you liked, all this time?"

What of it? He sounded bored. *I only wished to speak to you.*

"But you could have told everyone the truth!"

Perhaps. Or perhaps they would have found a princess a more credible witness than a talking horse. Either way, that is not how the godmothers' gifts work. We assist you in working through your troubles yourself, we do not magically erase every difficulty. I helped you tonight in ways you couldn't help yourself, but think of all that wouldn't have happened if I had spoken up then. Damon might never have been exposed, for one.

And I might never have grown close to Philip. Might never have loved him. All my anger at the horse melted away.

"Well that certainly explains how we moved so fast," Philip said, taking Arvin's history in stride more quickly than the others —perhaps because he had already suspected he wasn't an ordinary horse. "And how we avoided the poison."

"The poison?" Queen Eleanor looked at her son.

"Arvin knocked one of the men to the ground as soon as we arrived," Philip explained. "And he must have been the one carrying the vial of poison. It was crushed, and he and both of his companions breathed it in. They clearly got a larger dose than the viscount because I'm afraid they died almost instantly. Arvin somehow got us both far enough away, and the others were protected in the carriage. It wasn't a large amount, thank goodness."

I shuddered to think of the danger Philip had been in. I mouthed a thank you to my horse who appeared to take my gratitude as a matter of course.

"There are still a number of things that are unclear." Alyssa looked between Sierra and me with a creased brow. "It seems a large number of coincidences were required to provide such a perfect situation for Sierra's attack."

I shrugged. "I have no answer for that, although the person who might is standing with us."

"How did you arrange it?" Alyssa asked Sierra, as much curiosity in her voice as animosity.

"Why should I tell you anything?" A spark of Sierra's earlier defiance returned. "You'll just have me killed at the end of it."

"I give you my word that if you're honest with us now, you will not be killed," said the king.

Sierra gave him a long, measuring look and then shrugged, as if accepting that taking the chance on his sincerity was better than no chance at all.

$\mathcal{A}$t her acquiescence, the king gestured for the guards to leave. When one of them made a protesting noise, King Henry gave an amused glance toward Percy and Max. The guard glanced at the two princes and then across at Philip before giving a small bow, apparently satisfied his king had enough protection from one slim girl.

As soon as they were gone, Sierra began to speak. "There was no coincidence. My people spent many years on that island. Slowly we learned which of the native plants could be safely eaten and which could not. There is one freshwater weed that grows in the ponds there—it causes no actual harm, but it makes the stomach pitch and heave. Between the sea voyage and the pregnancy, it required only the tiniest pinch of the ground weed in Princess Celine's breakfast each morning to be sure she would find the journey intolerable. And when that was not enough to split the party and send Celine fleeing to Lanover, we sabotaged the ship."

"We?" King Henry asked.

"I am not the only one who spent many long months working my way into service and trust in the Eldonian palace. Those from the island who joined up as guards did the same, ensuring they were chosen when they volunteered to join the voyage. It is common in Eldon to allow men from the same family or town to be assigned to the same squad, so it was no difficulty to make sure they served together."

"We have the same custom here," Max murmured.

A sudden thought struck me. "The Arcadian squad which disappeared. Which town did the guards come from? Does anyone know?"

Max frowned, glancing at his wife. "Do you remember, Alyssa? I'm sure you pored over every document that could possibly pertain to them and their patrol when they first disappeared."

She frowned. "From memory, they didn't come from any one particular place. They were a squad formed from individuals born outside Arcadia who had chosen to make our kingdom their home."

"They were our people," Sierra interjected with a hopeful glance at the king, as if she thought volunteering information might win her extra favor. "Damon has been working on this plan for a long time. After he learned of the situation among the kingdoms from me, he brought others of his men here to Arcadia, dropping them off near the capital. They volunteered to join the guards, not revealing their shared origin, and formed a squad of outsiders.

"When the time was right, Damon picked them up from the Arcadian coast in our ship. They provided a great deal of information about Arcadie. Plus the 'honor guard' the prince brought with him were wearing their uniforms and carrying their equipment. It required only minor adjustments to make the uniforms look different enough. Damon wanted us to appear more prosperous and well equipped than we really are. He didn't want to arrive as a poor relation, looking for shelter, but as an equal—as much as it was possible."

"The emptied warehouse," Alyssa murmured. "And the nobles who were robbed."

Sierra shrugged. "We needed food, and Damon needed all the little trappings of nobility before he could appear before you. The things his parents took with them when they fled are hopelessly old and outdated now. Plus the robberies served his purpose in spreading fear and an impression of instability."

"I suppose this poison that has so baffled us came from your island as well," the doctor said, speaking for the first time. He had finished cleaning and bandaging my arm and was efficiently repacking his bag.

Sierra nodded. "Some of the plants we found were decidedly *not* safe to eat. Or even inhale."

"If a vial remains, I would appreciate the chance to study it," he said. "It may be possible for an antidote to be developed."

"We'll have her person, rooms, and possessions searched," the king promised.

"Thank you," the doctor said to him before nodding at the man beside me. "Philip."

Philip nodded back. "Aldric."

The doctor bowed to the assembled royals and departed.

Queen Eleanor, re-seated beside her daughter-in-law, rubbed her head. "It's been a long and rather terrifying day. Could someone please explain to me exactly what our nephew's plans were? It is clear he was a traitor from before we ever met him, but I cannot quite see how the two of you fit into his plans, Sierra and Giselle." She shook her head and looked at me. "How strange this all is. It will be quite an adjustment to remember that you are, in fact, the princess."

"I'm so sorry, Your Majesty," I said. "You opened your home and your family in the most welcoming manner, and both of your guests betrayed you. You are being more gracious than I could have expected."

Percy cleared his throat. "Two of their three guests betrayed them. Let me assure you right now, Your Majesties, that I am most definitely Prince Percival of Talinos, and I knew nothing about any of this until tonight. I only wish Giselle and I had met in more recent years so I might have recognized the deception."

I gave a tired chuckle. "Yes, indeed. This is definitely Prince Percy."

"I still cannot believe Mina's son would betray us so." The king sounded deeply grieved. "But I would like to understand his plan against our kingdom."

"I suspect it wasn't your sister's son who betrayed you," Philip said, "so much as it was Prince Friedrich of Rangmere's son who did so—although they were the same person. It seems clear now he was very much his father's son. The royals of Rangmere were always raised to be cold and strong—merciless, even."

"Friedrich was as weak as Mina," Sierra spat out. "Content to live out their lives, scrabbling for survival on a small island, when once they had been prince and princess with two kingdoms to command. Prince Friedrich was the elder son, not Prince Josef. He should have ruled Rangmere. Damon is the true heir, not this weak new queen who sits on their throne."

We all turned to her, astonished to see such sudden animation.

"That is not how succession works in Rangmere," Alyssa said. "Surely Prince Friedrich explained that to his son. When a king dies, all his sons compete in a series of trials, and the winner is crowned. Prince Friedrich was defeated by his younger brother who chose banishment as the cost of losing. He would have been within his legal rights to have his brother executed, so it was a mercy. Perhaps the only one old King Josef ever showed."

"Exactly," said Sierra, seeming to entirely miss her point. "Rangmere respects strength. This new queen is making the kingdom weak, destroying its foundations. How could Damon sit back and let it happen?"

"How did he even know of it?" I asked. "No one had even heard of your island before our ship found it."

Sierra shrugged. "We didn't know it then. But his parents had died, and Damon always knew he was destined for a greater future than one small island. First, though, we needed news of the outside world. We started working to repair our ship, intending to sail back here, when a better opportunity presented itself. Damon is a genius and saw the possibilities instantly. As soon as we saw a sail on the horizon, he wasted no time in choosing those of us best suited to leave—led by me, his most trusted friend." For a moment she looked proud before she remembered the reality of her situation and tears filled her eyes.

She dashed them away with an angry hand. "He loved me! He did! I know he did. Ever since we were children. We were raised together on the stories. We always knew we were destined to live as prince and princess. Damon refused to sit back and accept his fate as his parents had done."

A great sadness filled me as my image of the little girl playing dress ups returned, although now she stood on a sandy beach, her crown made of woven grass. How long had Damon been using her? Had his feelings ever been real?

"Those of us who were chosen sailed away, bound for Eldon as it turned out. When the repairs to our own ship were completed, Damon brought the rest of our people—the ones who remembered their true loyalty, at least—to Eldon after us. He harbored in a secluded cove and came to find me. I told him everything I had learned, including the way the delegation from Rangmere had dared to boast of their usurping queen and the ways she was destroying his kingdom.

"He is brilliant, there is no other mind like his. When he heard of Princess Giselle's planned trip to Arcadia, he formed the whole plan. He gave me my instructions and sailed for Arcadia to plant his men here and begin the long preparation that was needed."

A confused, defeated look filled her eyes. "He was

supposed to arrive, claim his place as a prince of Arcadia, and then fix Arcadia's problems. With his role as Lord Chamberlain, he could win the trust of the king, and then begin amassing the resources he would need to retake his true throne. Once he was established here, we were to be married."

I frowned. "But what did you suppose would happen when Celine and Oliver eventually arrived and exposed your true identity?"

She shrugged. "I would already have been a true princess by then, so it wouldn't have mattered."

I stared at her. "You don't think they might have been angry at you usurping my position?"

She looked uncomfortable, as if her eyes had been so firmly fixed on marrying Damon she hadn't considered any problems that might arise afterward.

"Damon would have protected me," she said. "I was only serving him. He needed me here as a princess. How else could I get close enough to poison the old Lord Chamberlain? And how else could he gain King Henry's blessing on our marriage?"

It was as if she had forgotten who Damon turned out to be and remembered only the image of him she had loved her whole life.

"So my grandfather never suspected your true identity?" asked Thomas, his voice reminding me of his presence in the corner of the room. His eyes were fixed on Sierra. "That was just lies from Damon? You killed him purely because he was the Lord Chamberlain, and Damon wanted his position?"

"Not just his position." Sierra sounded frustrated with our slowness of understanding. "He needed the palace in chaos so he could come in as rescuer. It was a brilliant move."

When I considered how nearly it had succeeded—as well as the resources the position would have given him access to—I had to reluctantly admit it was a clever plan. And the image of

Damon as rescuer brought the rest of the picture together in my head.

"But he never told you his true plan," I said. "The truth was you were just another pawn. The real reason he wanted you to swap places with me was so he could rescue me too. He intended to swoop in, romance me, use me to help make his version of the truth look convincing, rescue me, and then marry me. He proposed in the prison, and the handkerchief told me the proposal was genuine—although not his declaration of love."

Philip made a disgusted noise, but I kept my attention on Sierra.

"I believed Rangmere was using my ties to the other kingdoms to ensure my supposed crimes, along with my death, cut Arcadia off from her allies. But in truth, Damon intended to use my rescue and marriage to turn all those kingdoms into *his* allies. With Prince Max and his children dead, he would have been crown prince of Arcadia. And with the blame for their murders pinned on Rangmere, no one would have stood in the way if he led a campaign against his father's kingdom."

"He was cunning," Philip murmured. "I wonder how long it took him to forge the 'evidence' he found among the viscount's papers? He knew enough not to point the finger at Queen Ava initially—not when she's so well regarded here. But once the kingdom was in mourning, enraged by the merciless attack on their royal family, no doubt he would have begun to find evidence that suggested her involvement. I wonder how long he planned to string things out before it became *sadly* necessary for him to depose the queen and take her place?"

"The audacity of it," King Henry said in enraged tones. "He thought he could take the crowns of both kingdoms."

"And he might have succeeded," Philip said, "but he didn't account for Princess Giselle." I could feel his eyes on me, and my cheeks flushed. "She didn't fall for his flattery. She realized his insincerity, and she exposed him, saving the prince and princess."

He sounded warm and admiring, but it made me feel small.

"No, it was my pride and determination to prove myself that let him get so far," I said. "I should have insisted he reveal the truth as soon as I discovered he knew Sierra. But I was determined to be the one to unravel everything. I was playing at rescuer, just as he was."

Queen Eleanor crossed over to me, taking my hand gently in both of hers.

"It is not the same thing," she said firmly. "For one, you actually wanted to rescue people—he only wanted to appear to do so. Ask yourself—what would have happened if you had insisted on such a course? Would he have agreed? Of course he would not. And we have seen that he was willing to adjust his plan and kill you if you tried to stand in his way. It is fortunate for you, and for Eldon, that you didn't give him reason to mistrust you until the last."

She squeezed my hand. "And we all make mistakes, my dear. Sometimes grave ones. It is a hard lesson to learn, but one we all must accept." She threw a knowing smile at the king. "Older heads than yours have lived in foolish error for longer than the mere weeks you have been here. It is not our perfection that matters, but our growth, and how we learn from our mistakes. And I feel sure you will have learned from this." She sighed. "I suspect we will all be a little older and wiser after this."

"Thank you, Your Majesty," I said, tears pricking at my eyes.

"I am glad to know the truth of my grandfather's death," Thomas said wearily. "Although I can feel no rage against his murderer now I understand how she was manipulated by Damon. His is the true blame. But I notice he has not been dragged before us by Markus. Should we be concerned?"

Max looked at me, his eyes narrowing. "Where exactly were you when the men who attacked you vanished? Where in the park?"

Philip jumped in, explaining in more detail than I could have done.

As soon as he mentioned the fig tree, Max turned worried eyes to his father. "Is it possible? I thought no one but family..." His voice trailed away.

"Yes. No one but family," the king said grimly. "It appears Mina's stories to her son were complete indeed, although I cannot believe she ever thought he would use her knowledge in such a way."

"Your Majesty?" Thomas asked.

The king sighed and rubbed his face. "I suppose there is no point in maintaining the secret. The way will have to be destroyed now. The royal family has a secret bolt-hole which starts inside the park and exits far outside the walls. It was a last resort, a way of escape, in case of siege or attack. That is how the men who served Sierra were able to travel back and forth between Sierra and Damon without being seen, how they brought in the poison, and how they escaped when you injured them." He growled. "And no doubt, it is the way Damon has just used to escape my men tonight. And we thought we had him cornered."

He looked at me. "And thus you see the wisdom of my wife. Older—and I hope wiser—heads than yours still make errors."

"We will have to warn Ava," Alyssa said. "From everything Sierra has said, it sounds like he considers Rangmere his true kingdom. He has lost his chance to gain a position here, but I don't think he will so easily give up on Rangmere."

The king sighed. "I know you trust her now—and with reason. She has proved herself an ally these last ten years. But I must admit I do not like having to go to her and explain we let Damon slip through our fingers. She will have just cause to be angry."

"No one knows more of making mistakes than Ava," Alyssa murmured. "I think she will prove understanding."

"And I think we should also send a ship to this island," Max said. "Damon may have thought to take temporary refuge there."

Alyssa nodded approvingly at her husband. "And even if he did not, we may find some people there appreciative of rescue. Sierra said Damon took the only ship and left the island with those who remembered their true loyalty." She rolled her eyes.

"A ship will be sent as soon as it can be outfitted," the king said.

Their talk of Damon's escape reminded me of the final, impossible thing I had seen in the palace yard. I couldn't believe I had nearly forgotten it, but so much had happened in the last few hours.

I wet my lips. "I'm afraid there's some other bad news you might need to relay to Queen Ava."

Everyone turned to look at me.

"About Damon, you mean?" Alyssa asked.

I nodded. "It seems impossible but, given we have a talking horse in the room, I hope you'll believe me."

Of course they'll believe you, Arvin said, entering the conversation for the first time since he had been the topic under discussion.

I stared at him. Had that been a trace of threat in his voice? Several of the others gave him odd looks as well, so I hurried on.

"One of the guards wounded Damon, just as he was escaping. He gave him a deep gash in his leg. I was standing close enough to see, and the wound just closed back up. I've never seen anything like it."

Slowly everyone turned from me to Sierra. She looked reluctant, her loyalty to Damon so deeply ingrained she still had trouble throwing it off. As I stared at her, a sudden connection sparked through my brain.

"Was it the object?" I asked her. "You told me in the carriage that you used an object designed for protection—one that had only a little power left. Had the rest of its power been used to make Damon impervious to injury?"

She sighed and nodded. "It was a gift from his mother. She never told us where it came from."

"That's not going to make it easier to catch him," Max muttered, looking concerned.

"Don't worry, son." The king clasped him on the shoulder. "We'll talk to Ava, and between us, we'll find him. His enchantment won't stop us locking him away forever."

An awkward silence fell as we all digested the information.

"There is still one thing left to be explained," Thomas said suddenly, speaking the words burning in my mind. "What exactly is your role in all this, Philip? And why are you wandering around dressed like a servant, for goodness sake?"

I turned at last to look directly at Philip, eager for the answers to the questions that had long plagued me. But how did Thomas know Philip? And why was he surprised to see him dressed as a servant?

"You look familiar." Alyssa narrowed her eyes at him. "I've been thinking it all evening, but I can't place you. You certainly don't fight or ride like a servant."

Thomas barked a laugh at that. "I should say not. Have none of the rest of you met him before? Philip is from Lanover. I spent a number of years there with relatives when I was young, and he and I became close friends. He's the youngest grandson of the Duchess of Sessily. The fifth child of her only son."

I gaped at Philip. Thomas had been the friend from his childhood stories of mischief? And his grandmother was the Duchess of Sessily? Matriarch of the oldest and most respected duchy in Lanover, and their king's most trusted advisor. And she had been here in Arcadia—I had seen her myself.

"Grandson of the Duchess of Sessily?" King Henry frowned at Philip. "But what are you doing wandering around my kingdom dressed as a servant?"

"I've been here for some time, I'm afraid," Philip said apologetically.

"Celeste!" Alyssa suddenly exclaimed, triumphantly proclaiming the name of Celine's sister, the crown princess of Northhelm. "Celeste sent you, didn't she? But why didn't she tell us?"

I could see that every adult in the room except for Thomas and Sierra understood Alyssa's meaning. But I couldn't see why Celeste—who now lived in Northhelm—would have sent a Lanoverian noble to Arcadia.

Philip cleared his throat, hesitating a moment before giving in to the inevitable. "I was here to investigate among the servants. She wanted me entirely incognito." He grimaced. "I believe she thought someone would accidentally give me away if they knew of my presence. I've been ducking into buildings and behind trees like a jack-in-the-box whenever Thomas appeared, since I knew he would recognize me."

"I still think she could have told us," Alyssa muttered.

"I do hope you'll forgive me," he said to her with a charming smile. "You know Aurora runs her spy network for the good of all the kingdoms now." He used the name of the princess's alter ego as spymaster.

Suddenly Celeste's involvement made sense. I should have guessed from all of Celine's stories about her brilliant older sister that she would have used her marriage to enlarge her spy network, rather than leaving it behind.

Many other things I hadn't previously understood made sense as well. Why Philip had been suddenly 'too busy' to eat lunch with me on the day his grandmother arrived in Arcadia. If he had been afraid of Thomas recognizing him, he must have been doubly afraid of his own grandmother doing so. Why he had been so familiar with Thomas's story, and so full of empathy for his childhood. Why he had known his way around a noble's mansion and known to look for a hidden drawer in the viscount's desk. Even why he had been so interested in my oddi-ties when I first arrived.

"You saved Max and me, and helped save our children, so I suppose I shall have to forgive you," Alyssa said with a return smile. "But it seems to me there's someone else whose forgive-ness is more important." She gave a significant look in my direc-tion. "*You* weren't under an enchantment that prevented you from revealing your true identity."

Philip immediately turned and took both my hands. "I'm so sorry. I hated lying to you. But I'd made a promise to Aurora. She wasn't too eager to take me on, considering my rank, so I suppose you weren't the only one wanting to prove yourself. But then, the more I grew to love you, the more nervous I became. I could tell there was something strange about your history, and that you were no ordinary maid, but I still thought you a commoner, a true servant. I was afraid if I told you who I really was, it would scare you away."

I gulped, trying not to cry. "But why are you a spy? You're a son of the most important non-royal family in Lanover. You always seemed so disinterested in the life of a noble. Was that just a cover?"

He grimaced and rubbed the back of his neck. "It's true I don't have much patience for protocol and dancing attendance on important people—I much prefer a bit of adventure and new places to explore. I'm only the youngest which is why I was allowed to leave at all, and I was eking every last bit of enjoyment out of my freedom because it was only ever a temporary leave of absence. My family expects me to return to my responsibilities soon."

He let go of my hands and slipped both arms around my waist, looking at me with a hopeful expression. "Unless you might be prevailed upon to steal me away to an entirely new set of kingdoms? A princess of Eldon is a marriage alliance not even my grandmother could turn down."

The tears finally spilled over, making twin tracks down my cheeks.

His brow creased. "Don't cry. You're under no obligation to me. I would never want you to feel burdened by my love for you."

"They're happy tears," I whispered. "The handkerchief told me you weren't being truthful, and I thought it was when you said you loved me—but it was actually when you said you were a servant."

"How could you doubt my love?" he asked, horrified.

I mopped at my face. "I thought maybe it was only an infatuation, and you were mistaken in your feelings."

He removed one hand from my waist to gently wipe away my tears, lifting my face so my eyes met his. "My feelings for you are not infatuation, I assure you."

"I'm so happy!" I threw my arms around his neck. "You may not be Prince Percy, but surely my family can't say no to the Duchess of Sessily's grandson." I gave a watery chuckle. "Celine would never let them. And I don't want to go back to be shut up in a palace either. I've had a taste here of getting to know the people, and now I want to get to know my own people. I'm going to ask my parents if we can go exploring through the whole kingdom, meeting the regular people."

Philip's hands tightened around me. "I would love that."

Prince Percy cleared his throat. "And you may tell your parents that my parents sent me here to find an alliance in these kingdoms. Talinos already considers Eldon an ally and friend."

I looked around at our audience with embarrassment.

"Perhaps we should wait and finish this conversation elsewhere," I whispered to Philip.

"What conversation?" he asked promptly, keeping his attention on me. "All the important information has already been covered. It seems to me there's only one thing left to do. And you can't imagine I'm going to let anything so minor as a room full of people stop me, do you?"

"Oh," I said, my voice coming out as more of a squeak than I'd intended.

Philip gave me an affectionate smile and then lowered his mouth to mine in a gentle seal of promise. I forgot all about our audience. His lips promised all the years to come, and I could think of nothing else but him.

EPILOGUE

"Celine!" I rushed to the door to embrace my sister-in-law. "I thought you weren't arriving until tomorrow."

"We made good time." She embraced me back before looking nosily around my suite. "Obviously I wasn't going to waste a moment in coming after I got your letter. I still can't quite believe it! You were a goose girl for weeks and weeks!"

I grinned. "It does sound rather implausible, doesn't it?"

She eyed me, a knowing smile on her face. "And of course you're not in the least offended because you met your Philip because of it. At least tell me you weren't so addled by love you let Sierra off for all her crimes!"

I frowned. "It wasn't just me she wronged. She committed murder and conspiracy against the kingdom." I sighed. "But everyone in that room who heard her story could see how deeply Damon had his claws in her mind. I think he'd been brainwashing her since childhood, turning her into the perfect loyal servant."

Celine shivered. "The coldness of it. And the cruelty." She looked at me curiously. "So what did the king do with her?"

My mouth twitched. "After some consultation, we decided

that she herself had already demonstrated the correct treatment of an unwanted personal maid."

Celine collapsed onto the small sofa under the window, her eyes widening. "Don't tell me you made her a goose girl?"

I chuckled. "And no one who has been out to see her doubts the severity of the punishment. As someone who believes herself entitled to a throne, she's not adjusting to the reality of a gaggle of geese with much grace."

Celine laughed, her hand protectively cupping the small bump barely visible at her belly.

"I feel sorry for whoever has to guard her," she said when her mirth subsided.

"Actually, I think Colin and his brother quite enjoy it," I said. "And she's chained whenever she's in the park, so she can't do them any injury."

Celine wrinkled her nose. "Isn't Colin the boy who got you thrown in prison?"

I shook my head. "He didn't mean to do so. And I can hardly blame him since I did abandon my post constantly. I'm sure his brother is much better with the geese than I ever was."

Celine surveyed the room again. "This is a nice suite. I'm sure it's much nicer than your previous accommodations."

I nodded agreement, describing my broom cupboard room.

"You poor thing," she said.

"I was more than glad to have it, I assure you. Although I'll admit it has been lovely to be reunited with all my things."

Celine glared in the direction of my closet. "But can you bear to wear your gowns now that she's worn them all? I could burn them for you." She held her hands out toward my dresses.

"No, no." I flew across the room to push her arms down. "Remember you're not supposed to be doing that at the moment. And besides, I brought all my favorite dresses. I've compromised by having the palace laundry give everything a good scrub."

Celine lowered her hands skeptically. "I'm much more controlled now that I'm on land—and not being fed poison."

"It wasn't poison," I said quickly. "I'm sure it hasn't harmed the baby."

"Just don't let her catch sight of that girl," said a new voice in the doorway. "She's been fuming about the whole thing ever since we got your letter, and she'll never succeed in keeping her cool if she crosses paths with her." My brother Oliver turned to Philip, who stood beside him. "And with my wife, *keeping her cool* is a literal concern."

"I've heard about her remarkable new abilities," Philip said, sending me a private smile across the room.

"Philip!" Celine launched herself from her seat and threw her arms around his neck. "I couldn't believe it when I heard who my little sister had fallen in love with. And now we get to steal you away to Eldon."

He grinned and hugged her back. "How did my grandmother react?"

Celine pulled away and rolled her eyes. "With a long lecture to me about the responsibility we both have to Lanover, and the ways we can strengthen the trade relationship with Eldon."

Philip chuckled. "I'll take it she was pleased then."

"There may have been some dire remarks by your sisters, however," Celine said. "Something about you making good your escape from home."

Philip grimaced. "No doubt I will hear all about it when we get there."

Celine clapped her hands. "So you mean to bring Giselle back to meet your family?"

"Of course," he said. "And I hope you and Oliver will return with us."

Oliver nodded. "We've decided to make Lanover our home until the baby is born. No one wants to risk another sea voyage, even now we know of Sierra's meddling."

Celine gave a dramatic shudder. "No, indeed."

Oliver came over to give me a quick squeeze. "I'm proud of you, little sister," he said quietly.

I flushed. "I wish I were prouder of myself. I'm just relieved we were able to save Alyssa and her family."

Celine smiled over at us. "I told you she was lovely."

"And what of Percy?" Oliver asked. "Would he like to return to Lanover with us? He's been here in Arcadia for months now."

"He's traveling on to Rangmere," Philip said. "He seems to feel some sort of personal responsibility for not defeating and capturing or killing Damon in their duel. He wants to help Queen Ava track him down."

"I wish I could go and help," Celine said longingly.

Oliver gave her a stern look. "We are going back to Lanover, well away from any action."

She gave a small pout but didn't actually protest.

"I don't suppose you saw any sign of Daria, Cassie, or Daisy on your way over?" I asked.

Both Celine and Oliver shook their heads.

"Those poor girls," Oliver said. "I assume search parties have been sent after them?"

"King Henry and Queen Eleanor sent word throughout their kingdom as soon as the attack happened," Philip said, "and Aurora has alerted her entire network."

"If Celeste has taken the matter in hand, then I'm sure they'll be found in no time," Celine said.

"Search teams from their kingdoms are expected at any time." I crossed over to Philip, who slipped an arm around my waist and smiled down at me. "Their Majesties have been extremely concerned about Eliam's and Trione's reactions to Daria's and Daisy's disappearances, and we've promised Eldon's help in smoothing over diplomatic relations."

Philip nudged me. "You should tell them."

Celine sat bolt upright, her eyes lighting up. "Tell us what?"

"I had a visit from my godmother." I flushed slightly. "She wanted to bless my betrothal, apparently. But I asked her about the girls. She refused to tell me where we could find them, but she did at least reassure me they were alive and had each found safe shelter."

"I believe her exact words," Philip interjected, "were that they each had their own adventures to complete and kingdoms to save. Apparently we're not meant to interfere."

Miserable old woman, said yet another voice from the doorway.

Celine nearly fell off her sofa. She stared at Arvin, who had stuck his head through the door.

"Did I just hear you?" she asked him.

I rolled my eyes. "Yes, he talks to everyone now."

"But...but..." Celine gaped at me.

"Yes, I know," I said. "But don't say it, or we'll all get a lecture on working out our own problems."

"I always knew he was a miserable horse," she muttered.

I can hear you, thank you very much, Arvin said at his most dignified.

Oliver watched the horse with bemusement. "Does he often come into the palace?"

"All the time." I grimaced. "The servants have mostly adjusted to having a horse wandering loose inside."

Philip grinned shamelessly. "Lark's godmother had some things to say about him as well."

I do not wish to speak of that creature. Arvin glared at Philip, who ignored him.

"Ooh, tell me everything," Celine said.

"It turns out, Arvin wasn't gifted to Lark just to watch over her," Philip said. "While he was meant to assist her where he could, he was actually sent to our realm to learn some lessons of his own. And," Philip paused to grin, "she declared he has yet to finish learning them. So she refused to take him back to the Palace of Light like he was expecting."

Celine threw herself against the back of the sofa in gales of laughter.

Arvin directed his quelling glare at her, and when she didn't appear to notice, backed out of the room with a huff. I extricated myself from Philip's arm and ran out into the corridor after him.

Throwing my arms around his neck, I gave him a squeeze.

"Don't worry about them, Arvin," I said. "I'm sure you'll be able to return to the Palace of Light soon. You did save my life as well as Percy's and half the Arcadian royal family. And prevented a war in the process."

All things you could perhaps mention to your godmother, next time you see her.

I hid my smile against his neck. "I think she already knows. But I'm sure you'll master whatever lesson she still wants you to learn soon."

Arvin relaxed, bending his head around to whuff into my hair. *I like you much better than the others.*

"There you go then," I said. "That's a start."

He pulled away from me, the whites showing on his eyes. *You don't think* that *has something to do with it, do you?* He sounded horrified.

I considered mentioning his general disdain for everyone who didn't show him excessive deference, and the poor judgment he had shown on a number of occasions, but changed my mind. He seemed dedicated to the idea that you needed to work through your own troubles.

"Just know, you'll always have a home with me, as long as you're here," I said.

He relaxed again. *Thank you, Giselle. It is a relief to know that good breeding still exists. Now get back to your relatives before they come looking for you.*

I ran my hand down his neck one last time before slipping back into the room. Despite all his irritating features, I would miss Arvin if the godmothers did retrieve him one day.

When I rejoined the others, I found Celine standing near the door, her hand tucked into Oliver's arm.

"Apparently the housekeeper wants to show us to our rooms," Celine said. "I'm glad to hear the godmothers have their eye on Daria, Cassie, and Daisy. That will be a considerable relief to Teddy and Millie especially, I know. I can only imagine their family are beside themselves with worry. But none of them can be surprised to hear Daisy has gotten herself tangled up in a godmother adventure. And as we all know, there's no point trying to get in the way of one of those."

I bit my lip, not able to put the matter aside as easily as Celine. "I just hate to think of all the pain they will most likely have to endure in the course of such an adventure."

Celine gripped my shoulder. "But tell me, was all your pain worth it?"

I glanced up into Philip's smiling eyes. "A hundred times, yes."

She grinned and let me go. "Then have a little faith."

"You're right, of course," I said, and she swept out of the room with a triumphant smile on her face.

I turned into Philip who gave me a proper embrace.

"I'm so glad you already know Celine," I said. "I love her dearly, but she can be a bit much at times."

Philip chuckled. "She seems to have positively mellowed to me. Who do you think I got up to all that childhood mischief with?" He winked at me.

"I can only imagine." I shuddered. "Your poor parents." I looked up at him curiously. "I'm surprised you didn't end up marrying her."

This time he was the one to shudder. "No, thank you." He gave me a squeeze. "I like my fiery girls with a little more grace and natural restraint. Your brother is a brave man. Besides." He chuckled. "She's a year older than me, and both sets of our parents would have heartily approved the match. As you can imagine, both of those things were the kiss of death to any youthful romance between us."

I giggled into his chest. I could easily imagine how a young Celine would have felt at the idea of meekly marrying the parentally approved younger boy from the mansion next to the palace. And Philip would never have given up his chance at freedom and adventure for such a future.

"It's strange how these things work out," I said.

He pulled back far enough that I looked up at him.

"I think you mean it's perfect," he said.

"More than perfect." I rose up onto my toes so I could press my lips to his. "Because I want you all to myself. But I love that you know a small piece of my family already."

I pulled back. "Oh! I keep forgetting to say that you would be more than welcome to offer Harry a role in Eldon, in the stables or elsewhere, if you think he would be willing to leave Arcadia. I know you two have become good friends."

Philip shook his head without considering the question. "That's a lovely thought, but Harry wouldn't want to leave. And I wouldn't ask it of him."

I narrowed my eyes. "Wait a minute! I'm an idiot! Harry is one of Aurora's agents, isn't he?"

Philip glanced at my open door. "Not so loudly, thank you," he whispered before grinning at me. "How do you think I got assigned as coachman on the day we met? Aurora recruited him years ago. And he loves it here, anyway. He basically grew up in the royal stables."

I gaped at him. "I can't believe you never told me!"

"I didn't tell you because I was sworn to secrecy. I've told you every one of my own secrets—and I always will. But I can't tell other people's."

My eyes narrowed. "Well if we're talking about your secrets, why did you want to be a coachman that day anyway?"

His arms tightened, and a gleam sprang into his eyes. "I was here to investigate strange occurrences, and a royal ship suddenly springing a leak off the Arcadian coast seemed to qualify to me."

I gave him a light shove with my shoulder. "You mean you're incurably nosy and curious." My eyes widened again. "There are more agents than just Harry, aren't there? How many people around the palace were helping you? Is that how you got the key to the viscount's mansion? And there I was, just about dying of fright, thinking we were both going to be arrested and locked away forever!"

I swatted at him, but he laughed and caught my hand.

"Would you like me to inform you next time our criminal activity is unlikely to result in dire consequences?"

I wrinkled my nose, considering the question. "You know, it would have been a great deal less thrilling if I'd known."

He pulled me tight against him again. "That's my girl," he murmured.

I looked up at him. "I would have let you kiss me that night, if you'd tried, you know."

"Let me make up for it now then." He pressed a warm kiss down on my lips. "If you like I can tell you the many other times I nearly kissed you, and we can make up for all of them?"

His eyes twinkled down at me.

"I think that sounds like an excellent idea," I said.

"We can start with one minute ago."

"But you did kiss me one minute ago," I protested.

"Yes," he said gravely, "but I would have liked to kiss you twice."

So he did.

Discover what happened to Daria in The Mystery Princess: A Retelling of Cinderella, coming in early 2021.

But, in the meantime, you can find out how a woodcutter's daughter became a princess in The Princess Companion: A Retelling of The Princess and the Pea.

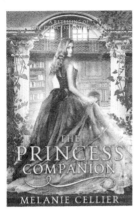

Or read more about Giselle and the kingdoms across the sea, starting in A Dance of Silver and Shadow: A Retelling of The Twelve Dancing Princesses.

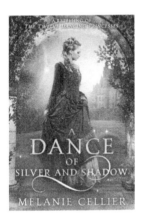

To be kept informed of my new releases, please sign up to my mailing list at www.melaniecellier.com. At my website, you'll also find an array of free extra content.

Thank you for taking the time to read my book. I hope you enjoyed it. If you did, please spread the word! You could start by leaving a review on <u>Amazon</u> (or <u>Goodreads</u> or <u>Facebook</u> or any other social media site). Your review would be very much appreciated and would make a big difference!

ACKNOWLEDGMENTS

I want to thank all the readers who have shown such enthusiasm at the prospect of returning to the Four Kingdoms and getting a glimpse of the ongoing lives of the original characters. I hope the return to Arcadia hasn't disappointed.

2020 so far has been a year like none of us expected, and there's every chance the rest of it will be just as tumultuous. As hard as it has been to concentrate at times, I'm so grateful for my small office, tucked away in my backyard in little Adelaide—a remote corner of the ends of the earth. There couldn't be a better place to retreat and dream of entirely different worlds where good always triumphs and true love brings universal rewards. I hope reading about my worlds gives you encouragement and an oasis as we wait in expectation of seeing such final victory in our own world.

In terms of specific thank yous, I feel like a broken record every time I write an acknowledgement section because I know the incredible value of my publishing team, and they never let me down. I would be truly lost without them. So, as always, the biggest of thank yous to:

My beta readers: My parents, Rachel, Greg, Priya, Ber, and Katie

My editors: Mary, my dad, and Deborah

My cover designer: Karri

My family: Marc, Adeline, and Sebastian

And, of course, a final thank you to God, who keeps me going through moments that seem hopeless or when I feel like I have nothing left to give. Your well never runs dry.

ABOUT THE AUTHOR

Melanie Cellier grew up on a staple diet of books, books and more books. And although she got older, she never stopped loving children's and young adult novels.

She always wanted to write one herself, but it took three careers and three different continents before she actually managed it.

She now feels incredibly fortunate to spend her time writing from her home in Adelaide, Australia where she keeps an eye out for koalas in her backyard. Her staple diet hasn't changed much, although she's added choc mint Rooibos tea and Chicken Crimpies to the list.

She writes young adult fantasy including her *Spoken Mage* series and her three *Four Kingdoms and Beyond* series which are made up of linked stand-alone stories that retell classic fairy tales.

Made in the USA
Monee, IL
03 July 2022

98948173R00187